WRITERS REPUBLIC

Winter's Gate

By Edie Campbell-Murray

This publication contains the opinions and ideas of its author. It is intended to provide helpful and informative material on the subjects addressed in the publication. The author and publisher specifically disclaim all responsibility for any liability, loss, or risk, personal or otherwise, which is incurred as a consequence, directly or indirectly, of the use and application of any of the contents of this book.

WRITERS REPUBLIC L.L.C.
515 Summit Ave. Unit R1
Union City, NJ 07087, USA

Website: *www.writersrepublic.com*
Hotline: *1-877-656-6838*
Email: *info@writersrepublic.com*

Ordering Information:
Quantity sales. Special discounts are available on quantity purchases by corporations, associations, and others. For details, contact the publisher at the address above.

Library of Congress Control Number:	2021903551	
ISBN-13:	978-1-63728-242-7	[Paperback Edition]
	978-1-63728-391-2	[Hardback Edition]
	978-1-63728-243-4	[Digital Edition]

Rev. date: 03/18/2021

ONE

K ate Willow hurried through her sponge bath. She struggled into her Ma's threadbare dress, pulled on heavy socks, and shoved her feet into cracked oxfords. The icy room caused goose bumps to rise on her arms and she grabbed a blanket from the bed and wrapped herself in it. Following her daily ritual, she scampered to the window, stepping over the rough floorboards that creaked, and pushed aside the limp fabric that covered the small panes of glass.

A light layer of frost covered the inside of the window. Kate blew on the window and rubbed a spot clear so the outdoors was visible. Then, using a hairpin wrote a message in the remaining frost. *Happy Birthday. Kate Willow Martin. September 17, 1937.*

Always in the back of Kate's mind was the belief she would be somewhere else on this day when she turned twenty. Fear kept her chained to the only home she had ever known.

Her dream of becoming a teacher burned bright within her, and she could only hope that somehow there was a way for her to accomplish her goals. Panic filled her stomach and lungs at the thought that she might not succeed in bringing her dream to fruition. She forced herself to concentrate on the window, focusing her attention on the frostbitten earth.

Her eyes traveled past the garden spot, with its withered bean stalks and puny pumpkins, past the irrigation ditch to the corn field, and beyond to the main road and the Clayton farm. Sometimes Augusta Clayton and his son, Big John, were in their barnyard, doing chores. They were fun to watch and she sometimes pretended she was there, working and laughing alongside of them. Kate thought Big John was a mighty fine looking man.

Disappointed that she'd missed them this morning, she scanned the terrain within her eyesight. On the west side of the house, behind the barn, smoke rose from a tin chimney. Pa's hired man, Jude, lived in the old house and tried his best to keep things in shape, but he was fighting a losing battle if Kate knew anything about it. Leon hated Jude, and was determined to get him off the place. The fact that Pa had willed Jude the house and five acres made no different to Leon.

There was a dozen or so farms scattered over 3000 acres. Her Pa had bought up 600 acres of the best irrigation land, following the Missouri river on the south side, and a small forest of cottonwood trees to the west. When Pa was alive it had been the best farm in the country. Now it lay neglected, crops going to seed, thistles and weeds growing on what had once been fertile fields. Pieces of broken barbed wire coiled over the ground; she watched them, fascinated, as they slithered and bounced in the heavy winds.

In a moment of whimsy, she fancied herself a director of an orchestra. Kate Willow, leading the music, following the movement of the wire in the wind. Her large body shed its bulk and melded with the air. The strands of wire twirled and bowed and swept gracefully to and fro. The music reached a crescendo, became violent, passionate, and the dancers crashed and melded together, clinging to each other like lovers, shaken and tossed about it by the passion of the frenzied gusts, only to become more entangled, until they were not individuals any longer, but merely bits and pieces of each other. And when the calm came, they crashed to the ground, there to grow old and rusty, with no one to remember their few moments of glory.

Kate took her diary from the closet and wrote with haste the scene she'd envisioned, and then turned her attention to the back yard where the depleted woodpile sharpened her anxiety. The coming winter filled her with dread. Leon hadn't hauled any logs to the yard. And it was time to butcher, they were running low on both pork and beef.

Kate sighed, resigned to the fact she couldn't change her brother. "But I can change myself. I must continue learning, and hope for the day I will escape from this merciless existence."

Reluctantly, she shrugged the blanket from her shoulders and walked to the door. It was time to get downstairs and stoke up the stove. Leon would be up soon and he expected a warm kitchen and a hearty breakfast.

Smoke from the chimney wafted through the rotting panes of the window, telling her Leon had built a fire in his room. She wasn't allowed to use her stove, and she swallowed past the lump in her throat, angry that his cruelties still had the power to hurt her. She gave a look of despair through the window, wishing she could fly south with the birds. In a hurry to get downstairs to her chores she almost missed the team and wagon lumbering slowly along the main road. The pieces of scrap metal that held the boards of the wagon together glinted cold and shiny in the early morning sun.

Kate knew the driver was Scrap Iron Nickleson; she recognized the team of bays. Pa had sold them to the Nicklesons shortly before he was killed. Scrap Iron must have done his trading early this morning. It was eight miles to Ryan and he'd been there and back already. The wagon was loaded with filled gunnysacks and cream cans.

She strained her eyes to see who was perched on the tailgate. Then exclaimed, "Oh my gosh! The wagon's stopping at our gate." Visitors were few and far between on the Martin place and Kate's eyes grew wide when the team pulled the wagon on down the road, leaving two girls standing by the mailbox. Kate ran from the room to warn Leon. He didn't like strangers poking around.

After she'd called Leon and told him the news, she bustled around, building a fire in the old cook stove and preparing breakfast. She cut thick slices of bacon from the large slab, peering out the window every now and then to see if the girls were really coming here. Who could they be? The little one cut through the wind, running hell-bent towards the house. Kate licked the salt and fat from her fingers, and hoped Leon would hurry, so she wouldn't have to answer the door.

The wind blew the girl's dresses awry and they wore no coats. The largest girl hugged a shawl close to her chest. She was struggling with a suitcase.

Shoulders hunched into the wind and heads bent down to escape some of the sting, they began walking up the lane towards the house. The frail woman lifted the girl down from the farm wagon into the cold gusts of the east wind. Taking the small hand in hers she pulled the child up the narrow-rutted road.

"I see the house, Mama." Mandy pointed ahead, and her nut-brown legs moved in excited, twirling dance steps.

"Yes," Angela said. "That's where I lived until I married your daddy." Sweat broke out on her face and she lifted the hem of her faded calico dress to wipe it off. She gasped as a sharp pain pierced her chest.

She forced her emaciated body into the fierce wind. Every few steps she coughed, spewing up mucous. The last of her strength fled her body and she sank to her knees. "Mandy, go get help. Tell them Angie has come home. Hurry." Mandy raced ahead to the house.

Fear of lying there overtook Angie and she began crawling in the direction of the crude monstrosity looming ahead. The sun poured its harsh rays over the house, exposing the ugliness of the unpainted stucco. Small windows were set haphazardly into its walls. She had fancied them as evil eyes when she was a child, and they appeared so to her now.

She was a scant forty yards from the house and she desperately searched for her brother. Her body sagged with relief when he stepped through the door, followed by the bulky figure of a woman.

A hysterical giggle bubbled up in her throat as she watched her brother, Leon, run crookedly down the dirt drive. He looked like that hapless idiot she had been forced to read about in school, the illustration in her literature book had shown Ichabod Crane with the same knobby knees, skinny legs, and sharp elbows as Leon.

Angie didn't recognize her sister, until Kate peered down at her and knelt to straighten her dress and wipe the perspiration from Angie's face. It was the eyes that brought recognition. She'd always been jealous of Kate's eyes, so large and wide, and the color of dew misted Concord grapes. What had the girl done to herself? There was no expression in her eyes, or on her whole face, for that matter. And never had she thought little Kate Willow would become so unkempt.

Leon carried Angie up the porch steps, and through the door. The cavernous rooms offered her no welcome. She shivered, as the malevolent atmosphere of the house, so damp and dark, penetrate deep into her thin bones.

Leon poured cream into his coffee, then tipping his cup, poured some in a saucer. He slurped it, and watched Kate as she removed the strips of bacon from the pan. Hot grease spattered up and he smiled when it landed on her hand, causing her to jump.

"Did you get Pa's princess all comfy in her bed?", Leon said. Kate nodded her head, not sure how he felt about Angie coming home. She hesitantly put his plate in front of him and moved quickly out of his reach.

Leon stretched his face into a foxy grin, relishing her nervousness. "Get you grub and sit down." He jerked his head at the chair next to his. He gobbled the eggs and shoved half the toast into his mouth. "Angie showin' up here puts a clink in my plans. Do you think she's fakin'?" "No, she really is sick." Fear for Angie gave Kate courage and she said, "She wants Dr. Larson to come see her. She asked about Pa's attorney, too. Do you think she knows about the will?"

Leon's green eyes narrowed into slits. "Don't you be runnin' off at the mouth about that will. This farm is mine, no matter what Pa wanted." He slid his leg forward, hooked his toes under the rung of the old wooden chair she sat in, and flipped it backwards. His eyes glinted in satisfaction when she screeched. "That's just a sample of what you'll get, if I find out you're tellin' Angie stories. Pa might have named her brat as his heir, but I aim to put a stop to that. I'm not allowin' it. This farm is mine."

Kate picked herself up off the floor and backed against the hot stove. Suddenly she grabbed the stove poker and shook it at him. "Someday I'm going to pay you back, Leon. You'll get what's coming to you. You're mean and hateful, like Pa."

Leon walked towards her, his steps slow and menacing. Spiteful green eyes tossed warning signals at her. His narrow face, usually so sallow, was flushed and wet. She watched as a glob of saliva coursed its way onto his chin, hovering over the deep hole in its center, and finally plopping onto the front of his shirt.

Kate's body began to shake as he advanced across the room. She saw his bunched-up fists, and fear clutched at her stomach. Against her will, vomit spewed from her mouth. Leon stopped and snapped, "You disgusting cow, go clean yourself up. Then get back here. I've got things for you to do.

Kate ran from the kitchen, fear propelling her up the stairs and into her room. She didn't bother to open the closet door, there wasn't anything in there that fit her. Only two dresses of Ma's were wearable, and today was wash day. Improvise, she told herself as she went to the wash-dish and wet the end of her towel. She scrubbed at the vomit stain with shaky hands and grabbed one of Pa's shirts and put it on over her dress.

When she returned, Leon was standing by the table, drumming his fingertips across the tattered oilcloth. A family of flies buzzed anxiously around the empty plate. One landed on the rim of Leon's milk glass and in an instant his hand snaked out and he crushed it between his fingers. She waited for him to speak, the silence seeming ominous; the crushed fly an omen of things to come.

"What do you want me to do, Leon?"

"I've got it all figured out. She mentioned her lungs were bad. Just like Ma." Kate saw his old resentment of their mother surface, freezing his face into a feral mask and quickly, return to normal. The familiar chill crept through her body and she shrank away from him. She scraped her tongue against her teeth, trying to get rid of the brassy taste of fear.

Leon hadn't noticed her agitation and continued talking, waving his hands and bouncing around the kitchen, caught up in his own importance.

"We'll treat Angie like the queen she thinks she is, get her to trust us. Then she'll sign guardianship papers leaving Mandy to me. When she's dead, I'll be in charge of Mandy and the farm.

He looked at his sister slyly. "You nurse her, soften her up, make that special tea every day and brush her hair, stuff like that. Just be careful what you say, she's a smart one." He hooked his fingers onto the straps of his overalls and walked to the window. "I'm going to get that five acres Pa willed to ol' Crip, too. See if I don't."

He glared at Kate. "Now you tell me what's going on with her?"

"She's so weak. I had to lift her into the bed and that cough is terrible. She's out of medicine. That's why she needs to see Dr. Larson."

"Tell her he's out of town. We're not helping her to get well. We're helping her to get dead and buried. Get it?"

"But she's our sister, we have to …"

"We? Who are you to say what we should do? I'm the boss here. Who else would put up with you? Huh, Kate? There's not a soul in this here valley that'd get within ten feet of you if they knew how Pa ruined you."

He clutched a hank of her hair and pulled it tight. "You do as I tell you. Get in there and butter her up but be careful what you say. If you do as you're told, you can bake yourself a chocolate cake later."

Kate's mind skittered. It was if Leon had magically detoured her thoughts to the past and she found herself helpless against the memories that attacked her. She fought against them to no avail. Her mind dipped and rose, circling until it centered in on the events of nine years ago. Kate's mind went back to the first time she had been rewarded with chocolate cake.

Ma had been sick all that winter. A chest cold forced her to lie in bed in her stark room, a grim, sour woman, refusing even the comfort another blanket would have given her.

Kate, eleven years old and used to looking out for herself, managed to get to school almost everyday by getting up earlier and doing her share of Ma's chores.

She lost herself in the many books and spent most of the recesses reading and studying. There was a fear in her that something would take away her chance to learn what she needed to become a different person, to go out into the world and live a life of freedom and equality. A place where no one knew her family and she would have friends again.

She thought wistfully of her first two years in school. She had been accepted then, but Leon had quietly destroyed her reputation by whispering lies to her friends and eventually they had stopped playing with her.

Her teacher, Mrs. Lowell, came to her one day and said lightly, "beauty and brains, too." She grasped Kate's hands. "I know you're having a hard time at home just now. If you want to cut back on some of the work, I'll understand."

"Oh no, Mrs. Lowell. I want to learn all I can. I'm planning to become a teacher like you."

"Bless your heart, child. If I can help you with anything, anything at all, please let me know." She smiled at Kate and left her standing there with a new warm feeling in her heart. Her newfound happiness lasted all day. After supper she washed the dishes and went to her room. She lay in bed, remembering the kind words of Mrs. Lowell and the warm smile that made her feel melty all over. She whispered aloud. "Mrs. Lowell likes me. Me, of all people." Her sigh was wistful, as she wished she had someone to share her happiness with. Kate fell asleep, looking forward to tomorrow.

A cold draft woke her and when she opened her eyes. Pa was standing beside her bed, wearing only his long johns. Frightened, she stared at him, wondering if Ma was worse. Suddenly, he reached down and tore the blanket from the bed, then flipped her nightgown up. His callused hands touched her body. Kate shrank back in fear, wondering what she'd done wrong. Forcing her thighs apart, he covered her with his body and jammed into her. The pain caused her mind to go numb and Kate lay under him in frozen terror. He smelled of cow dung and onions and his dirty sweat dripped on her head. When he finished, he left the room and returned with a big slice of chocolate cake.

He came to her room once a week every Friday, and always brought her a treat afterwards. Kate had never been so fearful. Her life had been predictable. Harsh, yes, but she had known what to count on. Pa's whippings, Leon's cruelties, Ma's coldness. These things had made up her life and she had set her mind to them, knowing the sting of the strap would soon go away, knowing Leon wasn't right in the head, glad that for all Ma's coldness, she never lifted a hand against her.

She lost her powers of concentration and no matter how hard she tried she couldn't remember her lessons. The intense curiosity ebbed away, and she lived her days in a trance state, silent hysteria blocking her throat and the fear in her so strong she appeared dull and stupid.

One night when Pa was on her, she'd looked at the window. Leon's face was plastered against the glass. He was still staring at her when Pa came back with some gingerbread and whipped cream. She gobbled it down, ignoring Leon, trying to fill the empty space under her heart.

Six years older than Kate, Leon had tormented her all her life. Now, he attacked her with renewed vengeance. She was forced to accept the blame for all his mischief. "I'll tell Ma about you and Pa if you don't do what I say and I'll tell the kids at school you're whorin' with your own Pa."

Shame created a cow-like appearance to the once lively eyes and her sprightly walk became slow and heavy.

She knew she was pregnant three weeks after he fourteenth birthday. Pa cursed at her, the words growling from deep within his throat. Ma died when she was five months along and Pa pulled her out of school, saying she was needed at home.

Pa delivered the baby much as he'd brought lambs and calves into the world. She remembered the smell of blood and sweat, the rough feel of Pa's hands and his grim, accusing face. She remembered the pain and her screams.

She saw her baby boy only once, when Pa placed him on her stomach to cut the cord. His eyes opened and they gazed at each other. Kate, for the first time, realized her baby was a real human being and her very own. He belonged to her. She could care for him, love him, talk to him and he was beautiful. She reached down to lift him to her breast, but Pa second guessed her. He picked him up and wrapping him in a quilt, took him away. Kate screamed until she fainted from exhaustion.

The baby was gone and never mentioned. One good thing came from it. Pa never bothered her again. The nightmare was stuffed into the shadows, along with all other secrets of the house.

The pain wreaked upon her young body and the intense fear and loneliness she experienced created a new Kate. An inborn sense of survival caused her to bury her feelings; she learned to live her days and nights without thinking of anything but the task at hand. She spent her days catering to the demands of the Martin men, and at night her exhausted body slept heavily. So complete seemed her metamorphous, Pa and Leon ceased to worry that she would ask someone for help. But unknown to Leon and Burt the passage of time caused her old dreams of teaching to again fill her mind. At the core of her being lived a tremendous amount of courage, and an exceptional intelligence.

As the months passed and the heartache became lighter, her longing to teach gave her courage to write to Mrs. Lowell, asking for her silence and telling her where to leave the books she needed to continue her studies. *"Pa needs me at home to do my Ma's work and he doesn't believe girls need an education. In fact, he's dead set against it, so please, do keep this secret for me."*

Kate studied in the morning before the others awoke. Always fearful of being caught, she hid the materials in the bowels of the pot-bellied stove that stood unused in her bedroom. It proved to be a good hiding place, and Leon, on his snooping expeditions, hadn't had the foresight to open the door.

Leon's abuse of Kate continued, and it was a rare day that she went to her room without a new bruise or lump inflicted by her crazy brother. Sometimes she would snap out of her lethargy and try to stand up for herself, but her moments of rebellion were few and short lived.

Now, laboriously climbing the stairs, her tired body doing what it had to do, she thought greedily of the chocolate cake Leon had promised her.

Angie leaned over the bed, gasping for air. She managed to grasp the cowbell and ring it. Where was Kate? Where was that dumb girl, anyway? If Pa were alive they wouldn't be ignoring her like this. With short, frantic movements she continued to ring the bell until Kate, puffing from the long climb up the stairs, dragged into the room.

"Help me Kate, dear God, help me." Kate rushed to the bed and lifted Angie up against the pillows, rubbing her neck and shoulders. "That's better, thanks. Where were you when I rang? I thought you weren't coming." She looked at Kate accusingly. "Today's wash day. The old washer makes a lot of noise and I didn't hear you 'till I'd finished putting the shirts through the wringer."

"Make arrangements for me to move downstairs to your old room, Kate. It'll be easier for you to take care of me, and I'll feel a lot safer, too." "I ... I'll see what Leon says. Maybe he won't mind." "Leon! What's it any of his business? I'm the oldest in this family, and I'll have that room whether he likes it or not." Angie's body was trembling and she was weak from her breathlessness, but anger gave her a pugnacious look, and Kate smiled to see the proud little chin pushed forward. Angie was a fighter, no doubt about it.

"Angie, please don't cause trouble. You don't know Leon. He can get real mean. Be careful what you say to him."

Picking up on Kate's agitation, Angie wondered about the fear she seemed to have of Leon. Where's the feisty little sister of nine years ago? A real go-getter, Angie recalled. Tough too. Took her whippings like a trooper. What had turned her into this frightened, zombie like creature? Suddenly, compassion entered Angie's heart, and she reached her hand out to Kate.

"Thank you, sister, for taking care of me." Kate surprised herself by answering bitterly, "Like you took care of me?' "I know. I was an awful brat. Pa spoiled me, I guess. I was his trophy, and I used that to get what I wanted."

"You're so beautiful, Angie. Pa was mesmerized by you."

"Pa was a strange man. He didn't love any of us, you know. I used to believe he had no feelings for anything. Even his animals. He just did what he had to do. How did he die, Kate?"

"All I know is he drove the Model T to the auction barn and the brakes bailed. Sheriff Henson said Pa should have junked it years ago."

"That's odd. You know Pa always kept everything in top condition." Angie pulled the covers up to her chin, shivering. "Who inherited this place?"

"Leon, who do you think?"

"Did Pa leave us anything?"

"No, Leon's got it all, he's lord and master of Pa's Little Kingdom."

"Ha, that's a laugh. Pa wouldn't leave Leon a dime. Have you seen the will?"

"No, I just know what Leon told me." She turned to leave, her lies smothering her so she had to gasp for breath.

"Can't you stay awhile? It's so lonesome here."

"I have to fix lunch. Leon expects it at twelve sharp."

"Isn't there anyone to help you, Kate? The place, the house, everything looks so neglected. Pa had money, is it tied up in court?"

"Leon says we should be self-sufficient, and not waste money on things any moron can do." Kate clutched the sides of her head, wondering how she could stop the endless questions. If Leon knew she'd talked…

"Angie, I hope you won't tell Leon I've said anything about the will. He … well, he wouldn't like it."

"I won't mention it, Kate. Look, don't worry; our talks are just between us. But I'm going to see to it that this house has a cook and housekeeper. You can't possibly do all this yourself. Leon shouldn't expect it. Tell him I want to see him." Noticing the fear in Kate's eyes, she quickly added, "Mum's the word. I love you, trust me.

Angie reached out and held Kate's hand. "Has it been terribly hard for you?"

"Not so bad," Kate lied, "except for Pa taking me out of school. I dreamed of becoming a teacher someday." She suddenly had the urge to confide in Angie. Perhaps it was the novelty of having another woman in the house, or did she just want to let Angie know she wasn't as dumb as she looked?

She decided Angie coming home was a miracle. Her first real birthday present. For the first time in years there was someone to talk to. Someone who treated her nice, and seemed to like her.

The words came tumbling from her lips. "After Pa took me out of school, I wrote to my teacher. We worked it out so she'd hide my lessons under a rock at the edge of the alfalfa field once a month. I sneaked out after dark. They never found out. I hoped someday to leave here and get my teacher's certificate."

"Kate, how wonderful! And so very brave." She pulled Kate closer to the bed. "I want to help you; I've neglected you for too long. You were a child when I left home. Nine, ten years old, goodness, it has been a long time. Come, sit here for a bit, and we'll make plans."

Sensing Kate's indecision, she said, "Don't worry about Leon. I'll tell him I needed you. Us women have to stick together, right?" She smiled at Kate and tugged at her until she was on the bed beside her.

"Now Kate, let's make plans for you. Did you know you can take a test and get your high school diploma? That would make you eligible to teach in the country schools. Or you could go on to college and earn a degree. Let's do it! Oh, this is so exciting. Just think, you could be Mandy's teacher someday soon."

"Now Angie, how would I look, going to school? I'm more suited for the circus."

"Let's get you started on a diet. Being overweight isn't permanent, you know. You're a beautiful woman, Kate. And yes, you do need to lose some pounds. Tomorrow, I'll make a list of the foods you should not eat."

Kate blushed. Talking to another woman, making plans and having fun was foreign to her. She was embarrassed by Angie's interest, yet excitement and hope began to course through her body. 'Woman' was not a word Kate had ever applied to herself. Her thoughts were focused on things rather than self.

Except for the desire to become a teacher, she paid no attention to her wants. Her life was such that she was not even sure what her needs were. She took what was given and asked for nothing. Now Angie had started all kinds of ideas popping up in her mind. Was Angie telling the truth when she said Kate was a beautiful woman?

She smiled at Angie and then, overcome by emotion, she turned her head and looked across the room … and saw herself in the looking glass that was propped on top of an old dresser.

At first, she wondered who the funny looking woman was. The ugly gray dress she wore was too small. It scrunched up around her knees, fitting into the crevices of her body. The bodice stretched so snug across her large breasts that they resembled two loaves of lumpy, lopsided bread dough. Fat arms pooched out of the tight sleeves. A red ring was indented into the skin under the hem of each sleeve.

A gasp escaped her as she realized she was the woman in the glass. Shattered by her image she blurted out, "You lied to me, Sister. I'm beyond repair." She gave Angie a bittersweet smile, and walked out of the room.

The ghost of Kate's smile haunted Angie until she fell into a deep slumber. When she awoke three hours late, her eyes fell on the plate of cold, greasy fried potatoes and shriveled pork chops. "That Kate," she murmured aloud. "She hasn't a classy bone in her body."

The pain in her chest filled her with fear. The afternoon stretched before her like a lifetime. By moving the pillows around, she managed to find a more comfortable position, and then leaned against them, letting her mind wander. Kate must be one of those women who like being walked on, she thought disdainfully. Imagine letting oneself become so unkempt. And wearing those ugly dresses of Ma's. Well, things had gone from bad to worse since she left here. It was up to her now to turn this sty into a real home. She refused to look at the shabby room any longer. She closed her eyes, images and thoughts filtering in and out of her head. She decided to let her mind take her where it would.

She had been Pa's favorite, but even so, he'd shown her no love or tenderness. There were no hugs or kisses for the kids of Burt Martin.

Pa had worked the land with a doggedness that amazed the most industrious farmers. He took no joy in his work, received no sense of fulfillment from his labors. He worked as if devils were at his back, brandishing whips.

Pa's method of doling out punishment was swift and non-negotiable. He would take the strap from its nail on the kitchen wall, run his right hand over the smooth leather, and silently with cold purpose, lash the helpless youngsters until he felt vindicated. When Angie was six, Pa had looked at her and decide she was a champion, there were no more whippings for her, but Leon and Kate had been bitten by the strap more times then she liked to remember.

Ma had no use for her daughters. She spent her days much like Pa, working at her cooking, cleaning with a vengeance. It was as if Ma hated her own sex. She had no friends and no vanity. Always she wore the gray dresses, and her hair in a tight knot. Her lips compressed in a straight line, and a perpetual frown carved creases between her eyebrows. A silent, grim woman who didn't believe in wasted words, she very seldom spoke to her girls, other them to give them orders.

Her one weakness was Leon. She'd treated him like a pet, Angie recalled, always stroking his head, and getting him out of his scrapes. Ma lied to Leon, calling him her little genius, praising him for deeds he'd had no part in. Everyone could see he was a real jackass, everyone but Ma, that is. She wouldn't admit there was anything wrong with him.

Angie and Kate were blamed for his misdeeds. Once Angie had tried to explain to Ma that Leon was different, but she'd used the word goofy, and Ma had pushed her down, and ignored her for days after.

She, like Ma, had always had a soft spot for her brother. Maybe because Pa had hated him so fiercely. Poor Leon. He'd always been a weird kid, with a cruel streak he couldn't seem to control.

Pa surely wouldn't have given his life's work to Leon. And why had Pa's brakes failed? She needed answers, but where to start? If only she weren't ill. And cowardly. Her heart ached with loneliness for her husband. "Noah, Noah," she sobbed. "We need you. Mandy and I need you so."

"Mama, don't cry." Mandy's soft voice startled Angie and she quickly wiped her tears. "I'm okay, honey. Mandy, have you noticed a telephone in the house?"

"I haven't seen one. I don't like it here, Mama. Can we go home now?"

"Not yet. I'm not well enough to travel, but be patient, I'm getting better every day." Angie held her child close to her. "I know it's hard for you to understand, baby. This isn't what your Daddy and I wanted for you. We had big dreams, and we tried hard to make them come true." She was silent for a few minutes wondering how to help Mandy understand.

"Remember when Grandma Senecah had a nervous breakdown?" Mandy nodded gravely. "Well, our country is having a breakdown, too. That's why Daddy lost his job. He went to another place to try to find work. We must be patient, Mandy, and pray for our country. And we need to be grateful we have a place to live. There are thousands of people sleeping in boxcars and under bridges, and in the fields, just anywhere they can find a space. Whole families have lost everything they owned, and have no place to live or food to eat." She smiled at Mandy. "Grandma Senecah recovered and our country is recovering too."

"Can't we go to Grandma's and stay with her?"

"They're very poor, and I don't want to be a burden on Daddy's family. If things go well here, we can help them, and Daddy won't have to leave us again. Be a big girl, and soon you'll have everything you want." She smoothed Mandy's collar and tucked her blouse neatly into her skirt. "Would you like to have an adventure and do me a favor at the same time?" Mandy's head bobbed excitedly. "Go to the Clayton's and tell Christine you are Angie's and Noah's girl. Give her this note." Angie put the folded paper into Mandy's pocket.

"Now listen carefully. Go out the back door, cross over the yard, behind the barn and take the path there, to the main road. They live straight across from us. It's the nice yellow house I pointed out to you when we got off the wagon. They have a girl your age and you can stay and play if they ask you."

Mandy left the room, her spirits high, and Angie could hear her calling for Tippy. She sighed, wondering where she'd gotten the gift for blarney. Mandy was appeased for now. Angie was proud of herself for being so good with Mandy. If only Mandy looked more like her. There was no mistaking the Indian blood in her. Sometimes it was downright embarrassing.

Maybe Christine would find time soon to visit. And Leon better come see her tonight, she had to get out of this stifling room and downstairs. At least the room down there was bigger and she'd be able to see the out of doors. If Kate fixed it up a bit and put a decent quilt on the larger bed, her days might be more tolerable.

Why didn't Kate come? It had been a good hour since she'd rang for her. She grabbed the bell and waved it in the air, over and over. The angry sound filled the room. Her breaths came in short gasps and she tired quickly.

Suddenly, she threw the bell across the room and curled her slight body under the sheets, lying quietly until Kate or Leon decided to check on her. She began to draw strength into her body through her will, and lay very still to conserve it. She would need her strength when she had the opportunity to confront her family.

THREE

The Clayton family gathered around the kitchen table for their mid-morning repast. Christine Clayton carried a large cast iron kettle to the table, and the appetizing aroma of beef stew soon had the men engrossed in their lunch with a few grunts and much slurping. The platter of home baked bread and crocks of honey and butter were soon depleted.

This was Christine's favorite time of day. She loved to cook, and enjoyed watching her men eat. Their day started at five in the morning and by ten o'clock they were ravenous.

She turned her sunny, freckled face to her husband. "Augusta, I need to go over to the Martins and see Angie today. She sent her little girl over with a note. We were good friends in school, remember? Her note sounded desperate, I guess she's ill. Have you heard anything about her?"

"Just bits and pieces, but look, girl, you be careful over there. I don't trust that bunch. I saw Leon last week running all over the east pasture, screaming like a banshee. He's crazier than ever since old Burt was killed. He's a bad one, and I don't want you or our June around him. I still think he had something to do with the Gordon's Essie getting hurt like she did."

"You think Leon is the one that assaulted her?" Christine was shocked.

"Well, it's the talk that's going around, and I don't discount it. I've been around that buzzard enough to know he hasn't any conscience. He doesn't care about anything but his own selfish wants. I hate to think what could happen to Angie's girl if she's living there."

Big John spoke. "He acted like a knot-head at Mr. Martin's funeral. His own Pa and all, and him acting like he was running for office. After a couple of hours, he started singing and telling those silly jokes. I don't doubt he's half-a-bubble off a plumb and the less we have to do with him the better."

"I'll be careful," Christine assured them. "I'll be back before June gets home from school. Angie wants to see me, and I need to make sure she's getting the care she needs."

Augusta leaned over and planted a swift kiss on Christine's cheek. "Take Big John with you. I'll feel better knowing you're not alone. You get ready and he'll be back to walk you over in about an hour."

Christine lingered at the table for a few moments, then began stacking the dishes, the same dishes her mother had used all through Christine's growing up years. In a moment of nostalgia she saw her face reflected in the plate, the face she had as a young girl.

She'd been full grown at twelve years old and liked to think of her elementary school years as a character building period. The kids at school teased her and called her Paul Bunyan's kid, but they'd liked her and the teasing was done without malice. Although she was sometimes hurt and lonely, her life at home was good, her parents, two sisters, and three brothers filled her life.

Christine saw herself as a ten-year old, big and gawky, leaning against the wall of the school, waiting for recess to get over. Angie had joined her, smiling and said, "Let's be best friends, Christine. Do you want to?"

She'd nodded dumbly, unable to believe Angie really liked her. But from that day on, they were together. She had a friend. She tagged along with Angie, Norm, and whichever smitten dude Angie decided to favor with her attentions. Until she met Gus. The day they'd announced their engagement, she'd overheard Angie tell a classmate, "Huh, he's just a dumb farmer, but she's lucky to get him, who else would want her? You can be my best friend now." The thrill of knowing Angie was jealous of her soothed any hurt she might have had at Angie's dropping her.

It was during her sophomore year she had met Augusta. His family had moved from Minnesota and bought the old Saunder's place. They'd bumped into each other in the assembly hall, and for the first time in her life, she'd had to look up at one of her classmates. A soft "Oh" escaped her lips as she gazed into his kind blue eyes. "How tall are you?", she spoke spontaneously.

"Six foot, three." His gravely voice thrilled her. "How about you?"

"Five foot eleven inches." Christine had fallen for him on that first meeting. He walked her home from school sometimes, but he was so popular a lot of the girls had crushed on him. He had his choices and dated a few of them. When he'd asked her to the school dance, she couldn't believe it at first. Her first dance, her first date, and with the best catch in the county.

Her pale-yellow gown had shown some of her magnificent bosom and a wide sash that buttoned in the back emphasized her small waist. The yellow gown brought out the highlights in her strawberry blonde hair. It had been a magical evening. Her classmates raved over her and she had lots of dances. Angie was with Noah, her latest beau. She had tried to get Augusta's attention, but he kept Christine close, and was over protective and a bit possessive of her. She became his girl and later his wife.

Spying John making his way to the house, she grabbed her jacket and ran out to meet him. She walked beside her brother-in-law, proud of her family, and proud that they lived off their land. Many of the years had been a struggle, and the depression and drought had been especially devastating for them.

There were times she had broken down and cried because of the never-ending winds and dust. Once she'd seen Gus standing by the corral, his hair and coat blown asunder, his fists raised at the sky, cursing the bloated gray clouds that refused to pen up and pour out their precious liquid.

With no market for their crops, they had still managed to stay self-sufficient. Augusta had planted potatoes and held back enough for seed the following spring. Their hogs brought only five cents a pound, so they used them for their own table and shared what they could with their neighbors. They'd gotten through the worst of it, and by God's grace they would continue to forge ahead.

John's voice broke into her thoughts as they struggled through the crisp, dead corn stalks on Martin land. "It's odd they didn't harvest the corn. Look at the fence lines." He pulled on the loose barbed wire. "This farm is one of the best in the county. Old man Martin kept it in top shape, too. Leon hasn't done a lick of work since the old man died. Well, I guess I should offer to lend a hand."

They had taken the short cut, across the fields and around the choke cherry patches. The corrals were just ahead. At first glance Christine couldn't believe what she was seeing. Gasping, she pointed ahead. "What's he doing?"

"What the hell?" John's voice exploded into the air. "Knock that off, Leon. Have you lost your mind?"

Leon jerked up and looked around, finally spotting John and Christine. He ran towards them. "Damn mare. She must be loco." Leon's voice crackled with excitement. "I've fixed her good. She'll never buck me off again."

Big John's face was livid. He snatched the whip from Leon's hand and raised it above his head. Christine yelled. "No! No, John, don't sink to his level. Oh, God."

John lowered the whip and began walking softly towards the mare, speaking to her with a gentle rumble. She lay on her side, both legs hobbled. Ropes were tied to the hobbles and John followed them with his eyes. He whistled sharply as he saw they were tied to the tractor. "The bastard! He must have pulled her legs out from under her and dragged her across the length of the corral, then put the strap to her." He wanted to plow into Leon and give him a good thrashing, but Christine was watching him. He managed to smile at her. He dug into his pocket and took out his knife to cut the ropes. As he removed the hobbles he continued talking softly to the mare. "Atta girl, Moonglow, do you remember me? I won't hurt you, girl, there now, there now." He knew she was done for, and so crazed he couldn't calm her down. The wild eyes, the foaming mouth, and the broken bones that kept the mare imprisoned on the ground, told him more about Leon than he wanted to know.

Leon stood back, his head pulled into his shoulders. He saw John make a sign for Christine to go to the house. They watched her walk away, and Leon breathed a sigh of relief. Everything was okay without that interfering woman. He went to meet John, eager to tell his side of the story. They stood eyeing each other for a moment. Leon grinned. He was still grinning when the big fist smashed into the middle of his face.

Kate opened the door and stared vacantly at Christine. The women stood silent, frozen in comical stances. Christine's hand was in the air as she was about to knock again. Kate's hand lay on her mouth ready to wipe off the frosting that had caught on it. Christine regained her poise and laughed. "Why, Kate, I … I'm surprised to see you. It's been years. We all thought you were in the city. I saw a woman in the yard a few times, but I didn't know it was you. I thought Leon had a girlfriend, or a housekeeper. How stupid of me."

Kate anxiously wondered if Leon knew Christine were here. Should she ask her in? "What … what can I do for you?"

"Oh, I've come to see Angie. She invited me."

"I don't know; I'll have to ask Leon."

"Leon knows I'm here. He's visiting with Big John at the corrals."

Relieved, Kate backed away from the door and invited her in.

Christine's head, still reeling from the shock of Leon's sadistic actions, made her way to a chair. She put her hand on it to steady herself. Stark terror pervaded her body, and she stood, motionless, waiting for it to pass. She wished she hadn't come.

She had a premonition of danger, a feeling so strong the fear squeezed her stomach into a tight knot. It was in Kate's bottomless eyes. Oh, God, what's happened to her? Those wide, violet eyes, so snappy and alive nine years ago, now devoid of any emotion. The eyes of a dead woman. She looked at Kate again, and the blood drained from her face. She placed her hand over her heart and gasped for breath. She senses, lurking in the depths of Kate's eyes, a pain so terrible she couldn't bear to look upon it.

"Angie must be anxious to see you. Come." They walked the length of the gloomy living room, into an equally dismal bedroom. Angie lay propped up on pillows, her emaciated body making a small lump in the huge bed.

Angie was overjoyed to see her old friend, and talked rapidly and continuously, giving Christine a chance to regain her composure. Finally, Angie turned to Kate and requested a tray of tea and cookies.

When they were alone, Angie grabbed Christine's hand and said urgently, "I don't know what's going to happen to me. I'm very ill. I'm worried about Mandy. Leon has offered us a home here with him and I wouldn't mind so much if you could keep an eye on her. She'll need a woman's advice as she grows older and you've seen Kate, poor thing, she'd be useless to Mandy."

"You're not seriously thinking of leaving her here, are you? With Leon?"

"He's changed, Christy, he treats me like a queen, and he's very fond of Mandy." Angie nodded her head. "I've been stuck upstairs all week. Leon was kind enough to move me down here and he visited with me last night. Yes, I remember how mean he was and all the nasty tricks he played on us, but he's grown up now. He inherited the farm, and wants to share his good fortune with Mandy and me."

Christine was dumbfounded. "What about Noah? Doesn't he want her?"

"I'm sure he does. I haven't told anyone this, but Noah left me, Christy. I came home because I was too ill to work and Mandy and I were down and out, but if he should come back, please, would you have room for him? Leon always hated him and I doubt if he'd let him stay here."

Christine's mind skittered about, searching for the right thing to say. "Now don't you worry. He's always welcome at our house. Try to get well, Angie. Have you seen our old friend, Norm Larson? He's the doctor in Ryan, now. I know he'll want to see you."

"Leon tried to get him to come out, but he said there wasn't anything he could do for me, and that he was going out of town. He wouldn't even fill my prescription."

Christine's brain clicked. Leon again. That fiend! "Do you have the empty bottle?"

Angie looked confused, so Christine reached over and opened the drawer on the bedside table; the bottle lay on its side in the back of the drawer. She quickly closed her fist around it and pullout out a handkerchief, as Kate came into the room with the tea tray.

Smiling at Kate, she said, "My that looks delicious," and began wiping the hanky over Angie's face. Her fingers trembled as they moved over the fragile bones and thin powder puff hair.

Why is it the people you think have so much potential, end up with so little? Angie, of all people, dying and in want, her man gone, and a child with no home. Angie had been such a beautiful girl, like a butterfly-small and quick, sassy and colorful.

You just expected someone like Angie to sail through life and live happily ever after. Yet, here I am, living a good life with the love of my wonderful family. Oh, Lord, get yourself together, girl, and get yourself home, before you go crazy too. She made her excuses and went to find Big John.

"I fell a hundred years old," Christine confessed to Augusta. They lay in bed, their long bodies touching, knee to knee, hip to hip. He hugged her closer. "Don't go back there. John told me about the mare. Broken ribs and a cracked leg. John had to shoot her. The man's dangerous. Promise me you'll stay away from them." She promised, to ease his worry, and they fell asleep, holding each other.

During breakfast the next morning, she told her family of her impending trip to town. "Is there anything I can pick up for you?"

"I've had a hankering for some of that good strawberry ice cream they make at the Carter Creamery." She smiled at Gus. He was a fool for that ice cream. He really needed a new winter coat, but they had decided to make do for another winter. After seeing how the Martins live, she felt incredibly blessed.

The Ford V8 started right up and she stepped on the gas, anxious to see Norm before he began his house calls.

Norm poured coffee into two cups and said bluntly, "What's troubling you Christy?"

"You know Angie is home? I visited her yesterday." He listened closely as she poured out all the facts and her fears.

He looked at the empty pill bottle. "She must be suffering terribly. I can drive out there, but Leon could keep me from seeing her."

"Something has got to be done. What about Mandy? If Angie dies, what will Leon do to that child? Norm, if you could see what's happened to Kate. She's a zombie. All these years, she's been cooped up there, with Burt and Leon. There's something evil in that family, and I think it's Leon." Christy was breathing hard, her emotions raw.

"It's best to stay out of it. You know folks around here mind their own business."

Something in Norm's voice caused Christy to look at him closely. "You know something about them, don't tell me no. I'm on to you. Out with it, Norm. The girls need our help."

Norm rubbed his jaw, thinking of the promise he'd make to his dad years ago. Then, shrugging, he said silently, "Sorry, Dad," and turned his attention back to Christy.

"Burt Martin came to see my dad when he was still practicing medicine. I was about twelve then and had gotten sick at school. I was resting in the patient's dressing room. I overheard Burt ask dad to declare Leon insane and put him in the asylum. Dad said he could do that only if Burt signed commitment papers. Burt refused to put his name on the papers. He stomped out of here and never came back." Norm paced up and down the small space of floor, and shuddered.

"When Mrs. Martin became ill he called another doctor. After I started to practice, he sent word to me to look in on Jude once, but of course he didn't know I'd overheard the conversation."

"He knew Leon was insane!" Christy clutched Norm's sleeve. "So, do something. You could get him committed?"

"Unless he goes completely berserk, my hands are tied. The only way to put him away is for Angie or Kate to sign commitment papers."

"But they won't do that. Angie thinks he's grown into a wonderful person and Kate is so afraid of him she would never dare to think of such a thing."

"There's another trail we might follow. I remember Rob mentioning that Burt was coming to town to make a will. He said he thought the old man was going to leave the farm to his granddaughter. I could ask Rob who the rightful heir to Burt's estate is."

"Oh, Norm, do you think that would do it? What would Leon be guilty of?"

"We might be able to get him arrested for fraud, or something." Norm picked up the empty bottle again and said thoughtfully, "I'll take some medicine to Angie, and if Leon is there and stops me from seeing her, I'll give it to you. Can you sneak it in if I fail?'

"You bet. I'd love to put one over on that … words fail me."

"Watch yourself around him, Christy. Revenge is sweet, but in this case, too risky."

"Dr. Norman Larson, you are a dear. I need to get home, but why don't you drop out Friday for supper. It's been awhile."

FOUR

Jude lurched across the room and set the gunnysack in a corner. He looked about for a piece of string to tie the top of the sack together. Finally, he settled for a frayed shoelace. All his packing was done. He wouldn't need much at the county farm.

A heavy sadness settled over Jude. He glanced around the two rooms that had been home to him for twenty-two years, and found he couldn't swallow past the lump in his throat. He'd been twelve years old when Burt found him in the back woods, weak from hunger, and exhaustion.

He regretted having to leave his books behind, the books he had educated himself with over the years. When Jude accepted the fact he could not change his deformed body, he'd decided to exercise his mind. To his great delight, he discovered his mind was sharp and soaked up knowledge like a sponge. The more he learned the more he wanted to know. He'd come to understand himself by reading the philosophy of the Masters, and had developed a good understanding of himself and his place in the world.

Marcia, his mother, had no use for him, but had done her duty as she saw it. The constant flow of men in her life had been an education in itself. Some of her friends tolerated him. Others ignored him. He put up with it until his twelfth birthday. That night she brought him a present, a new daddy. There was a mutual hate between them from the moment they laid eyes on each other.

"Hell Marcie, you told me he was sick, but shit, he's a damn cripple." Then he'd shouted at Jude, "Get me a drink, boy, and make it snappy." Jude hobbled to the kitchen and found some lemonade. He could hear the man hollering at his mother. "Hot damn, I can't stomach that kind of thing. I'm telling you, Marcie, either that cripple goes or I go."

His mother was crying and pleading with her new husband when Jude reluctantly returned to the room. The man took one look at the pink lemonade and knocked Jude backwards into the wall. The ensuing convulsion left him dazed and disoriented for hours. He grabbed some grub and a blanket and headed for the country. Even when he was starving, he couldn't make himself go back.

He made a promise to himself … to never let anyone treat him like that again, even if he died. And he had almost died. After four days without food, he'd decided to call it quits, and curled up under a cottonwood tree.

Jude remembered thick, short arms lifting him up and carrying him to a wagon. He'd been carefully stretched out across some hay bales, and driven to this house. He'd watched the man called Burt carry in armloads of wood, and build a fire. Burt left, and returned with towels, blankets, food and water. Burt had done all this without speaking, then he'd made up the bed, and put some stew on the stove. "Eat" he'd told Jude gruffly, "then sleep. I'll be back tomorrow."

Jude started working for Burt. He received thirty dollars a month, and his house and food. He felt lucky, though he knew Burt took advantage of his circumstances, he also gave him respect. Jude liked paying his own way and the two odd characters formed a friendship of sorts.

When Burt was killed, Jude had accepted the news stoically. It wasn't until Attorney Holden informed him he had inherited the house and five acres surrounding it that Jude broke down and sobbed. Burt had also left him fifty dollars a month, to be paid from the income of the farm, and his food. He was to continue working as usual.

It took him three months to realize Leon was trying to chase him off the farm. He didn't receive his pay, or any food. When he asked for his wages, Leon had screamed at him in a fit of rage. "Listen here, Crip, I didn't hire you, and I don't give you nothing. I'm thinking of movin' the new chicks in here coms spring. You'd do good to remember this is my place now. What I say goes, and I say you go."

"This house and these five acres are mine. You can fire me, but you can't kick me out."

"Maybe not, but I can make you wish you were somewhere else, you deformed lunatic."

Jude took his usual walk around his acreage that evening. The cottonwoods were beginning to lose their leaves and his right foot dragged some of the red and gold foliage along the path. He bent down and scooped up a handful of the heart shaped blades. He was at peace as he walked through the forest. The animals were his family. They were used to Jude, with his odd, lurching walk; his rich voice happily recited poetry as he hobbled along the well-worn path.

When he came to the grand dad of all the trees in the forest, he stopped and embraced it with his good arm. It was too large to reach around, so he pressed his twisted body against the trunk. Jude often spoke aloud to alleviate the loneliness of his days.

"Leon is out to get me, and I can't fight back. How I wish I had your strength, your endurance, and could see this through. So far it's been little things I was able to handle, but I can't take a chance on the farm being destroyed. He's poured tar over my winter wood, tipped my outhouse over, and last night he started a fire in the brush outside my house." He was silent, remembering the near disaster. Tippy's barking had warned him something was amiss, or the whole place could have burned down.

"I'm finally convinced Leon is plumb craze; I have to leave to save Burt's farm." He patted the tree and tuned out his anxious thoughts to listen to the sounds wafting through the air.

A blue jay scolding a small flock of sparrows, hundreds of crickets filling the area with their special brand of music, soft breezes chasing each other in and out of the tree limbs. Jude was thrilled to hear a meadowlark burst into song: "baby needs new sho-es, baby needs new sho-es". He smiled and walked home, to prepare his last meal in the house that he had called home for so long.

Burt had kept him apart from the family, so he didn't really know Leon. What he did know was from observing him, and what Burt had told him. A conversation between him and Burt suddenly came to mind. They had been working side by side in the corn field, when Burt said, "I half ta go ta Ryan tomorrow, you work da corn alone?" Jude nodded. They continued to pull the ears of ripe corn from the stalks. When they reached the end of the rows, June had been surprised to hear Burt blurt out, his Swedish accent enhanced by his anxiety.

"I'm going ta make me a vill. Haff ta see a new lawyer, da one from back east."

"Are you feeling okay, Burt?"

"Yeah, yust vorried. Leon, he's a bad 'un. I make sartain he cannot haff dis place ven I die." He glanced at Jude and there was fear in his face. "I tink he vants ta kill me."

Jude nodded his understanding. Nothing was out of bounds for Leon.

"I tink I leaf my place to Angie's girl. Angie's man, he not vot I vanted for her, but it is done. I tink dey'll do good. So he iss Indian. What am I? I come from da old country."

As Jude sat on his porch that evening, his thoughts returned to Burt. He wondered what sort of life he had lived as a boy. Burt had mentioned once that he had come to America from Sweden as a child. He talked about Ellis Island and said he knew his first sight of New Youk was a magical moment. He had waved his hands at his neat lush crops, silently telling Jude he received the same satisfaction gazing and working at his accomplishments. Jude recalled a book about Swedish immigrants. Many of their children were farmed out to work for their bed and food. The youngsters worked from dawn to dusk, receiving meager diets and harsh treatment. Many died during the bitter winter months. Only the strongest survived. Burt certainly could have been one of those boys.

Jude knew that he had to do something to stop Leon. Because of Burt Martin he had a home and plenty to eat. Now everything he and Burt had slaved for was in danger of being destroyed. He sat quietly for a few moments, running different solutions through his mind. Then his eyes brightened and he said aloud. "I'll ask Norm Larson what to do. Someone needs to know that Burt suspected Leon would kill him."

He'd spoken aloud, as he often did, so he didn't hear the light rustling in the trees beside the house.

He was struggling to lift himself out of the rocking chair, when he became aware of cold metal pressing against his right ear. He moved his eyes to the side and saw the barrel of a pistol. Leon was standing behind him, grinning, his finger on the trigger. Jude twisted around to better see his tormenter.

The evil on Leon's face hit Jude like a hot blast from a furnace. His mind lurched and a swirling mass of colors spun furiously around his head. Jude saw the hate busting out of him from the pores in Leon's body. An aura formed around Leon, ugly dark grays jabbed with slashes of red; the slit of a mouth opened and spit poured out the sides. The slit said, "You're gonna get it now, Crip." Leon pulled the trigger and Jude sank into swirling depths of confusion and blindness. His afflicted body, at the mercy of his dread disease, thrashed violently on the porch floor.

Leon watched Jude's quivering body with avid interest. He jumped up and down screaming. "Don't mess with me, freak. You're on dangerous waters when you mess with Leon Martin." Leon knew he had a shit eating grin on his face, but it felt so good to get revenge on ol' Crip. And there was more to come, too. He wouldn't stop until he'd driven Jude off the farm.

He headed for home, Jude forgotten. Maybe he would get the truck and go to town again tonight. The urge to feel another little girl made him tremble. The last night had been so scared she'd peed her pants. He licked his lips as pictures of all the girls wafted through his mind. They were so soft and trusting and his for the taking,

Jude tried to pull himself up, but his legs wouldn't obey him. Scooting closer to the porch rail he grabbed it, trying to lift himself. He attempted to put his good leg under him for leverage, but couldn't seem to move that leg either. Gingerly, he put his hand on his thigh and pinched it, hard, but there was no feeling. He hit himself and didn't feel the punch. Frightened, he lay back and took stock of his body. He tasted blood and realized he'd bitten his tongue. There were slivers sticking in his shirt, pricking his skin. His nose hurt, and he massaged it lightly. "I must have hit the floor hard; can't believe that I lived through that one." He wanted to add "it might be better I hadn't," but he refused to let the subtle whispers in his mind surface.

The evening had turned chilly. He scooted across the porch, anxious to get into the warmth of his home. Opening the door, he noticed the fire was still burning and there was plenty of wood to last through the night. He lit the kerosene lamp, grateful for the reassuring glow it cast around the little room, with his last bit of strength he managed to pull the mattress onto the floor and roll onto it. Watching the flames cast their magic around the room, his thoughts were of loving families, and he pictured himself as a normal boy, sitting before the fire with a Mom and Dad. His mom was sewing, and her beautiful face smiled at him. His father was cleaning his rifle, and sharing hunting talks with Jude. Thus, he lulled himself to sleep, his acid tears on his leathery cheeks.

He awoke at the first crow of the rooster, and groaned. His head ached, there was a shooting pain in his right shoulder, and his tongue was swollen. "So you're a mess, what's new?" He answered himself. "I'll tell you what's new. I can't walk, and I've got to piss." He spied the wash dish, but grimaced, and shook his head. He rolled onto his stomach and pulled himself to the front door. He dragged himself through it, and on to the end of the porch. Damn buttons! He left the overalls open when he finished; he'd have to change clothes somehow. And eat. For the first time in years he felt vulnerable and helpless, and frightened. Would Leon come back? Whatever it took, he knew he had to get out. He wished Burt were here.

Mandy ran along the narrow path, as silent and swift as the Indian brave in her Daddy's book. He had an eagle for a friend, she thought, but I have Tippy, and she smiled at the collie who ran beside her. The path wound around behind the corrals, and Mandy became a pinto pony, her black mane blowing behind her. She shook her head and neighed, making pawing motions on the sod. Using a dried-up corn stalk for a whip, she hit at her legs and whooped, all the while running, intent on her errand.

There was the main road ahead, and there was the Clayton house in the distance.

They'd invited her to spend a few hours with them. It was wonderful to get away from the Martins. Mama spent all her time in bed, and Uncle Leon frightened her, he looked at her funny sometimes it made her stomach hurt. Aunt Kate was nice, but she was so busy running after Mama and Uncle Leon, she hadn't any time for her.

Suddenly aware of Tippy's whining, she watched as he ran ahead, making yipping noises. When Mandy reached him, he was licking Jude's face. The sight of Jude lying in the middle of the lane didn't faze Mandy. Life was full of changes and unexpected happenings. She immediately fell upon her knees and inspected Jude closely.

"I think you better get up, mister."

"I … can't, my legs. I can't walk. I'm trying to get to the road and catch a ride to town." Jude wasn't used to children, and didn't know how much she would understand. He felt half-dead, his head and chest a mass of pain. It had taken hours to get this far, and he'd been about to give it up and crawl under a bush and rest there while he tried to figure out a way to help himself. He rolled onto his back, willing his heartbeat to slow down. When he looked at Mandy he saw she was studying him intently.

"I'm going to the Clayton's to play with June. I'll get you some help."

Jude nodded. Dizzy from exhaustion and fear, he was relieved to turn his life over to someone else, even a little girl.

"Thank you. Are you Angie's girl?" He winced at the harsh tone of his voice.

"Yes. I'm seven. My name is Mandy. Well, my real name is Amanda, but people mostly call me Mandy." She turned to Tippy and ordered, "You stay here, and take good care of the man."

Augusta parked the Ford alongside the road and walked over to where Jude lay. Poor sucker, life sure handed some folks a bum deal. He tried to look nonchalant as he bent over to pick Jude up. "I'm taking you to see the Doctor." Augusta carried him to the car and had him "all stuffed and ready for the oven," he cheerfully told him, while wrapping a blanket around Jude and arranging him as comfortably as possible in the back seat.

Augusta had seen Jude from time to time, working in the fields, but they'd never spoken. Burt wasn't neighborly, and folks had learned to leave him alone. The neighbors talked some about Jude's lameness, and some used him to scare their kids into behaving. As the years passed, they just forgot about him most of the time. Gus was trying to figure out what to say to him, when Jude asked. "The little girl, Mandy, will she get home safely?" His voice was still harsh from the dust he'd eaten.

"She's staying with us for a while. My wife will take good care of her." He was surprised by the question, and his heart warmed towards Jude. He liked a man that showed concern for the little ones. "I'm taking you to see Dr. Larson, that okay with you?"

"That's fine, I know the man. Burt had him over to see me once when I had pneumonia."

Jude was in a state of euphoria. He transcended the pain, wanting to experience fully all the new and wonderful things that were happening to him. This was his first ride in a motorcar, he'd received his first smile from a child, and he was passing the time of day with a neighbor. He drew upon the books he'd read and tried to present himself as a gentleman, a learned gentleman. He wished he could take a pipe out of his vest-pocket and light up. He smiled, hurting his face. There was no vest hanging in his closet, but if the day continued like the last hour, shoot, he might go home and find a whole new suit.

FIVE

D r. Norman Larson drove in grim silence. Finally, about to burst with anger, he spoke aloud. "I can't remember when I've been so damned mad! I'd like to wipe Leon Martin off the face of the earth."

After tending to Jude's bruised, he'd closed the office, called Nellie's Eatery and had sandwiches and coffee delivered. In all his years of practicing medicine, he'd never had a case as bizarre as this one. He'd left Betsey to help feed Jude while he went to the office and called the sheriff, and then went back to the emergency room to tell Jude the bad news.

"You're lucky Leon shot wild. Do you think he was trying to kill you?"

"I don't believe so. He gets a big kick out of tormenting me."

"Your cuts and bruises will heal, but I don't expect you'll ever walk again."

"Well, Doctor, it wasn't something I did very well, anyway."

"My God, man, after what you've been through, you can sit here and joke about it? You're a better man than I am."

"Gunga Din." Jude smiled, waiting to see if the doctor caught on.

"You've read Kipling?" Norm was pleasantly surprised.

"I've read everything I could see, even labels on gunny sacks. Burt brought me books. I've had a lot of time to read. Books are my best friends, and I can't imagine what my life would be without them." Jude was sitting in a wheelchair. Norm's nurse, Betsey, had taken a light blanket and draped it over and around him, leaving only his head, neck, and good right arm exposed. Norm was stunned at the difference it made in the man. He hadn't realized what a good-looking man Jude was. He searched around in his head for an apt word to describe him. Aristocratic? Yes, and sensitive. Also, a bit sensuous with the long, full lips and black brows and lashes. One never really saw Jude, only his deformities. Norm was ashamed of himself. He admitted silently he would never have seen beyond the physical façade to the intelligent human sitting before him if it weren't for the blanket and an astute nurse.

Jude broke the silence. "I told you I was packed to move to the County Farm. Is there someone who could give me a ride?"

"I can't let you go out there. It would interfere with your treatment. I'll find someplace for you to stay, in fact, Betsey's scouting around right now."

The phone interrupted them, and as Norm reached to pick up the receiver, he said to Jude, "I want you to wheel yourself into the hall and look at yourself in the mirror." Jude looked at him incredulously. "Go on, go on. Dr.'s orders." He turned his back on Jude and answered the phone.

During his conversation with Burt's attorney, Norm managed to drop all the facts and bits and pieces of information he had gleaned from Christine and Jude. Rob hadn't heard of Angie's illness, or that she'd returned home. He also wasn't aware that Leon was claiming to be the heir. "Burt willed his entire estate to Amanda Senecah, Angie's daughter," Rob informed Norm. "Leon isn't mentioned in the will."

That evening Sheriff Henson and Attorney Rob Holden met with Norm and they laid out a plan to put Leon Martin away for good.

So here he was, driving out to the Martin farm, with the distasteful job of telling Angie and Kate. It was asking a lot of them, but he hoped they would agree to help snare Leon. If the girls wouldn't sign the commitment papers then the men would have to resort to trickery. As things stood now, they didn't have enough proof to get him arrested. The three friends had already decided Leon Martin would be behind bars before nightfall. Whether it was prison bars or the State Asylum they didn't know yet, they only knew he had to be stopped. The children of Ryan would live in a safe world again, and Angie, Kate and Jude could live a normal life.

As he turned into the drive, he psyched himself up to play the country doctor. He intended to give Angie a check-up anyway, but it was also an excuse to look around and sort of feel things out. God, he hoped luck was with him, and he could get into the house before he ran into Leon.

Kate heard the car door slam and looked out the window. Thank goodness Mandy had come home to see Angie. Kate called her and asked her to answer the door. "Tell him we're not home," she instructed Mandy. "Don't let him in or Uncle Leon will be mad at you." She hurried up the stairs to hide.

Norm took one look at Mandy and fell in love with her. "Hello there. You must be Mandy. How are you?" He shook her hand playfully. "I've come to see your mother. Would you take me to her?"

"You can't come in. I'm not supposed to let anyone in the house."

"I'm here to help your mother, Mandy. I hear she is ill and I'm a doctor. Don't you think it would be a good idea for me to give her a check-up? You can help me if you'd like to."

"Mama doesn't feel good, she's been in bed ever since we got here. I'd sure like to see Mama get out of that bed."

"Lead the way, boss." Mandy led him across the living room and into a dark hallway. "I better tell Mama you're here." She opened the door and Angie saw Norm standing behind Mandy.

"Oh, Norm, I've prayed you'd find time to see me. I was starting to give up on you."

"I came as soon as I could leave the office. I thought you'd forgotten your old friends." He walked to the bed and took her hands in his, continuing to chat cozily with her while his eyes took in the visible signs of her degenerative condition: Cyanotic; rapid respiration. He watched the pulse point in her neck beating furiously. There was a fine coating of perspiration on her skin. "I need to examine you. Mandy, will you run to the car and get my medical bag out of the back seat?"

He turned to Angie when they were alone, and said seriously, "Why haven't you gotten treatment? Do you want to die and leave that lovely daughter of yours alone?"

"But, I have sent messages to you, every time I knew Leon was going to town. He said you were busy the first time, and just last week he stopped by to see you and they told him you were on an extended vacation."

"We need to talk about Leon. After I examine you though."

Angie, her face white and strained, stared at Norm. "I believe you. I really thought he had grown up. I believed he was sincerely glad to have me home. He's ruined Pa's farm, but worse, Norm, you should see Kate. She'd been cooped up here for years, and she's terrified. It all fits now. I've been trying to figure out what was going on here. And Jude, I'd forgotten all about him. When can I see the attorney? I'll make sure Jude gets his money, and of course he can stay in his own home. To think Pa left his estate to Mandy! It … it's hard to believe."

"You must be careful," he admonished her. "You and Mandy could be in danger if he even thinks you knew the terms of the will. Did I tell you Burt excluded him completely? Yes. He willed Mandy the entire estate, with you and Noah as her guardians. Noah is to run the farm, and Kate is to be taken care of however, you choose. Rob Holden is the administrator."

"Do we dare bring Kate into this? She's so frightened of Leon, I'm afraid she might let something slip. Kate doesn't seem to grasp things; she's very vague. But this thing about molesting the girls, Norm, you're wrong about that. We're a respectable family." She reached a shaky hand towards him. "Please, you mustn't let this get around. It couldn't have been Leon, he's just not like that. The girls must be lying."

Norm was stunned. Talk about Kate not grasping things! I guess some people never change. Angie's the same silly, self-centered snob she was at sixteen.

SIX

Leon ran through the forest, dodging between the trunks of the cottonwood trees. Stretching into a lope he headed towards Jude's place. Jude was history and about time, too. What had Pa wanted that ugly cripple around for anyway? "When I'm done with him he'll rot in jail."

Leon slowed to a walk and crept close to the shack. Looking around for Jude and seeing nothing, he commenced digging in the soft dirt by the back corner. "Ah, that should do it. I can just see ol' Crip's face when they show him what he's got buried here."

He reached inside of his shirt and pulled out a small sugar sack. Shivers rippled through his body as he thought of the little girls these items had belonged to. The one today had been especially sweet. She'd struggled at first when he'd pulled her shirt off. He'd needed the shirt. It had her name embroidered on it and that's what would trap Jude. After she'd gone limp from fear he'd pretended to let her go, and then tripped her. Rubbing himself against her rear-end, he'd whispered in her ear, "Tell them Jude hurt you." Before he disappeared into the thicket of trees, he'd pinched her hard on her inner thigh until she'd screamed shrilly. This was one assault he wanted reported.

Quickly, he wrapped the shirt around the sack and buried it. A few leaves over the top and Jude would never notice. Where was the Crip anyway? "I must have scared the hell out of him last night when I shot that pistol. Bet he's hiding from me. Yesserie, everything's going like clockwork. I'm a genius, just like Ma said."

He slipped out of the yard quietly and headed home. A smile remained on his face until he saw a car coming towards him. It was Doc Larson. Shit, what was he doing here? Norm stopped the car and Leon sidled to the window Norm opened.

"Hello, Doc. What brings you to this neck of the woods?"

"I heard Angie was home, decided to pay her a visit, for old time's sake. You should have let me know she was at death's door." Norm saw the pleased look that flitted across Leon's face. Just for a second, but I saw it, Norm thought grimly.

"I've been wanting to get you out here to see her, but Angie wouldn't have it." Leon could see Doc was all broke up over Angie's condition. He said sorrowfully, "Maybe she's just pinin' for Noah. Maybe she'll take a turn for the better." He peered at Norm, trying to look hopeful.

"Sorry, but your sister is dying. I've changed things at the house a bit. I do hope it won't inconvenience you. I've asked Kate to move into the room with Angie, and Mandy is going to Christine's. Angie needs around the clock care and good nourishing food. I'll see if I can round up a cook when I get to town."

Damn, the Doc sure took charge ... well, he'd go along with it, wouldn't be for too long, the way he talked.

"I'm obliged. Nothing's too good for my sister. Feel free to give her what you think she needs." The two men shook hands.

Spasms of delight passed through Leon's body. God, he felt good. Angie dying. Things are going his way, finally. With Jude in jail and Angie in the grave, he'd have all Pa's money. These uppity-up neighbors would look at him different then. They'd see he amounted to something. He could see them now, bowing and scraping for his attention.

After Pa's funeral folks paid him a lot of attention and he'd liked that. Some of his neighbors had come to visit, but then they'd forgotten him again. Max Gordon had come to the farm to offer him a hand; Leon grinned as he remembered the joke he'd told him. Max had gotten all red in the face and turned on him. "You're the most twisted son-of-a-bitch in Carey County," he hollered at Leon. "Stay away from me and mine."

Leon spent the next week spying on the Gordon farm. He'd watched their comings and goings and noticed that Essie, their youngest girl, always got to the mailbox at 4:15pm. She took the shortcut home, crossing over a small section of the Martin sheep pasture. Leon hid behind a pile of rocks, and when she walked by he'd caught her from behind and thrown her down on her belly. She hadn't even seen him.

He stroked his crotch and grinned. "I was as frisky as the best bull in Pa's pasture." He'd finally managed to do the things the boys at school had snickered over, the thing Pa had done to Kate. It was good, he admitted, except he didn't like the ending. After the good feelings, he lost his strength. It left him weak as a woman, and made him feel soft in the stomach. He'd stumbled around like a bumblehead all that evening.

Soon he'd have control of Mandy. Angie had to sign those papers and he'd better get home and start working on her. Kate was worthless these days. He might give her a good lickin' tonight. Show her who was boss around here.

Upon reaching the house, he went immediately to Pa's study, and rummaged through the desk drawer, looking for the papers that would give him legal custody of Mandy. They just needed Angie's signature. He brushed his hands over his pants and shirt, smoothed his hair and put on his loving brother look. Jauntily he stepped down the hall to visit the soon to be late Angela Marie Martin Senecah.

The sisters were playing checkers. At his knock, they hid the game under the bed, and Angie slipped under the covers. "Remember, your half-dead," Kate quipped, as she answered the door.

Leon went to the bed and kissed Angie's cheek. "How's our big Sis today?" Angie groaned, and Leon turned to Kate. "Get lost. I need to talk to Angie."

"I … I'm not supposed to leave her alone. Dr. Larson says it's imperative I stay in the room with her."

"What did I tell you about usin' them big words? Imperative. Humph." He turned to Angie, "She thinks she's a big shot."

"Please, Leon, I want Kate to stay. I don't feel so scared when she's with me."

Kate flinched under the murderous look Leon threw at her. She sat in the chair in the corner. "I'll be right here. You and Leon have your visit."

"Did you go to town today, Leon?" Angie's voice was a whisper.

"Yeah, not too much goin' on, lots of talk about that molester." At Angie's questioning look he said, "You don't know about that? Well, someone's going around town scarin' little girls. I think the sheriff is gettin' too old for his job. Or maybe this guy is just smarter than the law." It made him feel good to say that so he repeated it. "Yeah, I'll just bet this guy is smarter than our good sheriff." He looked around, "Where's our girlie Mandy?"

"At Christy's, till I feel better. I hope you don't mind. Kate told me how much you like her," Angie lied.

"Fine, fine. I told Doc Larson, anything for my pretty sister. That reminds me, I have some papers for you to sign." He shoved them in her face.

Angie's heart dropped when she saw the papers Leon held in front of her. Guardianship papers? If she didn't sign he might become suspicious. She'd have to stall and hope fate would step in and stop this. "Why should I turn my daughter over to anyone, Leon?"

Leon was dumbfounded. Doc Larson hadn't told her she was dying. He hadn't thought of that. He scrambled around in his brain and said weakly, "Oh, just trying to make things easier on you. Don't want to wearin' yourself out worryin'."

"I'm so tired, leave the papers and I'll read them later." She forced herself to take his hand and squeeze it. "Thank you for being so thoughtful."

"Kate, you help Angie get those papers signed." He laid the papers on the table and left the room. A few minutes later he jerked the door open and looked in. Both girls were as they had been. Satisfied, he decided Angie really was tired, after all she'd had a medical examination a few hours ago. He'd see her first thing in the morning.

Leon went to Pa's study and slouched in the worn chair, then straightened up and put his feet on the desk. He picked up Pa's pipe and a can of Prince Albert and fixed himself a smoke. Feeling fidgety he danced around the desk and across the room until he stood in front of the picture of his parents.

He studied them a few moments, noticing for the first time the remarkable resemblance between them; both short and stout, with long grim faces; heavy brows over long narrow eyes. Where had he gotten his height? He looked like both of them. He must be a throwback to some tall relative.

"Ma, Pa, how ja' do?" He made an exaggerated bow, then stood up and stared at them. "Ma, I miss you sometimes. I depended on you to help me out of my troubles. You did a good job until you went and got sick on me and spent so much time in bed. Just left me on my own, and I hated you for that. Always coughing and asking for favors. It made me nervous, Ma, and one night I just kind of sleep walked into your room and held a pillow over your face." He moved his eyes to the left of the picture, narrowing them at the man who stood so sedately beside Ma.

"Well, Pa, it's a darn nice life I have now, without you. The best thing I ever did in my life was to fix your brakes. No more razor straps, Pa. No more boxed ears. You can't hate me now, Pa. You're dead, but you had looked ahead, hadn't you, Pa? You didn't leave your worldly goods to your only son. For shame!" He pulled the picture from the wall and held it close to his face and stared into Pa's eyes. "Did you really think I'd let you get away with it? Of course, you did. Dumb, goofy Leon! How wrong can a man be? I'm taking this place, Pa, every last acre, including Jude's. Nothing for Angie, nothing for Jude, and Mandy will be mine. You had Kate. I'll have Mandy. Like father, like son."

He dug into his pocket and took out his knife. With a flick of his wrist the blade snapped open. He could feel the meanness creep into his mind, and he put the picture to his lips and kissed Pa, then stabbed him in both eyes and cut across his throat. "A fitting end for a man that wasn't fit to have a son." He placed the photo in the stove and watched it burn. Weakness washed through him and he sank to the floor. He laughed, exulting in his power. He tasted his tears before he knew he was crying. Crying for Pa.

"You back so soon, Doc?" Leon's displeasure was evident. He didn't like people coming around, snooping. Things weren't going his way today. Angie hadn't signed the guardianship papers, Kate wouldn't leave Angie so he could talk to her, and the new cook had practically thrown him out of his own kitchen.

"I came out to see you, Leon." Norm put a confiding ring in his words. "You see, there's new evidence on these child assaults and it points to your farm."

"What do you mean? What kind of evidence?"

"A seven-year-old girl was assaulted in Ryan. She named Jude as the assailant."

"Jude, huh? Well, that don't surprise me. You know Pa wouldn't let him around my sisters. Say, I saw Jude yesterday afternoon. Late, it was, about 4 o'clock. He was burying something beside his house. Maybe we should go have a look."

Norm watched Leon closely. He saw the avid eagerness, the trembling hands and loose legs. He shivered. The chilly October air that he'd always loved, not seemed unfriendly and sinister. He breathed deep, and said, "Get in, why don't you? We can talk here in the car. It's warmer." Pretending to like Leon was one of the hardest things he'd ever had to do. He hoped to God he could pull this off.

"Due to the nature of the assaults, yes, there's been more than one, Sheriff Henson asked me to get the women off the farm." At Leon's negative gesture, he quickly added, "He has reason to believe there could be danger to them, you know, shooting, or Jude might try to use them to escape. He insists everyone leave, except you, of course. He could use your help. If you don't mind, that is."

He watched the emotions play across Leon's face. First the negative power play, then the paranoia. Finally, the excitement and what he'd hoped for, self-importance.

"I'll be glad to help out. When will the Sheriff be here? What does he want me to do?"

"The first thing is to get the women into the car. I'll take them to town. The Sheriff is parked out by the cattle guard, waiting for me to give him the all-clear signal. Then he and his deputy will drive here to your place. You're to stay away from Jude's place until they get here. Jude could be dangerous, and we don't want you getting hurt." That should do the trick, Norm thought, flattery was a powerful tool with a man like Leon.

It took Leon ten minutes to get the sisters out of the house and into the car. "No sooner said them done." He looked at Doc to see if he was impressed. Norm nodded his head and said, "Good job. Couldn't ask for better. Oh, you'd better send the cook away, too." He patted Leon on the shoulder. Now to get himself and the women away. "We'll be going along, then. You be careful and don't go near Jude."

Leon nodded and sat on the porch steps to wait for Sheriff Henson.

Norm didn't begin to relax until they were off the Martin place and on the main road to town. It had taken a lot of luck to pull this off. When the report came into the Sheriff's office on the child assault case, the three men knew they couldn't wait any longer. Too many kids were getting hurt. Norm was thankful that Jude was in Augusta's car at the time of the assault. He would have had no alibi and the girl had named him.

Angie rode in the back seat with her legs stretched out on the cushions. Kate had propped pillows around her and Angie was comfortable and happy to be going somewhere. She asked Norm, "However did you manage to talk Leon into letting us go with you?"

"Personalities like your brother's thrive on flattery. He actually thinks this is his idea. He's hated Jude for years, and since he believes himself to be the undisputed ruler of his universe, he feels as if he brought Jude's downfall to fruition."

"But, Norm, why would Leon hate Jude so? He's never been anything but Pa's hired hand."

Norm remained quiet for a minute. He wasn't' sure if the girls were ready to hear the truth about their brother. Finally, he said, "Leon is jealous of Jude. Burt liked Jude, and worked by his side. He talked with him and treated him like a friend. Leon can't handle that. He needs to be number one or he loses his sense of power. People like Leon must be first in everything, and their greatest motivation comes when they're fighting to win. Since they have no moral center, anything goes. There's no compassion or empathy for anyone, so whatever they have to do seems right to them."

"You keep saying 'they'. You're really talking about Leon in a roundabout-way aren't you?" Angie's voice was angry and sharp

"Leon is a very sick man, Angie. He needs to be committed. You girls may have to sign papers to that effect."

"Won't they put him in prison for his crimes?" Kate's fear of her brother was evident in the trembling of her voice.

"There's no proof of his crimes. The evidence was found on Jude's property, and although we know Leon lied about Jude. We can't prove that Leon planted the evidence himself. He told everyone he inherited the farm, but he didn't sell it, or take anything off of it. Though he tried to con you, it didn't work. No crime there. Just talk. If he had anything to do with your parents' deaths, well, he'd have to confess to that."

He saw Kate shrink into herself as he talked; she was fearful that Leon couldn't be charged. Well, she had plenty of reasons to be, living out there with him all these years. He wanted to reassure he, but had promised not to tell the girls they were setting Leon up. If it worked, they'd know soon enough. Kate was leaning against the window, watching the countryside, and he realized she was angry, and extremely vulnerable. He glanced back at Angie and a sigh of relief escaped him as he saw she had her eyes closed and appeared to be resting.

The difference in the sisters was extreme. Both wore shabby clothes, but Angie's fit her slender form perfectly, while Kate seemed to have poured herself into a garment with no style. Norm realized all of a sudden that the dress Kate wore wasn't hers. It was too short and made for an older woman. Her shoes were cracked and awkward looking. Had Leon denied her life's necessities? The poor girl had suffered under Leon's hand, that was clear. Yet, she seemed to have more class than her haughty sister. There was dignity in the way she held her head. Kate turned and met his eyes at that moment and Norm's heart skidded around leaving him with sweet feeling and new longings.

Norm sighed with relief when he pulled into Betsey's driveway. "You'll be staying here. Betsey has your rooms ready. Try not to worry, and Angie, you get to bed." Angie acknowledged his orders with a nod of her head. Kate remained quiet and Norm smiled gently to assure her. "Leon won't find you here. Enjoy yourself as much as possible. We'll see you this evening."

Kate and Betsey helped Angie into bed. She curled up in the comfortable four-poster bed and was soon asleep, a smile of contentment on her lips. Kate watched her sleeping sister, struck anew by her daintiness and beauty. Angie appeared so fragile, almost ethereal. She kissed her cheek and went to find her room, wishing she had a nice dress to wear.

Kate was taken aback when she entered the room Betsey had given her. She walked tiptoe over the cream carpet and smoothed her hands over the Cherrywood furniture. Someday, I'll live like this, she vowed. The large canopied bed beckoned to her invitingly. She reached down and lightly touched the soft yellow and green sprigged spread and curtains surrounding the bed. How wonderful! So soft, so beautiful. The colors of daffodils, sunshine, grass, and trees.

She sat down on the silken settee gingerly, as if it might break and thought of the car ride and the feelings she'd experiences when she realized she was free from the farm.

She'd drank in all she could see, the cozy little homes, the scattered farms, and so much land and sky. She hadn't been off the farm since Pa took her out of school. The experience was heady, but not as frightening as it seemed when she only dreamed about leaving. No, there had to be good things in this larger world. She wouldn't go back, she decided. Maybe she could get a job. There must be some way she could forge a life for herself, but in the back of her mind, there awaited Angie, Mandy, Tippy, and the livestock.

She began to feel restless, used to working all day, and paced around the room. It was nice to be alone, but she needed something to do. Ah! A bath and in a real bathroom. She ran the water and began to undress, ignoring the long mirror that hung on the door. The mirror was a magnet, and unable to resist, she lowered her naked body onto the edge of the bathtub and slowly raised her eyes. She peeped at the glass and gasped. A deep flush spread over her body, and she continued to stare at her over-ripe form. She put her hands under her breasts and lifted them high. Dropping them, she sucked in her stomach. Her face burned from embarrassment. Guilt washed over her when Ma's admonitions popped into her mind. *Keep yourself covered. Don't look, just wash. Nice girls don't touch themselves there.*

She'd denied her body since Pa had come to her room, and never looked at herself. If Angie hadn't come home, with all her vanities, if Kate hadn't bathed her sister and slathered lotions on her skin, she would never have been curious enough to risk looking at herself.

Angie repeatedly told her how beautiful she was, not that she'd really believed her, but it had started a kind of excitement within her, and hope. Now her curiosity was at its peak and she stood up, turned around and inspected herself critically. Well, she was no Angie, that was for sure, but her body didn't look as fat and unshapely as it felt. "It's Ma's clothes," she said to her image. "They're tight and uncomfortable." How would she look in a dress that fit her? Would she be pretty? She lifted her eyes to her face.

Wide violet eyes stared back at her. They were fringed with long black lashes and topped with curved black brows. Her honey colored skin was smooth and fine pored. Thick black hair hung to her waist. There'd been no time to comb it this morning. "I wish I had a nose like Angie or Leon." Their noses were narrow and straight. Hers was wider and turned up at the end. She traced around her full, wide mouth, suddenly thoughtful.

There was no resemblance to anyone that she could see. Except the dimple in her chin was like Ma's. She couldn't do anything about her body right now, but she could wash her hair and look presentable and clean. Quickly, she stepped into the tub, resolving to enjoy all these grand things around her while she could.

When her hair was dry, she snuggled into the soft, fresh sheets, reveling in the warmth and richness of the downy blankets and the feminine spread. For all the Martin money, her folks had been miserly. They'd bought serviceable items, nothing pretty or even comfortable. She stroked the soft fuzz on the blanket and fell asleep, still unable to believe the changes her life had taken.

"Don't worry so, Angie, you'll be able to manage the farm. At least 'til Noah gets here." Kate was weary, tired of reassuring Angie, weary of her complaints.

"Kate is right," Betsey said, "and Rob Holden will give you good advice."

"I hope he can answer my questions. For instance, where did Pa get all that money? It certainly didn't come from farming. Where was his money during those darkest days when the banks failed?"

"I can't answer you." Betsey shook her head and stood up. "We'd better get dressed, everyone will be here soon."

"Who are you expecting?" Kate was nervous and didn't want to see anyone.

"Oh, just Norm, Attorney Holden and Sheriff Henson. Maybe Gus."

"I think I'll stay in my room. I'm not used to all this visiting and it gets on my nerves."

Surprise showed on Angie's face. She'd never known Kate to go against anyone's plans. "You need to be here, Holden is bringing the will, and they'll have news of Leon. Poor Leon," she added. "I hope he's bring treated well." The sisters climbed the stairs and went into their separate rooms. Kate couldn't understand Angie's worry over Leon. She hoped to never see him again, and she didn't care what they did to him.

Only since this visit had she realized how deprived her life had been. Visiting with Betsey and Angie had been a traumatic experience. She'd been tongue tied, and ignorant. She was missing large pieces of information, general things that anyone who'd lived here would know.

The scary part of all of this is that I spent eight years in isolation, and didn't fight for myself. Why did Pa and Leon keep me hidden away? Her mind answered her; they were afraid you'd tell. You had to pay for their evil.

After combing her hair and smoothing her dress, Kate descended the curved staircase. She was afraid. Afraid of making a fool of herself, of embarrassing Angie. And most of all afraid they would look at her and see her as Pa and Leon had seen her.

"I thought we'd be more comfortable here, grouped around the table." Betsey led them into the dining room. Kate dropped into the first available chair. She felt better at once, knowing the table covered most of her body. Norm sat across from her, Angie on his right; Gus took the chair next to Angie. Betsey sat at the foot of the table and Rob at the head. Sheriff Henson plopped on a chair next to Rob. "Is everyone here?" They all looked at the empty chair. "I invited Jude. He might be here soon, but let's get on with it." Norm grinned at them. "The tension's so thick I could cut it with a knife. We're all friends here, just trying to iron out a few wrinkles." Betsey bit her bottom lip, that Norm and his cliché's.

Rob spoke first. "I have copies of your father's will with me." He handed them across to Kate and Angie. "Come in to my office tomorrow and I'll go through the finer points with you."

"Thanks, but what about Leon? Where is he? That's what this get together is all about isn't it?" Angie tossed her head, holding Rob's gaze with her own.

"That's another story. I'll let the Sheriff tell you about Leon." The group turned their heads to listen to Sheriff Henson. Red suffused his face as he began speaking.

"I don't know where to start. Right at the beginning, I guess. After Norm drove off with you women, my deputy and I went on up to the house. Leon was waiting for us, as nice as you please. We talked for a bit and then he took us to Jude's place. He pointed out the spot he said he'd seen Jude burying something."

The sheriff paused for a moment, remembering the frenzied delight on Leon's face when they'd dug up the evidence. "The stuff was there just like he said. Pieces of clothing belonging to the assaulted girls, a few pieces of ribbon, and a bracelet." Henson was extremely uncomfortable and wished to hell they'd thought some other way to entrap Leon. He worried that the women were not strong enough to handle the news they would receive shortly. It had been partly his idea to tell them this way, now he regretted it. His gut told him this was wrong.

"He was out for Jude's blood, and wanted us to break into the house shooting, but we calmed him down and knocked on the door. No answer, of course. I should remind you that Jude was in my office at that time. Leon got excited, insisted we go look along the path through the woods. Evidently Jude takes walks there two, three times a day. Well, we did, but no Jude. Leon fidgeted around the place, shouting obscenities as the non-existent Jude, and we finally coaxed him into riding back to town with us. Told him Holden needed to discuss the will. He calmed right down and went with us to the law office as planned." He looked at Kate and Angie.

"This isn't going to be pleasant for you, but it was the only way we could think of to find out just what Leon had done. We needed to know what crimes he had committed." Henson left out the most bizarre parts; like when Leon had fingered the clothes and objects they dug up. A shiver ran down his spine as he recalled the look of utter bliss that had passed over Leon's face, the trembling hands stroking the fabric, his breath harsh and saliva dripping out of the corners of his loose mouth. Sheriff Henson sat down with a thump and asked Rob to continue the story.

Rob remained seated, rolling a yellow pencil between his fingers. "Leon walked into the office expecting to see me. I was there, but hiding in the file room where I could see and hear everything. What Leon saw was the back of a man in a wheel chair. The man spoke without turning around. "Are you looking for me?"

"No, I'm meeting my Pa's attorney here, about some property I inherited."

"I say you've found your Pa's friend instead."

Jude spun his chair around and met Leon's eyes. I could see Leon jump. His confusion was visible. He stepped closer to Jude and peered at him. Fright and disbelief played tag across his face.

"Heh, heh," he laughed, "I thought you were someone else there for a minute. Heh, heh." He wiped his mouth with his shirtsleeve and sat down.

Jude said, "I am Jude Bainville. You didn't know I had a last name? Yes, but still the same ol' Crip you love to torment. As you can see, I win again. I'm alive and I might not be kicking, but damn you, I am alive. You paralyzed me, you see. The rest of me is better than ever however.

The pencil snapped and Rob turned to Norm. "You're the one to tell the rest of the story." He turned to the others. "Norm and the Sheriff were there by this time, waiting in the doorway."

Norm was uneasy. It was wrong to tell Angie and Kate these things in front of others. Rob and Sheriff Henson thought it would be better if everyone heard the story at the same time. The girls would have their support, and it would all be over that much sooner. Not to mention the fact that they were taking the law into their own hands, being judge and jury to Leon. He cleared his throat and began telling his story.

"Leon realized his plans were disintegrating; he couldn't believe it, and all the hate he carried for humanity welled up and spilled over. He was totally confused, groping for understanding. Comprehension comes slow to Leon. I watched these emotions warring within him, turning his face dark, almost purple, and then dead white. The rage continued building. It grew until it reached his brain and exploded, and his mind cracked. Leon grabbed his head and screamed at Jude, "I'll kill you. I'll kill you this time you freak, you twisted monster. I killed Ma and Pa; I'll kill the little girls, too, and you'll fry for it, you hear?" He sank to the floor sobbing. "Ma, Ma, help me. Please Ma. I've been a good little boy. I'm your good boy, Ma. Don't let them get me."

Norm reached shaking hands into his pocket for his hanky. Angie was looking at him, horrified, Kate had a closed look on her face, and the others stared at him, stunned. He dreaded this last part of the story, and gulped in a deep breath of air. The delicious aroma of Betsey's home-baked bread wafted around the room, and he took comfort from the homey smell.

"Leon continued to cry out to his mother for a spell, his moods fluctuating between a deep rage and self-pity. Then he was on his feet, running around the room in frenzied, jerky movements." Norm gulped and continued with his story.

"Jude felt sorry for Leon and motioned for us to help him. We moved towards him, and then stopped aghast. He had stripped off his overalls and was standing on one leg, hopping up and down, flapping his arms and crowing. I spoke quietly to him. He stared at me for a few moments and said, "You tricked me." He moved back to the corner of the room and huddled into it. He sat on his haunches and sucked his thumb. Then, giving us all a shy smile, he hid his face between his knees and drew his last breath of reality. When he raised his head the four of us found ourselves looking into a face of a child … a child with vacant eyes and a wet mouth."

Silence filled the room. The friends stared at each other, speechless. Angie's shrill voice grated on their nerves.

"Where is my brother? What have you done with him?"

"He's at the State Asylum by Judge Barstow's orders. I signed the papers declaring him insane and in need of evaluation. They'll observe him for thirty days, then he'll be committed or taken to jail to await trial." Sheriff Henson answered Angie and wished he could say something to comfort her. She appealed to him, maybe it was her helplessness. He was a sucker for the soft, weak ones. But Angie was angry and she flared out at him. "How can you arrest Leon? You don't have any evidence. You can't prove he killed Ma and Pa."

"He'd be arrested as a suspect for the child assaults, the murder of your parents, and one count of rape. Now leave it alone, its's in the hands of the law."

It wasn't all fun, being a law officer. Here this pretty, little thing was about to have a tantrum and he didn't know how to handle it. There was only one thing to do. He said, "Well, duty calls. I'll go make out my report." He picked up his hat and left.

Norm reached over and touched Kate's hand. "Are you doing okay?" Surprised, she nodded, and wondered what he'd say if she asked him to get her a plate of cookies. Her body clamored for food, sweet food. After inspecting herself in the looking glass she'd decided to lose weight; somehow or other she had to achieve something, just for her.

Angie's soft weeping broke her muse, and she was about to reach over and hold her hand when Angie began speaking.

"It's hard to think one's good friends could believe such terrible things about my family. I refuse to believe it. There's no way you can convince me Leon hurt those girls." She wiped her eyes with her lace edged handkerchief and smiled gently.

Kate's anger began in her stomach and slowly built up into her head. Angie was trying to con them, bent on saving Leon. Well, she wouldn't let her get by with it. "Aren't you the least concerned about these girls that have been hurt? Are you really going to pretend that none of this is real?"

Angie glared at Kate and said, "Of course I'm concerned about the girls. Who wouldn't be? I just don't think it should affect our family. It has nothing to do with us, really."

"It's always affected our family, always. You know it. You've always known. You're ready to deny this like you have everything else. I'm not going to let you do it, Angie. If you do anything to help Leon, I'll fight you. I'll spill all of the nasty secrets you've been afraid to admit." Kate's voice grew quiet and firm. "Pa and Leon kept me isolated on the farm for eight years. Where were you when I needed you?"

She stood up and placed her hands on the table. Leaning forward, she looked at each of them. "I'm the one that knows what our brother is capable of." Enunciating each word, she said, "Leon tormented me, brainwashed me, and did things to people and animals you couldn't conceive of, you, with your nice little lives, in your safe cocoons. I was left alone with Pa and Leon. I was just a little kid, Angie, just a little kid, like the one's he's been hurting here in town."

She brought her face closer to Angie's. "I would like to see him hang. And believe me I'll do anything in my power to help the Sheriff do just that." She turned from the table and walked heavily out of the room.

When she came to the staircase, her body spun into action and she ran up to her room and shut the door with a bang. It was a relief to be away from them all. She was angry with herself. Why hadn't she run away from home? Reported Leon's unnatural behavior? Was she really that stupid she didn't know he was a criminal?

Her behavior this evening had surprised her. I can't believe I actually said all those things in front of everyone. What kind of a person am I? Kate suddenly felt bereft and frightened of a future she was not prepared for. Weakness swept over her, her legs began to tremble, then her arms and hands. Soon her whole body was shaking. Sobs erupted from her mouth.

She ran to the window and flung the curtains apart. She imagined herself standing at her window at home, in the cold morning air, wearing one of Ma's ugly dresses; and the cold stove glinting in the early dawn, while Leon, in his room, lay warm and cozy, waiting for her to go down and heat the house and fix him breakfast.

"I prayed for escape," she spoke aloud. "And my prayers were answered. Am I going to be a weak kitten and fall apart? No, I am not. Not ever. I will take this new chance and make something of myself. I'll carve a life out of the debris."

Kate didn't hear Norm come into her room and jumped when he touched her shoulder. "I couldn't leave until I knew you were all right." He smiled into her eyes and began stroking her hands. She jerked them away. She was not used to caresses and she felt extremely uncomfortable.

"Please, Dr. Larson, I want to be alone. I – I'm not used to being around people." She turned from him and gazed out of the window again, willing him to go. Instead, he sank into a chair and watched her. Love struck him dumb. He'd never been in love before, and yet the moment he'd heard her speak, he'd known she was what he wanted.

The image of himself came into his mind's eye. Slightly pudgy, five foot ten inches, wire spectacles. Not the picture of a girl's dream. Plus, he was going on thirty years old, while she was barely out of her teens.

"You know, Kate, your Dad let everyone think you were away at school. We believed it. But it's not too late for us to help you. I'm here for you if you need me." He was hopeful when she smiled, and he decided to go a step further. He put on his glasses and crossed his legs.

"Can you talk to me Kate? About your feelings? If you would purge yourself, get all the bad things out in the open, you'd heal so much faster."

The anger in Kate simmered. Smug, self-satisfied son-of-a–so and so! What did he know about her life? Sitting there parroting platitudes. How could he understand the evil in that house? Did he really want to know about her? A need for retaliation and overwhelming desire to wipe that gentle loving look from his face swept over her.

Using all the control she could muster, she asked him politely to leave. She locked the door behind him and the years of hurt and anger, the confusion and bitterness erupted. She was only partially aware of the sobs pouring from her throat.

Much later, in the deep hours of the night, she awakened and was aware of the cleansing that had taken place within her. She had a feeling of relief so deep she wanted to weep. The old ache was there in her heart, but the guilt and shame were gone. "It wasn't my fault. It had nothing to do with me or my actions." She fell into a restful, dreamless sleep.

SEVEN

The sisters met at breakfast, anxious for their meeting with Attorney Holden. Kate kept her eyes down, pretending to read the will. Angie acted as if nothing untoward had occurred between them. Angie spoke first.

"I'm glad you're okay, Kate. I missed you this morning. I had to get dressed by myself. Could you button me?" She turned her narrow back and Kate pushed twenty-four tiny buttons into their holes. "And my hair, could you just do it up in the back?" Angie sat still while Kate silently arranged the blond fluff. Angie hoped Kate would get over her bad mood before they met with Rob. They needed to put up a good front; thank God Rob hadn't reacted when Kate pulled her martyred act.

"Well, it's off we go, come on girl, let's go hear the good news. Mandy an heiress, imagine that."

When Rob finished explaining the will, Angie, flushed and triumphant, kissed Kate on the cheek and hugged herself.

Kat sat in glum silence. Pa had disposed of her in the cruelest way. Not by ignoring her as he had Leon, she could have handled that, but by giving Angie the authority to do as she wanted with her. Like an old suit he didn't care for, just wear it out and toss it to the next in line. She should be used to Pa degrading her, but the arrow pierced deep, the hurt fresh and raw.

Her life was her own responsibility. Not Pa's. Not Angie's. The choice she made now would make the difference between a life or an apology for living. If only she had the guts to stand up for herself.

"I want to contest the will. I need an attorney. Will you represent me?"

Rob nodded gravely. "I was hoping you would stand up for your rights. Of course, I'll be happy to help. It would be ethically wrong for me to represent you, but I will give you the name of a good attorney."

Angie wailed, "Kate, why? What's the matter with you? Why are you doing this to me?" She turned to Rob, patting her hair and smiling provocatively. "You don't mean it, surely? Why would you even consider it? She doesn't need to go to court, I'll take care of her." Facing Kate, she said softly, "I love you, Kate. I'll see you have everything you need, and of course it goes without saying you'll make your home with us."

It suddenly struck Kate that Angie didn't have the capacity to see beyond herself. Pa had hurt them all in one way or another. Angie's helplessness and silly patter were a defense. It was her way of coping with the disappointments and fears of life. She reached out and took Angie's hand in her own. "I don't want to be taken care of. I don't want you to give me a home. I want my own money. I deserve it. I intend to leave here, and I intend to take my money and build me a life. I earned it, believe me."

"Maybe this can be settled right here between you today," Rob suggested. He asked Kate, "What do you think is a fair settlement?"

The words stuck in her throat. It would sound preposterous, but she it said it anyway. "I need one hundred thousand dollars." The words were too loud, but clear.

Angie gasped, "You must be mad!"

"It's what I need."

"That's ridiculous. What would someone like you do with that much money?" The moment the words were out she wanted to take them back. *I didn't mean it really. I don't think of Kate in that way, do I?* Images flitted through her mind. Kate running to answer the bell when she rang it, bringing her tea, mending her clothes, bathing her, holding her when she cried. Angie was deeply ashamed. She tried so hard to be thoughtful, but it seemed as if she was naturally selfish. She knew Kate had been treated abominably by Pa, and knew of her fear of Leon, but she hadn't realized she, too, was exploiting her, using her to fetch and carry, thinking only of her own comfort. She turned to Rob.

"Pa was wrong. She is entitled to a share of the inheritance. We've all been unfair to her. Give her the money." The smile Rob threw at her warmed her heart.

Kate wanted to hug Angie, but she was overcome with emotion. The false bravado she used to stand up for her rights suddenly evaporated. She was too weak to get out of the chair.

Rob took a packet from his desk. "Sit down, Angie, I have information here about your parents you might be interested in. You Martins were raised in a family that harbored many secrets. Mysteries are exciting, but when you're personally involved, they can be devastating. Now, I don't know the whole story of Burt Martin, but my inquiries have brought forth information that affects you both."

At their questioning looks, he said, "In order to protect Mandy's interests, I had to be sure this money was Burt's to give away." He rushed on, aware of the apprehension that was settling on their faces.

"Burt worked for a family called Carstairs, in Philadelphia; his life was hard. His boss was a brutal man. He actually hooked your father to a plow when he was short of horses one spring. Burt Martin pulled that plow until he'd dug up fourteen acres of new ground. The people who remember the family say Burt never spoke a word against the Carstairs. Instead, he sought revenge in a more, subtle way. He courted the boss' only daughter; her parents didn't know until it was too late.

They told them the news when she was four months pregnant. Cartairs grabbed his rifle and was chasing Burt when he suffered a stroke. He was put to bed where he lingered for two years, before dying. Burt took over the management of the farm and married the daughter.

The baby was three years old when his wife left him and the child. Burt soon sold the farm. There's no information on him until he appeared in Montana. He needed someone to care for the child and run his home for him.

He ordered himself a mail-order bride from Ohio. Eunice answered the ad. They married and bought the farm you were raised on." He nodded at Angie. "That baby is you, Angie. The Carstairs daughter was your biological mother."

Tears stood in Angie's eyes. Kate squeezed her arm. "Go on, Rob. Finish it."

"This is sketchy. Eunice became pregnant and had Leon within the year. He was a mess from the beginning. Somehow things didn't connect right in his head. Eunice doted on him. Burt hated him. As you already know." The silence in the room was blatant. Rob stopped speaking to pour them all cups of coffee.

"No one has been able to find out where Burt got the money. The sale of the Cartairs' farm brought some, but not near the half million Burt brought into me. There were no bank robberies or embezzlements. It seems the money is clean. He must have hidden it on the farm somewhere. When he brought it to me shortly before his death, I went with him to the bank and helped him set up his accounts.

"Now we come to you, Kate. I don't know how you'll feel about this, but I need you to know about yourself." She nodded at him, her eyes wide and frightened.

"It seems your mother got an itch for a farm hand that worked for Burt. When Burt took his annual trip to Granite City, Eunice and Phillip Sutton had a short affair. When Burt came home, the hired hand was gone and Eunice was pregnant. With you. Burt was actually your stepfather, Kate."

She felt the joy come in little ripples and as she realized that her Pa wasn't her father, she felt the ripples explode into a great flood of gratitude. She was spared from the greatest of all sins. "He's not my Pa! He's not my Pa!" She repeated it over and over until Angie, not understanding, quieted her and the two sisters sat quietly, holding each other and thinking their own thoughts.

"I hope I can get word to Noah, he might come back to me now that we have all this money," Angie thought.

Kate was filled with the satisfaction of getting revenge on Burt. Finally, he was paying for his brutality to her. He would have a stroke if he knew she had so much of his money. She smiled at the thought.

Rob called the bank to make arrangements for Kate to deposit her money.

She paid her first visit to a bank and opened an account in her name, Kate Willow Sutton. She was so happy. "I have a new life. I have a new name. And I have a bank account. One hundred thousand dollars. Oh my!" She was beside herself. "What will I do first?" She didn't know. "Where will I go?" She couldn't think. Who could she talk to? Norm. She'd talk to Norm, he'd tell her what to do. No, she was on her own now, she was free, and could decide for herself. Of course! She needed clothes, she would find a shop and buy a new dress.

Kate's mood plummeted as she looked at one dress after another. She decided not to bother and turned to leave when a hand touched her arm and asked softly, "Would you like some help? It's difficult to make up one's mind when there's so many to choose from."

"I've never shopped before. I don't know what size to get, or anything." Perspiration coated her face and she could feel it running down the thin fabric of Ma's good dress.

"Well, no wonder you're having a hard time of it. I've been shopping for forty years and I still have trouble. Come with me, I'll take care of you." Kate followed her to a back room, where she was told to strip and wait. Soon the woman was back with a tape measure and proceeded to measure Kate up and down and sideways. "My name is Beulah. I own the shop. I won't steer you wrong. I'll choose some things and bring them in to you."

Kate loved the lingerie most of all. Never had she imagined such soft dainty underwear, and nightgowns. She bought enough clothes to see her through until she lost some weight. She added boots, shoes, mittens, hats and scarves.

She walked to Betsey's proud of the new green wool suit, the silk stocking and new heels. She rubbed her cheek on the fur collar of her new coat. She decided what her next step would be.

Kate decided to go home. "Just for a while," she told Angie. "Someone has to take care of the place. We can't expect Augusta to do our work much longer. I can take care of the animals through the winter. I want to do this, Angie. I need to. I have my reasons. I've made arrangements for you and Mandy to stay with Christine and Gus. They can use the extra money and you'll recuperate faster in their warm home."

The weeks had flown by. Kate was busy from dawn to dusk and she grinned as she surveyed the immaculate barn and yard. The fence posts stood proud, their wire stretched tight, and the woodpile was growing daily. It had been too late to save the hay crop, but she'd bought hay from neighbors and grain at the elevator in town. The livestock would be fine for the winter.

Leon's neglect had taken a toll on the horses and Kate went into the shed to mix the solution for one of Pa's thoroughbred mares, Miss McTavish. She had a puncture wound in her front foot, and Kate was afraid lockjaw might set in. Big John had enlarged the wound with a knife so it would drain. Now all they could do was soak Miss McTavish's foot in disinfectant twice a day and keep the wound clean.

Thank God for John. He worked with Kate for two hours every morning and most of every afternoon. Christine had offered his help when Kate found the horses so neglected and their stables totally rotten with manure and moldy hay. He was glad for the work. "I'm saving for college," he'd told her. "I aim to be a veterinarian. Farming for a living isn't for me."

He came into the shed now and took the solution. "It's looking good, Kate. You go on in now. I'll see you in the morning." Giving her his lopsided grin, he strode out the door, his shoulders brushing the frame. Big John was a big man, all right. Kate thought it ironic they'd been neighbors for years and never met. He hadn't known she existed.

Tippy whined and Kate patted his head. "Are you wanting go in, boy? Too cold out here for you?" She slipped her hands into her mittens and stepped into the frosty afternoon. The cold wind sent shivers through her, in spite of the warm sheepskin jacket. "Race you to the house!" She and her collie ran pell-mell along the path.

A smile of satisfaction crossed her face as they bounced into the cheery kitchen. Tippy went straight to the stove and lay on the rug Kate had put there for him. The first thing she had done when she came back to the farm was move him into the house. The last few winters had been hard on him, and it made her happy to know his last years would be spent in comfort. He was good company.

She used great care in dishing up her chicken stew, careful not to take too much. Her hard work and light meals were paying off. She was getting smaller each week. She felt better, too. No fried foods or sweets were allowed on her plate. It had been incredibly difficult at first, and her body had cried out for the cakes and icings, but she'd gotten past that now, and she pictured a slimmer, prettier Kate in her near future.

Kate used only three rooms in the house, the kitchen, study, and bathroom. She had decorated them, ordering her supplies from Montgomery Wards. After painting and papering the walls, she had taken the best furniture from the other rooms, laid rugs on the floors and made pillows for the soda and chairs. The large study became a sitting room and bedroom. The fireplace, unused for so many years, was now the focal point of the room, and Kate and Tippy spent long evenings in front of it. Kate used the winter nights to study, and increase her knowledge of current events. Her books were proudly displayed on shelves beside the fireplace. She was constantly ordering more reading material, and learned to drive so she could shop in the little bookstore in Ryan. On her last trip to town she'd bought a radio. It opened up a whole new world to her, and she listened to it for hours at first, awed by the magic of the voices in a box. Soon she was forming opinions and learning more than she ever thought possible.

As she learned more of the world, she found her thoughts turning to her mother. She'd never called her Mother, only Ma, but she liked the word mother. In the back of her mind, when she'd decided to come back here for the winter, there was a need to search for something to prove her validity. There must be something here to show her mother as a real person, not that work-ridden hag, but a woman that had once laughter, loved, and dreamed.

She began her search upstairs, searching quickly through the five bedrooms, but the cold was so severe, she went down and warmed herself at the fire, then put her coat on and went to the one bedroom on the main floor. Angie's stockings were draped over a chair back, and various cosmetics were scattered on the dresser top. Her sister's things made the room homier and Kate was glad she'd left them.

Her back ached but she diligently went to work, searching every nook and cranny, but found nothing. Where to look next? Ma must have had some personal things, but where? Where would a woman hide something from a man like Pa? Sometimes when Pa had a problem, he'd say, "I'll sleep on it." Wouldn't it be funny if she'd hidden something in the mattress? Kate folded the coarse sheets and blankets as she removed them from the bed. There was the bare mattress. Suddenly impatient, she pulled it to her then managed to heave it to the floor. There was nothing under it. She looked at the old bedsprings with distaste. They were rusty and dust and spider webs clung to the coils. I'll throw it out, she decided. It was the bed she'd slept in when Pas was coming to her room. This had been her room, then, until Ma had become too ill to climb the stairs.

She gave one more searching look around the room, unwilling to give up, wanting, needing something of her mother's. She noticed a small bulge in the linoleum, beside the wardrobe. Her heart quickened. Running across the room she began tearing at it. The pieces crumbled, cold and crisp like old toast.

The package was bigger then she'd expected. Ma had used a scrap of old yellow checked oilcloth to wrap the keepsakes in. Kate was impatient to see if anything pertained to her. She carried the treasure back to the study and sat beside the fire. Hesitant, now, she tremulously began looking through Ma's hidden cache.

The first thing she pulled out was a letter, and she read it at once. The return address read Phillip Sutton, Gen. Delivery, Marshallville, Montana. There was no greeting; a cold, bare letter, written by a man who was bitterly disappointed to find his life complicated by the consequences of his actions.

'I have received your note and am understandably upset by your unexpected condition. I will only say I took what was offered. I pride myself on being an honorable man and if you decide it's best to leave your home and join me, then of course I will take you on. What you do with your two children is for you to decide. They may come with you, if you wish. I would, however, much rather be responsible for just the two of us and the child you are expecting. I will wait for two weeks to hear from you. If you have not contacted me within that time, I will get on with my life. Phillip Sutton.'

Poor Ma. How she must have suffered. For the rest of her life, no doubt. What had she seen in a cold potato like him?

She shuffled through the pile, and saw the picture. He had written on the back, 'My love forever, Phillip.' She studied the photo, he was handsome, tall and slender. His thick black hair fell in waves over his forehead. She could understand how Ma was taken in by him. Her own resemblance to him amazed her. That must be why Ma hadn't liked her. He'd hurt her deeply. Mad had a lot of pride.

"Yoohoo! Where are you?" Angie's cheerful voice startled Kate. Quickly stuffed the papers under the chair seat. "Oh, there you are, do you feel like company?"

"Of course, I'm glad to see you." Kate grinned, happy to see the rosy cheeks and smiling face of her sister. "You look great. Are you feeling better? Is Norm giving you some new medicine?"

"I do feel better, in fact these last few days I've had lots of energy. I've been taking walks and doing some housework. Christine won't allow me to stay in bed and she sends me to get the mail each day. Then I help with the dishes, and play with Mandy, who, by the way, sends you her love. Oh, Kate, I'm sorry I worked you so hard, on top of all the other work and problems you certainly didn't need me to boss you around."

Kate's heart leaped with joy. Angie was trying to change. "Don't blame yourself. We're what our folks raised us to be. We have to change the parts that don't work for us." She thought for a few minutes. "Angie, I wanted to come here to sort myself out. I need the hard work to help dissolve the terrible anger I feel. And it's working." She looked shyly at Angie and stroked the top of her thigh. "I … I'm trying to lose weight. I think I've lost quite a bit. I don't eat sweets anymore."

"I can see you have. I'm so proud of you." Angie tried to ignore the jealous stabs that were pricking her heart. "I don't know what all happened to you; if you want to talk about it, I'll be here for you. It's time I acted like the big sister I am."

Should she tell Angie? We're all we've got, she realized, just Angie, Mandy, and me. The sisters talked, stoking the fire periodically, and refilling their coffee cups. Kate told her story first, everything except the baby. She couldn't talk about that yet. Then Angie talked. "It's my fault Noah is gone," she said. "I complained all the time, blaming him for not supporting us the way I thought I deserved." Her eyes were wet when she added, "I think he is and always was unfaithful to me, and the suspicions drive me crazy."

"Why Angie, I had no idea Noah was like that. What makes you think so?"

"I don't have any real proof, but it's the way he looks at other women, and the times he stays out so late. It's a sixth sense, something a woman can feel when her man's tomcatting."

They talked far into the evening, and when it was time for Angie to go home, and Kate to do the milking, they parted with tears and promised to help each other through the difficult months ahead.

It was 8:30 pm when Kate finished her chores and went to the kitchen to fix her dinner. She'd gone six hours between meals.

Jude wanted to go home. He'd been enthusiastic at first for the chance to live in Mrs. Jolly's boardinghouse, and liked her and the residents. But he missed the sounds and smells of the woods. He was waiting for Norm to answer the message he'd sent him. Norm was no doubt still mad at him for not going to Betsey's. They'd had words over that, but Norm had to understand he wasn't a social person. Nor likely to become one after all this time. Where was the man? As if on cue, Norm drove into the yard.

"You want to do what?" Norm was as mad as he could get. Here he thought Jude was settled, and now he'd come up with this hair-brained idea. "How will you manage out in the woods? Man, you can't steer that wheelchair on cow paths."

"If you'll let me explain," Jude yelled back. "Ben Claybourn will be with me. He'll take care of me, and the outside work. I can do most of the work in the house. The two of us can handle it easy."

"I know Ben. Seems like a good enough fellow." Norm rubbed his hand over his jaw, trying to think of a good argument, but Jude grabbed the ball again, putting him on the defensive.

"I need to see about getting my back wages. I have $200.00 coming. That'll be plenty to build me a ramp on the porch and store up groceries for the rest of the winter, and hire a boy to help Ben with the woodpile."

What Norm had thought was impossible now seemed totally workable. How does he do it? I should know by now he always has an answer for everything. One thing's for certain, Jude has an ugly temper.

"Give me a week. That's next Wednesday. I'll pick you and Ben up in the morning and take you home, that will give me time to check out your house and take care of any repairs. I just hope this Ben can take good care of you. I'm still not convinced this is a good idea." Jude let him have the last word and Norm walked to his car feeling as if he'd been hit with a jackhammer.

He'd wanted to see Kate again, and now he had a valid excuse. Instead of going to his office, he turned onto the Horseshoe Trail and headed to the Martin farm. The eight-mile drive seemed endless. About a mile from the farm, he suddenly had an attack of self-consciousness. Driving with one hand, he tried to smooth the cowlick on the crown of his head. He glanced in the mirror. The cowlick was standing up, waving like a flag in the wind. Damn! He reached behind him and fumbled around until he found his hat, and jammed it on his head.

At first glance he thought Kate had hired a hand, then he recognized her by the long braid hanging down her back. She looked happy, and beautiful. Too beautiful to be pushing that wheelbarrow piled with wood. He told her so as they walked to the house.

"I'm working hard on purpose, Norm. It's my way of releasing all that anger I have stored up. I'm cleaning myself out while I'm cleaning the farm up." She waved her hands at the neat yard and corrals. "I'm proud of what I've done. It's starting to look like I always dreamed it would."

"You can afford help; promise me you won't take on too much. I don't want anything too happen to you. You're very dear to me, you know."

Kate was ashamed at the irritation she felt. Why couldn't she simply accept his concern?

"I don't want to be wrapped in cotton. I need to experience life; not watch from a window." Kate sensed that if Norm had his way, he would spirit her off to a cozy hide-a-way and take care of her, attending to her every need. What most women dream of, I'm sure. Kate sighed. There was no way she would let anyone take control of her life again. Not ever.

She invited Norm in for a cup of coffee and they walked towards the house.

"You've lost weight." He felt threatened by her new independence and her glowing health.

"That's the other reason I'm doing most of my own work. Big John helps me with the really hard stuff." She smiled at him, happy he had noticed her weight loss.

They went into the kitchen. Kate could see Norm was impressed.

Norm looked around the clean cozy room, sniffling the rich aroma of chicken boiling. "You're a woman of many talents, Kate."

He told her of Jude's plans to move into his house again, and she nodded in agreement. Angie and she had discussed Jude. She liked what she'd heard of him, and was anxious to meet him.

"I used to see him walking, whistling conversations with the birds. We weren't allowed to talk to him. I'd pretend to understand what he was saying and what the birds said in return. Then I'd write in my journal. I write all my imaginings in it." She poured coffee into the thick cups. "I sensed the goodness in Jude, but was afraid for him, because Leon hated him so much. He would brag about the mean things he did to Jude." She lifted shamed eyes to Norm and whispered, "he's such a monster."

The scratching at the door interrupted Kate and she went to let Tippy in. They went into the study and sat on the floor in front of the fire. The collie laid his head on her lap. She stroked his sable coat. "Leon hurt everything on the farm. But for some reason he loved this dog. Tippy is the only animal on the place that doesn't have scars from Leon's mistreatment. The funny thing is, Tippy wasn't crazy about Leon. Leon didn't seem to mind. He loved him anyway."

Norm had a lot to think about as he drove home that afternoon. It shouldn't surprise him that Leon loved that old dog, but for some reason, it did. He'd dig out his books tonight and see if he could get a new perspective on the man.

Kate poured the milk into the cream separator and sniffed the air. Mmm, smells like snow. Her chores were done and the workers would be driving in soon. She'd called John last night and before an hour had passed, he'd rounded up a crew of fifteen men, eager to work on Jude's house.

With a can of cream in one hand and bucket of milk in the other, she walked to the house, enjoying the hard, crisp noise of the earth under her boots.

"I'll make pots of coffee for them," she decided. She filled large baskets with hard-boiled eggs, biscuits, jam and butter. Then feeling magnanimous, she threw in a fruit cake. The coffee smelled good and she poured herself a cup.

Angie had agreed they should help Jude, and offered to furnish his house. Kate had drawn plans for the men to follow. She'd added two rooms to the original structure. Jude's room was to have bookshelves on two walls and a big window facing his beloved forest. She had ordered a wool rug and curtains. Angie helped to choose the right colors and styles. Ben's room was smaller, but boasted a cupboard to hold his wood carving supplies. She had called Mrs. Jolly to ask what kind of man Ben was and she'd planned his room accordingly. Small pot-bellied stoves, one for each bedroom, would be delivered tomorrow.

A car horn broke the stillness and she ran to the window. It was Angie in her new LaSalle. She ran in quickly and made a beeline for the stove.

"You look like a movie star," Kate said, handing her a cup of coffee.

"I'm just so revved up, wanted to see your plans for the house. However, did you manage to find a crew willing to work in this weather?"

"People are hungry, work is scarce, and they were glad I asked them. I think they'd build those rooms in the middle of a snowstorm."

"Big John was all excited last night when you called him. I think he has a thing for you."

"Oh phooey, he's just a good friend." Kate turned pink and fussed around the stove. "You'd be the one he'd want Angie. Honest, you look so pretty these days."

"Who, me? Lordy, I'm only ten years older than the guy. He's your age." She studied Kate for a moment, taking in her new slimmer figure, and arresting face. Extremely beautiful. Tall and willowy. God, this girl had it all, even the eyes, magical eyes, watching her now with intelligence and warmth.

"Kate," Angie said haltingly, "if I tell you something you won't take it personal, will you?"

Kate shook her head in reply. "It's just that Christine and Gus want John to stay on the farm for a few years yet. They would be hard pressed without him. They're afraid he might get hung up on some girl and leave home. He talks about you so much I think Christine is beginning to worry. If you ask me he'd be lucky to have you."

"Oh, Angie." Kate laughed. "Tell them not to worry. John and I really are just friends. I appreciate his help, and enjoy having him here. He's like the brother I wish we'd had." But her feelings were hurt; didn't they think she was good enough for him?

"Let me see what you've done with Jude's kitchen." Angie studied the plans, admiring Kate's creativeness. "I wonder if we could find someone to bring water into the house? If the ground isn't too hard, we could bring pipes into the kitchen. The old pantry could become a bathroom."

Kate hit her head with her hand. "I never thought of a bathroom!" Oh, Angie, it would make all the difference for Jude. It could be done. Though it's cold we haven't had a freeze yet." She hugged Angie and they were laughing and spinning around the floor when the knock sounded. The construction crew had arrived.

Fifteen men worked day and night, sleeping in shifts in Jude's house. Kate and Angie cooked their meals and kept them supplied with plenty of hot coffee and cocoa. They finished on the morning of the sixth day. They'd done the impossible.

Kate made out checks for each worker. Both girls were deeply touched when the men shook their hands and thanked them. Angie surprised everyone by presenting a bonus to each man. They went home with light hearts. There would be full cupboards for fifteen more families, Kate thought, a warm, happy feeling in her heart. It was the first time she had helped anyone outside her family, and she vowed to make a habit of it.

Gus and John rattled into the yard in Gus' old pickup, filled to overflowing with furniture and boxes donated by Jude's neighbors. Christine drove up with two of her neighbors and they all pitched in with the work. Kate and Christine laid down the rugs and hung the curtains. Angie decided where the pictures would look best, and set up the lamps. The rest of the ladies unpacked groceries and cleaned the old coal stove.

There was an icebox in the kitchen now, and Kate ran out to the well and pulled up the bucket that held Jude's milk, eggs, and butter. She dumped out the milk, and placed the eggs and butter in the new icebox. I'll see that Jude has fresh milk and cream, and meat. She'd bring them over later this evening.

Christine banked the fire and the women stood in the kitchen admiring the cozy room. The pine cupboards gleamed, the windows sparkled happily, proudly showing off their new starched linen. The old floorboards had been covered with a blue and white linoleum, adding just the right amount of texture and color to bring the room into focus. The women sighed with pleasure and moved into the living room. The paneled walls glowed softly; the new, overstuffed furniture lent elegance to the large room. The desk Augusta had given to Jude stood by the new window, and someone had brought over a globe and an entire set of encyclopedias.

When Christine had passed the word around the community that Jude was coming home, they'd been overwhelmed by the gifts and hand-me-downs their neighbors had given him. "We're thankful to Jude for putting Leon away. We can breathe easy again, knowing our girls are safe." Angie was relived no one held her or Kate responsible for Leon's actions.

EIGHT

A heavy blanket of snow covered the earth. Kate's throat tightened with wonder as she drank in its pristine beauty. She dressed hurriedly; like a child she wanted to go out and play.

She slipped into the back yard, catching her breath as the cold air numbed her face. Tippy yapped, running in circles in the snow, and then shoving his nose under the soft fluff. Kate caught him in a hug and wrestled him to the ground. "Let's go!" She scrambled up and ran ahead, lifting her legs high, exultant in her freedom.

Would she ever become accustomed to living without the restraints of mad men? Even here by herself, with Leon in the asylum, her skin prickled with fear and nervousness. Disgusted with herself for letting old habits ruin her freedom, she scooped up a handful of snow and rubbed it over her face.

She lay on her back, listening to the quiet. Small flakes touched her face softly, like angels' fingers.

Fierce anger filled her heart as she thought of Leon and the miserable life she had lived with him, and before him, Pa and Ma. She'd never been a child; never been anyone's little girl. Now she didn't know how to be a woman. A couple of the contractors had flirted with her, and she'd been repulsed by them. Just as she had been with Norm.

The sun poked its yellow head through the angry clouds and warmed her face. Her spirit floated in the air, meeting the sun, exultant and free. She gave herself up to the weightless, ethereal moment. A moment was all she had, as the memories of Leon kept creeping into her mind. That was one of the battles she was fighting daily, and today she was losing, but it was getting better and there were times now when she forgot to be so cautious, when she could let herself go and be truly joyful.

Her thoughts turned inward and she heard the whispered words: *You're ruined Kate, ruined. Whorin' with your own Pa. No one will come near you, you're ruined.*

Kate shook her head and sat up, confused. The back of her head was wet from the snow, and she snorted, "Fool!" and went in to change clothes.

Kate finished her chores and housework. It was time for Norm to drive in with Jude and Ben. "We'd better get over there and shovel the drive, so Jude can get his chair up the ramp," she told Tippy. Glad to have a job to do, to keep her mind from going off in tangents, she got the scoop shovel and headed to Jude's.

She checked the inside of the house and smiled to see Big John had been there this morning and started fires in all the stoves. The rooms were warm and inviting ready to welcome their owner. Just as she finished shoveling a wide path to the ramp, Norm's car pulled into the yard. She hastened to clean off the ramp, then ran down to help the men move in.

Jude looked as if the sky had fallen and hit him on the hear.

"Ha!" Norm said. "For once you're speechless. Never thought I'd see the day." He leaned back and gave his friend a pat on the shoulder. "Come on, now, don't you want to see your new home?" He lifted Jude out of the car and into the wheelchair. Ben followed, and wheeled Jude up the ramp on the front door. Kate turned to Jude, smiling. "Welcome home, Jude. I'm so glad you've come back." She gestured at the house, "Do you like it?"

Jude stared, transfixed, at the dwelling before him. He knew it had to be his house and yet it was so different. Larger, and the new siding and windows had turned the shack into a fine-looking house. "Like it?

It's magnificent. I don't know what to say. Is it really my house? Why did you do this?"

"It's yours Jude, all yours. We just gave it a face-lift. I… I'm really sorry you suffered so at Leon's hands."

Norm sensed that Jude didn't trust them; he was afraid someone was going to take his place away from him. He motioned for Ben to wheel Jude into the house and to the desk. He handed the desk key to Jude and told him to open the drawer. Jude did so and saw the papers; Norm spread them out on the desktop. "You like to read, well, read these." He walked over to Kate and they sat on the sofa and waited. "I need to show you something later," Norm whispered to Kate.

It was difficult for Jude to take all the good news and digest it at one time. He had the deed to the house and the five acres, plus an income of a quarter share of the farm's profits for the duration of his life. Turning his chair around he looked at Norm and Kate. He simply said, "I thank you from the bottom of my heart." Norm thought, he looks like a lord. There's blue blood in that boy, I'd stake my life on it.

Kate was impressed by Jude's dignity. She rose and skipped towards the kitchen. "I'll fix us all some coffee while you look at the rest of the house. Jude, your bedroom faces the forest, and yours," she turned to Ben, "is on this end."

Jude and Ben began talking, exclaiming and giving whoops of joy over their rooms. Ben happily ran out to the car to bring in his carving knives and wood pieces and promptly put them in special places in his new cupboard. Jude ran his hands over the bookcases, and read the titles of the books his neighbors had given him. After inspecting every corner and closet, they went into the homey kitchen.

Jude was again speechless. He shook his head, words seemed so inadequate and when Kate opened the pantry door, and he saw the blue and white bathroom, he knew he was going to lose it. He groped for his hanky and blew his nose, while Ben wiped his eyes with his shirtsleeve. They all sat around the table and drank coffee and filled each other in on all that had happened to them since Jude had left home.

Kate said her good-byes and Norm followed her to the door. He took an envelope from his pocket. "This letter came for us. It concerns Leon. You and Angie read it and let me know what you decide. Keep in mind, there's no obligation on your parts, where Leon is concerned. You need not see him if you choose not to."

"I don't intend to," Kate answered coolly, stepping out into the snow. "Norm, I know you mean well, but I don't want anything to do with Leon. Ever."

She didn't want to discuss Leon. Why did Norm always ruin everything? She thought of him as a snoopy old gossip monger with his nose in everybody's business. Yet, if it weren't for him, she might still be under Leon's rule, Angie would be dead, and Jude would be living at the Poor Farm. She owed him so much. If only there was some way she could repay him and rid herself of the obligation she felt to him.

Snow began to fall, thick, swirling flakes, causing a barrier between her and the house. She could see the gray outlines of the trees. She put her hand on Tippy's neck and let him lead. "We must be almost behind the corrals. Yes, here's the posts."

She decided to follow the corral until she came to the front of the barn. The snow was slushy, and she remembered she had pulled a patch of gooseberry bushes out of the ground here during her cleaning frenzy. She stepped forward to put her hands out to break her fall. She was using her arms to push herself up when her hands came in contact with a smooth cold object. Curious, she ran her hand over it. There was a metal strip attached to the box, so she put four fingers under it and pulled. She stared at the rather large wooden box in astonishment. Carrying the box, using the corral fence as a guide, she was soon at the front of the barn. She would see the light from the burning fireplace through the window of the house.

This is likely to turn out to be a long blizzard, Kate thought, and went into the barn to throw extra hay into the cow stanchions. She took the ax from the wall and chopped holes in the water troughs. Making her way to the other end of the barn, she checked the horses and fed and watered them. Then taking a rope, she tied it to the outside of the barn door. When she got to the house she tied the remaining end to a large hook on the porch pillar. She would use the rope as a guide back and forth to the barn if this storm continued.

She'd forgotten the scoop at Jude's, damn it. Now she'd have to get another shovel before she could get to the woodpile. She was fine for the night, though, plenty of wood in the house, and more stacked on the back porch.

It was 9:00 pm before she could sit down and open the box. She'd taken a bath and donned her new flannel nightgown and velvet bathrobe. The robe was purple with gold braid around the collar and cuffs. How she loved it. She slipped her feet into the matching slippers and felt very grand. The slippers had little gold heels on them and she paraded around her studio like a child playing dress up.

It was so much fun being a grown up and having her own money and privacy. Why, she could run naked in the house if she wanted to. Which she didn't do, but she might try it someday. Freedom was a heady experience and, Kate determined, it was a great gift. Not to be abused, but cherished.

Reaching into Burt's box, she took out a paper at random and began reading it. The blood drained from her face. It couldn't be! What had Pa done? Frantically, she searched the papers again, sure she had misread them. A ball of fear tore through her body as she remembered the hell of her fourteenth year. Numbly, she read the papers again. There was no mistake. Pa had given her baby to the St. Peter's Orphanage in Marshallville. He's only ninety-five miles away, she thought hysterically. Alive. I can't believe this. She was sure her baby died or sometimes she thought Pa had killed him, but mostly she hadn't let herself think of him at all. It was the one part of her life she hadn't shared with anyone, not even Angie. Dread surrounded her and her life suddenly seemed gray and bleak. Her new confidence and accomplishments faded as the fear grabbed at her. She needed to call someone to talk. She was afraid if she gave in to the terror she'd be lost and never find her way back.

Norm answered on the second ring. "Kate! How is it at your place? Are you all right?"

"Yes, I'm just checking to see if you got home okay," she lied. She hung up quickly unable to confide in him. I can't tell Angie, it would upset her too much. She was glad she'd called Norm, though, the boring conversation had restored her balance and she was able to think coherently again. To be honest about it she had worried about Norm driving home in the snow storm.

She went to bed and lay still, staring into the darkness. When she slept, the nightmare visited her again. The old gray goose stood on a knoll. He was flapping his wings and scolding the younger white goose. They were watching her and the white goose ran for her as the elder gave a loud honk. She was a child, running, her legs pumping up and down in desperate motion. Her breath, ragged and quick, burst from her mouth in sharp explosions. She turned her head back and forth searching for a place to hide. The white goose was gaining on her. There was only a puff of breath left in her body. Suddenly a cupboard appeared before her. She opened the door and crawled in. The goose searched for her in vain, honking a warning. She cowered in the cupboard, listening to the accelerated beats of her heart.

She awoke disoriented and afraid. It was the nightmare she'd had many times over the years. The nightmare is a warning, she told herself. An omen. Pa was dead, but Leon wasn't finished with her yet. Her body moved slow and heavy, like the old Kate, the fat, useless Kate. In desperation. she reached over and turned on the radio. Gene Autry's 'There's an empty cot in the bunkhouse tonight' filled the room and Kate hummed along, forcing her mind to concentrate on the day ahead.

"Let's get the chores done, Tippy. It's stopped snowing but I'll bet it's as cold as Jack Frost out there." The dog happily listened to her talk all the while she was getting dressed and making coffee. Just as they were ready to go outside, someone knocked. She opened the door and a smiling Ben stood there, holding a bucket of milk and a jar of cream. She stared at him, open-mouthed.

"I used to be a farm boy," he drawled, "and I said to Jude, this is no weather for a nice lady like Miz Kate to be out in. I'm fixin' to do your chores 'til you find a good hand."

She sent the milk and cream home with him, along with a pan of muffins she baked while they talked over coffee.

"Now don't you go out in this bitter cold, you hear?" He left by the back door, promising to see her again that evening when he did the milking.

She was fully restored to normal by the time he left. That visit was a God send. She was ready to tackle the rest of Burt's box and she began by shaking her fist at it.

The contents of the box surprised Kate. There was an insurance policy on his first wife. He'd pinned a heart shaped locket onto the papers. She opened the locket and saw pictures of Pa and a woman inside. The woman smiled prettily at her and it was like seeing Angie. The next thing she drew out was a deed for a piece of property in Marshallville and then a bank book from a Chicago bank with $75,000 showing on the balance line. There was a pile of receipts, records of farm profits, and some personal effects.

At the bottom of the box were two snapshots. The first one she looked at showed a farm couple dressed in work clothes. A young boy stood in front of them. Could this be Pa and his folks? Their stony faces and old clothes told a story of self-righteousness and deprivation. Had these stern-faced parents used the strap on Burt? Were they the reason he was so anti-social and cruel?

They seemed old to have such a young son. She turned the picture over. Someone had scribbled Olaf and Hannah Martin and Burtram, across the back. Kate put that picture aside for Angie, too.

The last photo was a small snapshot of a baby boy. He looked familiar. Kate turned the photo over and read the words 'Kate's boy, 16 months'. Desperately searching through the pile of receipts, she found three from the orphanage. They were all dated in December of three consecutive years – 1931, 1932, and 1933. She looked at the picture again and a warm feeling crept into her heart. His large eyes were shaped like hers and she hoped they were violet. She held the picture close to her breast, and rocked back and forth on the sofa, humming a lullaby to her lost baby.

The orphanage was no longer in business. The last person she had talked to had given her some hope, but even that sounded too bizarre to be true. She had contacted other orphan homes but they had not accepted any child from St. Peter's.

The information she had gotten from an old housekeeper of St. Peter's said that some of the kids had been sent to the Marshallville State Asylum. She shivered in horror, but when Angie said she was going to see Leon, Kate knew there was no choice but to go and check out the flimsy clue.

The ride to Marshallville was a torture of memories for Kate.

"Since Leon has been found insane and can't be arrested, we have the right to decide where he should go. Sheriff Henson says that as long as he is confined the law is satisfied. If you don't go with me, I'll do it alone," Angie said.

So, Kate had no choice, she couldn't tell Angie about her baby and she couldn't let Angie take such a trip in the cold of winter all by herself.

"Regardless of what you think, Angie, I don't trust him. He's putting on an act. He's not so crazy he doesn't know what he's doing. I'd rather see them arrest him and let a jury decide his fate." Angie just smiled and patted Kate's arm. She didn't take Kate seriously and it would be a cold day in hell before she let her brother stay in a place like that. The nerve of Norm and his cronies playing such tricks on poor Leon. There was sure to be a way out of this and she would find it!

The wind fought their every move, as they strove to climb the cement steps. Kate pushed the door open and they entered a cold entrance hall. The door to the Superintendent's office was closed. They stared at the sign. Paul Duggin, Superintendent. Angie knocked timidly and they went into the room, noticing the opulent furniture, such a contrast to the barren hallway. A roaring fire burned in the stove. Angie handed the man the letters he'd written them, by way of introducing themselves. "We're here to see about Leon Martin."

"Ah, yes; a sad case." He shook his head sorrowfully. "If you ladies will sign these papers we can make him a permanent resident." He had a way of pursing his lips that irritated Angie. Kate picked up the pen.

"Wait," Angie said. "We want to see our brother before we do anything this drastic. And read the medical reports."

"Oh, my dear lady, you can't be serious. We have an unwritten rule to keep the patients and their families apart." Duggin shifted uneasily in his chair.

"I'm serious, be sure of that. He's our family. We have a right to check on his well-being before we sign him over to you." She dabbed her eyes and said, "I just can't believe he's really that ill."

Her disbelief had its desired effect on Duggin. He'd seen other families who were blind to the defects in their family, so he went to the door to call for a nurse. He directed her to take the ladies to see Leon Martin.

Her face registered surprise, but she made no comment. Curtly telling them to follow her, the nurse pointed her shabby shoes to the east wing of the long hall. They walked through the din of the mad. Men and women were languishing on barren floors; the air was redundant with the shrieking harangues of the patients. Kate noticed a young woman, her hair tangled and ratted like a bird's nest, beating her head against the bars on the window. An old man lay on his back, naked, peddling his legs in the air. A woman reached out her claw fingers to Kate, moaning, "Give me my cat, oh, poor kitty."

Kate shuddered. Her concern for the patients raised her above her own fear as she became aware of their plight. That they could live in such horror and survive was unbelievable. She could smell their soiled underwear and see the urine stains on the women's long stockings. Some of the men had wet trousers and others were barefoot. There were no vestiges of human habitation here.

"Our animals couldn't live like this!" Anger and helplessness made her voice loud and strident.

They turned into a small dark hall and descended stairs into a damp area under the asylum. These were the dungeons, the nurse explained. "Them as is dangerous is put here." She motioned to a cell, no bigger than their woodshed.

"Here's your brother."

Angie reached him first and she gasped, "Oh, my God" and sagged. Kate caught her and stood her against the wall, holding her up. There was no place to sit and the floor was so filthy, she hated walking on it. "Buck up, Angie, you don't want to faint in this mess." Then steeling herself, she turned to look at Leon.

He was naked, sitting on his haunches. His feet and legs were blue from the cold. His clothes were thrown haphazardly around the cell. Kate couldn't see any bed and she wondered where he slept. His eyes were shut and he seemed to be asleep. Dried food and grime covered his body. Something that looked like oatmeal lay on the floor by his feet. Other globs of spilled meals were scattered around the floor. The cell was thick with flies. Small insects wove their way over the lumps of food. Leggy spiders crawled on the wet walls.

She looked at Leon again and noticed the bruises on his head and arms. Unable to keep her eyes focused on her brother she turned her head and noticed the cell next to Leon. The nametag above the door ready Cyril Bench. A pathetic version of a man was standing there holding onto the bars of the cell door. He grinned at her, and she was close enough to him to see the insanity and wickedness that lived within him. She jerked her head back to Leon.

He opened one eye. He stared at them for what seemed like hours, then opened the other eye. Angie came forward. "Hello, Leon." She tried to think of something to say but the words stuck in her throat.

"Hello, Leon," he mocked. He continued to stare at them, his eyes narrowed, his teeth showing through pulled back lips.

He looks like a mad coyote, Kate thought. But she said, "Why have they put you here? Where are your clothes?"

"I'm a good boy," he sniveled. "Tell them, Kate, tell them I'm good."

"Yes, I'll tell them." Suddenly struck with the horror of what she was seeing, her stomach rebelled and she felt the urge to vomit. A familiar reaction to Leon. Fear of him threatened to overcome her and she remained out of reaching distance of the cell.

She motioned to the nurse. "How did he get those bruises?"

"The guards had no choice. He was in an open ward and attacked one of the residents. They had to pull him off of her and he fought them."

Angie shook her finger in the nurse's face and shouted, "You can't treat people like this. It's inhumane. That's my brother, and I want him cleaned up and dressed. Now, do you hear? Now!"

The nurse back away, mumbling, "You'll have to talk to Duggin 'bout that." She turned to leave and Kate called to her, "Please, could you tell me the person he attacked? Was she young?"

"I'll say. Ten years or so. He raped 'er. Right in the open ward, in front of 'em all."

"A child? So, you do have children here?" This had to be a nightmare.

"Why sure. Kids go crazy too. But this girl wa'an one of 'em. She came in with the orphans. 'Ta orphanage closed up. We got five of 'em."

"That orphanage, was it St. Peter's?" Her voice shook.

"Sounds familiar. Come to think on it, you kind of remind me of a little fella here. The eyes, I think. I thought he might be yours but his last name is Martin." She turned and trudged down the hall with a no-nonsense look on her face. Kate stood paralyzed and watched her disappear around the corner. Helplessly, she turned to Angie.

Angie was talking softly to Leon. "We have to go, but we'll get you out of here, I promise."

As they walked away, he began squawking and crowing. They know, without looking, he was standing on one leg, flapping his arms. Kate wanted to tell him he didn't have anything to crow about, but she began crying instead. She wondered why she cared.

One of her daydreams had been to see Leon hurt, as he hurt others, but not like this, not to be treated like a filthy beast. Even at his worst he'd resembled a man. It's the cage, she thought, the cage has taken away his humanity.

Her own needs would have to wait, but at least she had an unexpected verification that her son was indeed here. She'd come back for him. Soon. Maybe tomorrow.

Angie insisted on seeing Duggin again. Leon needed their help. Kate agreed something should be done. After seeing what he had become, she admitted he couldn't stand trial.

"What are you thinking of doing, Angie?"

"I don't know what to do, but we can't leave him in this mess. Let's see Duggin and see what we can do for now. When we get back to the hotel maybe we'll figure out something."

Duggin was waiting for the women. If he played his cards right, he would fatten his wallet from these two. Rich Bitches! He hated the families of the residents. They liked to think they were above all this. Wrinkling up their noses, walking on tippy toes.

"Come in, Mrs. Senecah, Miss Sutton." He watched them closely. They were shaky and near tears. Good.

"Now if your satisfied that Leon is in need of our care, just sign these." Confidently he pushed the papers to the edge of his desk. "Since this is a state hospital, the care here can be free. Most all the patients here are funded by state money. However, for a little consideration, I can make life here a bit nicer for the patients. Most families are happy to oblige." He waited for the little blond to reach into her purse. Instead she looked at him with scorn.

"The State of Montana will be hearing from me, I assure you. My sister and I will be back tomorrow and I expect to see my brother dressed and in a room. And make sure he's clean." She looked down her patrician nose at Duggin. "You made the biggest mistake of your life when you tried to bribe me. I'll see you live to regret it."

Duggin's pop eyes stared at the door long after they were gone. How could he have been so mistaken? Sweat dropped from his forehead. He'd been called before the board twice already. This time they'd probably give him the sack.

He bellowed out the door for the nurse to bring Leon Martin to his office. Two guards threw Leon into the room and closed the door. Duggin walked over and turned the lock. Leon lay huddled on the floor, his face awash with fear. Duggin grinned.

"Well, Leon, you should feel right at home tonight." The razor strap whistled as it sliced through the air, as swift and sure as rattlesnake.

"Pa! Pa! Don't hit me, Pa." Leon screams seeped through the locked door and drifted down the hallways and into the cells and rooms of the inmates.

The weary nurse sighed with relief. The loonies would be quiet for the rest of the night. They know what Duggin's up to. She shook her head wisely, but who'd believe the likes of them? And they might be crazy, but they weren't stupid. No, he was safe from them. She wasn't above tellin' on him herself, though. He was a bad 'un. If you ask me, he's crazier 'en ta lot of 'em. Her shaggy head shook emphatically as she made her rounds.

The hot baths and dinner restored the girls to normalcy and they sat in the plush chairs, talking.

"You amaze me Angie. One minute you're weak and helpless, then suddenly you're a warrior, standing up to that despicable Duggin. I wouldn't have the nerve."

"I was so outraged at the treatment of all those poor souls and to see our own brother living in such filth. Kate, I know he's an evil man, but he's a human being." The pallor of Kate's skin disturbed Angie and the tired droop to her mouth.

"What do you say I call Norm and let him help us decide what to do? Maybe he'll know of some other institution. I understand how hard this is for you. You're the one he betrayed so cruelly, but I remember him as a child. He could be so sweet, sometimes. I think all he ever wanted was for Pa to love him."

"I'm all for taking Leon out of this place, but he's more than sick, Angie. He's insane. Criminally insane. He hurt another little girl and he did it in public." Kate's voice rose shrilly. "You can't just concentrate on the things being done against him. You have to remember the horrible things he's doing to others."

She put on her coat and scarf. "I'm going for a walk. I feel restless." On her way to the door, she wondered how far Angie would go to save Leon. She turned to Angie and said, "He's had his eye on Mandy, too. Remember that when you're making arrangements for his comfort."

The cold was sharper then she'd expected and she hurried around the corner to a coffee shop she'd noticed earlier. Slipping in the door she shrank into an empty booth by the window. It was good to be alone for a while. Kate missed her dog and her cozy rooms. The masses of people made her uncomfortable, it was hard to get used to all the new things she had to cope with now that she was on her own.

Not that she'd change it, no, just this thing with Leon had upset her. Her son was just a few miles away and Leon had taken priority again. His face swam before her. The narrow, cunning eyes, his thin cruel mouth. Please, God, he would be out of her life forever, and soon. But here was Angie, acting like an old mother hen about him. But then, Angie was a person of the moment. She might love him today and hate him tomorrow. She'd do anything to avoid a scandal. Kate breathed a sigh of relief. Angie would send Leon away to protect her good name. Kate had learned to love her sister dearly, but she was aware that Angie's moods were as changeable as a chameleon.

She glanced at the clock above the counter. 5:00pm. There was the whole evening and night to be gotten through.

The waitress brought her coffee and Kate heard herself ask, "Have you had something you heard repeat itself over and over in your mind?"

"Oh sure, who hasn't?" Janis, the waitress, wasn't surprised at the question. People said all kinds of dumb things when they were away from home. This little gal, though, she was really nervous and there was a sadness in her eyes. "It's time for my break, if you don't mind I'll sit here with you." At Kate's nod she plopped into the booth and introduced herself. Soon they were chatting like old friends.

When she left the café an hour later, she knew exactly what she was going to do. Would Angie understand? Maybe, but she'd worry about what people would say later. Kate didn't care what they said. She wanted her boy more than anything in the world. Angie would have to live with it.

Kate marveled at the difference a friend could make in one's attitude. Janis hadn't blinked an eye when she told her about Leon. Or her baby.

"You're a tough one," she'd said, "just keep doing what's right. That little boy of your's deserves a good home. Anyone can see you're a good person and you'll be a fine mother. Just be sure you tell him the truth. You weren't to blame, and don't go being heroic to save your Pa's image. God knows we've all got rotten relatives."

Kate started to interrupt, but Janis continued. "And as for your brother, you can't do much about him. Why not let your sister take care of that? After you pick up your kid tomorrow morning, stop by. I want to get a look at your little fellow."

The hotel was quiet. The sleepy-eyed clerk nodded respectively as she went by. Kicking off her boots she sank her feet into the spongy carpet, reveling in it richness. Running lightly up the stairs, immersed in her delicious feelings, she was suddenly knocked backwards onto the floor.

"I'm sorry lady, clumsy of me." He bent down to help her. She recognized him first. "Noah, oh Noah, it's you."

"Kate? Wow, you're all grown up. Angie is here then? I thought I saw her at the window. I came up to see if I could find her, then decided I was nuts. I mean what would Angie be doing at the window of a swell hotel like this? But you're here? Angie's here?" He couldn't stop babbling. She laughed and said, "Calm down, Noah. Let's get you to Angie. Oh, she'll be surprised." Soberly she added, "She needs you now. We both need you." Taking his hand, she led him to their rooms.

Kate went in first to prepare Angie for her husband's unexpected arrival. Angie squealed and ran to Noah and wrapped her arms around him. "Wait 'til I tell you ... you'll never guess what's happened. We're fixed for life. Pa left everything to Mandy. Oh, Noah, we can be a real fam ..."

He caught her as she sagged in his arms. "She's fainted, Kate. What's happening? God, get help."

Her heart pounding in fear, she called the desk and asked for a doctor. "My sister's fainted and her skin is funny, blue and clammy, please hurry!"

They carried her to the bed and covered her with a blanket. Noah began rubbing her arms and hands. "She's so cold. Has she been sick?"

"When she came to the farm, she was terribly ill, but Norm gave her medicine and I thought she was fine. She's been doing too much. I should have known all this would be too much for her. How could I have been so stupid?"

They waited in the sitting room while the doctor checked Angie. Kate filled Noah in on the news, telling him all that had occurred with Pa and Leon.

"Leon's been loco since he was a pup. I never wanted Angie to go back there. I didn't want Leon around Mandy. Mandy! Is she okay?"

"She's great. Mandy's a good kid. She's staying with Christine and Gus while we get this mess straightened out. Mandy's been waiting for you. Every day she walks to the bridge to look for you."

The doctor came out of Angie's room, smiling reassuringly. "She's fine. Just too much stress and not enough rest."

"She was blue. Her skin had a blue tinge to it. Isn't that serious?"

"Lack of oxygen," he said gruffly. "I want you to see that she takes at least three rest periods a day. And no undue stress. If she learns to limit herself, she can live fairly comfortable with her disease for a time."

Noah and Kate gaped at him. "What are you talking about? What disease?"

"Surely you know your wife has heart failure. I'm sorry, I assumed you knew. She's been under treatment by your family physician, she tells me."

"She didn't tell us." Kate remembered Leon mentioning it, but she hadn't believed it, especially when Norm had used a deathbed scene to trap Leon. "She knows. It's why she worries so about Leon and is letting Mandy stay at the Clayton's. She's very brave, keeping this to herself." She began to cry softly. Noah hugged her and went to sit with Angie, his face a picture of sadness and guilt.

NINE

Kate hastily scribbled a note to Angie, stating she'd be back soon. Stealthily she left the room, and hurried down the stairs and out into the blustery weather. She let the car idle while she thought over her plan. Janis had told her that deliveries were made to the institution early in the morning, and she counted on the back door being unlocked for the delivery men. She crossed her fingers for luck and drove slowly to the asylum.

She followed a road that wound around the big building to the back and stopped a few feet from the door. If she remembered right, this was the end where they kept the children. So frightened she could barely breath, she forced her body out of the car and crept to the door. She turned the knob. Luck was with her it opened easily. Silently she walked along the hall, hearing her heart thump with each step.

Suddenly she lost the little confidence that had helped her sneak in. Could she really do this? What if she were caught? Kate stood in the hall completely immobilized.

A piercing scream poured out from the ward and it galvanized her into action. She ran toward the children's room and came face to face with the old nurse. They stared at each other in surprise.

Kate pulled the picture out of her purse. "I'm looking for my son," she said simply. "Can you help me?"

"My ol' eyes ain't what they should be." The nurse had liked Kate when she visited her brother yesterday. "There is one little fella here, kind 'a looks like you. You plannin' to sneak 'em out of here?" At Kate's nod she sniffed. "It'd be a smart thing to get his chart first. That way they'll never know he's missin'."

"Will you help me? He was taken from me at birth. All these years I've thought he was dead."

"I'll find your boy, you'll have to get the charts, I don't see so good." She told Kate to look in the office and added that Duggin wouldn't be in for another hour. Handing her a large key she said, "Use the side door. He'll never know anyone was there." The nurse smiled as she thought of the many times she had gone in and had a little nip and him never the wiser.

Kate ran to the office, frightened, but excited, too. Maybe she could pull this off. The door squeaked when she pushed it open, but she stepped in and went to the wooden cupboards. She opened the drawers and saw they were filled with papers. Where to begin? Then she realized they were stacked alphabetically. He must be listed under Martin, but Leon and a woman named Nellie were the only names there. Continuing to open drawers, her eyes moving frantically over the papers, she finally found it. The kid's charts were laying alone in an otherwise empty drawer. She picked up a chart labeled Boy Martin. Quickly stuffing it into her purse, she started to leave, and stopped, startled, when she heard sobs. They were coming from the part of the office where she and Angie had met Paul Duggin. Nervously, she sidled to the front and peered into the gloom.

At first glance, she couldn't believe what she was seeing. Leon lay huddled on the floor, moaning and sobbing. Unable to stop herself, she moved closer and peered at him. Her hand flew to her mouth as she gasped. He was covered with bloody welts; he'd been beaten almost to death. The putrid odor of his body made her retch. It was all she could do not to run off and leave him there. The thought passed through her mind that if she didn't help him, he'd be dead with the hour.

Damn him, anyway! She beat her fist on the desktop. Leon, the despoiler, forever interfering with her life. She looked at her abuser, cold and beaten, lying on the floor, all his power gone, and she saw herself, cold and beaten, on the floor, Leon standing over her, his snaky eyes agleam with maniacal delight.

She grabbed the desk, holding on, trying to think of what to do. The telephone. She picked it up and called the police.

Kate backed out of the office and locked the door behind her. She flew up the hall, searching each room until she found the nurse. "Did you find him? Do you have my boy?"

"Mebe you can look, my eyes ..."

"Never mind. I found Leon in Duggin's office; he's been whipped almost to death. I called the police. They'll be here any minute. You'll have to talk to them. I'm getting my boy out of here." She shoved the key at the nurse and ran.

The kids were jammed into one small room, next to the open ward. Kate shuddered. The bitter wind blew through the window panes. The kids stood beside their beds, shivering, their haunted faces pinched with cold. She wrapped blankets from the beds around them, remembering her own misery when she had suffered in her cold room. One of the orphan girls ran to help her. She seemed to be the leader of the group as the kids let her wrap them up and smiled at her.

"Who are you?" Kate asked.

"Betty. What are you doing here? Are you somebody's relative?"

"Yes, I am looking for my boy. He's six years old. Are there more of you?" Betty shrugged. "I think there are a couple more, they went to the toilet."

Kate looked at each child, hoping to recognize her son, but she became overwhelmed by the eyes of the children. Hopeful eyes. Belligerent eyes. Vacant eyes. Some that were simply sad and bewildered. They were all watching her waiting ... for what?

Her heart was breaking and she turned to go when the boy came into the room. A boy with large violet eyes and dark wavy hair. Ma's dimple in his chin. Her son. She reached out to him and smiled. He flinched. She drew her hand back, sorry for scaring him. "I won't hurt you. I'm your friend." She knelt on the floor and smiled at him. "My name is Kate. I've come to take you home." He studied her solemnly. She took his hand. "We're breaking out of here, hurry." She started to walk to the door, pulling him along. Suddenly he broke free and ran to his bed. He lifted-up the mattress and pulled out a brown envelope. Then he ran to her and nodded his head. Mother and son ran out the back door and drove away.

Kate drove to Janis' café. Before they got out of the car she reached over and smoothed his hair. He shrank against the door. "You don't need to be afraid of me," she said gently. Holding out her hand, she waited for him to respond. His great eyes sized her up, not sure of her yet.

"Let's eat. You'll love Janis. She's our friend." She mentally kicked herself for talking so simplistic.

Kate ordered pancakes and eggs for him and coffee and toast for herself. Her nervousness was obvious. She felt gawky, not knowing what to do next. Why doesn't he talk? I don't even know his name. "Honey, what is your name?" she asked, looking at him hopefully. He didn't respond. Sighing, she went ahead and ate. He did the same. He ate with gusto, cramming food into his mouth until his cheeks resembled two small balloons. She giggled at him and puffed up her cheeks, and he smiled at her. He ate everything and then drank the large glass of milk Janis brought to the table.

Kate hadn't told Angie or Noah about him. She had planned to leave him with Janis while she stayed at the hotel until she found a way to break the news to Angie. Now she found it impossible to leave him. She just couldn't do it. Hopefully, Angie wouldn't get too upset, but there was no other choice. He would go with her. Suddenly she thought of Jude and wished she could talk to him. "I need to go home." The image of her cozy rooms and quiet fields filled her with longing. Yes, she and her son would go home today.

Janis untied her apron and threw it under the counter as soon as her helper came in. Sometimes they didn't show up at all and she'd be stuck with both shifts. There must be a better way to make a living. She joined Kate and shoved a newspaper at her. "Read this advertisement. It's a house, real cheap. I drove by it this morning and it's a steal. Nice. If you can afford it, you and the kid can always come to Marshallville if things don't work out at home."

Kate let the idea simmer in her mind. Owning her own home made sense, especially since Noah was back. Could they all live harmoniously together? She wasn't ready for a noisy, bustling home yet. There were a lot of obstacles she still had to work through. It was hard for her to make decisions. Pa or Leon had always told her what to do. She was too dependent and the struggle to achieve autonomy was a constant struggle. If she lived with the others would she get caught up in their lives and become lost again? She wasn't alone any more. She had her son. What was his name anyway? "Please, will you tell me your name." He looked at her and shook his head.

"I don't know what to call him." She grinned helplessly at Janis.

"Did you get any papers or maybe there's something in his suitcase?"

"There's no suitcase. Papers?" Kate hit herself on the head. "Of course, how stupid of me. I have his charts." She fumbled with her purse and brought out the chart. His name was Conner. Conner Burtram Martin.

"Hello, Connor. How about if you and I buy us a house?" He nodded emphatically. The two friends and the little boy went out to Janis' car.

They parked across the street from the house and watched the people milling in and out. "It's a funeral party," Janis explained. Kate thought the house was lovely and decide to buy it without looking at the inside. Janis took her to the bank and she made the arrangements. From there she went to the garage and bought a new Dodge sedan. Kate hugged Janis goodbye and took Conner with her to the hotel.

Angie was sitting up in bed, looking pretty and happy. Kate explained briefly about Conner and told them she was going home. Angie, her head full of visions of dining out and taking in the latest shows, passed over Conner's sudden appearance into their lives. She and Noah would be staying at the hotel until she was strong enough to travel. Kate bid them goodbye.

Before they left town, Kate drove to a clothing store and bought clothes for both of them. She bought recklessly, outfitting Conner and herself from the skin out. On impulse, she bought shirts and heavy wool socks for Jude and Ben.

At "Walters Fine Books and Notions" she chose a copy of *Anthony Adverse* for Jude, and a harmonica for Ben. Conner helped select the books he wanted and for herself she chose *Tender is the Night*, *The Good Earth*, and *Robert Frost's Collected Poems*. She added a modern dictionary to the pile and after some hesitation, a Bible. The back of the new sedan overflowed with their purchases. Flushed and happy they headed home.

Dr. Norman Larson and Attorney Rob Miller pulled up to the curb outside the asylum. They were to meet Noah there. Norm had arranged to send Leon to an institution in Minnesota. There, he would be taken care of and treated with as much dignity as possible. A rich man's prison, Norman thought, but it's what his sisters want for him and they can afford it. At least he wouldn't be running around assaulting young girls. Norm had changed his mind about Leon's chances for recovery. He would have liked to see him hang for the murders of his parents, but there wasn't enough proof and the state wouldn't arrest a crazy man. What if Kate is right and he's putting on an act? Fear touched him for an instant as he realized Leon could very well be playing a diabolical game with them. They might be playing right into his hands.

It was done. Angie had hired a private car on the Great Northern train and three men to deliver him to the private clinic. When the men returned, and made their report, she would pay them. It was the best they could do.

Paul Duggin was sitting in jail for abusing the patients and pocketing Montana State funds. That poor nurse had talked her head off and shown the authorities the fresh welts on Leon's body. She wanted to meet her maker with a clear conscience.

Jude wheeled himself to the south window in his kitchen and looked over at the Martin house. The workmen were there and he nodded in satisfaction. The new heating system was already installed. They were doing the finishing touches now. Kate was turning the upstairs into living quarters for Angie and her family. She and Conner would continue to live in her rooms on the main floor.

When Kate called him from Marshallville, he'd been glad to have the chance to thank her for having a telephone put in his house. He and Ben were still pinching themselves, finding it hard to believe they were set up so good. Jude wanted to do something to repay Kate for her kindness, so when she had called and told him what she needed done to the house, he'd offered to see to everything. She'd accepted gratefully. He was proud that she'd taken for granted his ability to do it.

Most people thought because he was lame, he must be dumb too. Or deaf. He grinned, remembering all the folks who bent close to his face and hollered when they spoke to him. Like that waitress in the coffee shop who put her face within a hair of his and hollered, 'Coffee?'. The devil must have bit him that day because he couldn't resist roaring 'coffee' right back at her. She'd jumped a foot and served them with a red face, pointedly ignoring him. Norm and Rob had convulsed with laughter and all in all it had been a lot of fun.

A horn honked and Jude looked out, surprised. He hadn't noticed the mail truck coming up the drive. Ray had started delivering Jude's mail when he heard he was in a wheelchair. Jude was constantly surprised by the goodness of people. He'd made some good friends and had company often. Norm and Gus came most frequently, but he had visits and good wishes from many of his neighbors. Wheeling his chair out on the porch, he thanked Ray for bringing it by. He noticed a pink envelope with blue writing and lots of curlicues and wondered about it.

You're turning into a real wimp, he said to himself as he rolled over to the stove to warm his hands. He remembered working outside in colder weather than this and not even thinking about it. He didn't want to get soft. He loved his new lifestyle, but if things changed on him, he sure wanted to have the toughness it took to live rough again.

He went to the desk and sorted his mail. Bills in this cubicle. Literary information in the top drawer. Advertisements and catalogues in the bottom left. There was the pink envelope again. For some reason, he was hesitant to open it. "I don't know who'd write to me, unless Kate decided to follow up her call with a letter." He laid the envelope on the desk and covered the bottom half with a thick rendition of Shakespeare. Then taking his bone handled knife in his good hand he expertly slit the envelop open and retrieved the contents.

His eyes went to the signature first. 'Your mother, Marcie Lindsay'. He licked his dry lips and read the letter.

'Hello, Jude. I have seen yur name in the paper and thot I wood tell you I am very sick. I am sorry I wasn't a good mother to you, but I tried. My landlady will write ware I am and send this to you.'

Jude had mixed feelings for his mother. She had been a victim of ignorance and he knew she had done the best she could for him according to her knowledge of what was right. He had no illusions about her, though and he had to figure out what it was she really wanted. Yet his spirits were lighter as he went about his work; he was proud she had turned to him for help. Then he wondered what she would think of him if she saw him again. It was twenty-two years since he'd run off and he honestly hadn't thought of her that much. He'd like to make a good impression. Let her see what she'd missed.

He wheeled his chair into his bedroom, where he'd had a full-length mirror hung on the wall. Ever since Norm had sent him to the hallway to look at himself, he'd taken pleasure in his handsome face. Course it was the blanket covering his deformities that did the trick. Before, he'd washed his face, ran a comb through his unruly hair and went about his business. He'd never paid attention to his face. His body was always in the way. The misshapen body, the stunted arm, no bigger than a child's, the spindly leg, short and bent at the ankle so his foot turned inward. Truth to tell, he liked being in the chair. Jude preened, proud of his dark brows, his full mouth, and the clear tan color of his skin. He was a handsome bugger, all right.

There were some women in Ryan that liked him too, one in particular. She'd hang on to his chair, all gushy and rolling her eyes, casting him suggestive promises. Jude enjoyed the little flirtations; they made him feel normal and happy. He was lucky, as he had no sex drive. The paralysis had closed off that part of him, so he could enjoy himself without the agony of unfilled dreams. He smiled at himself, and wondered who his father was. Norm was undoubtedly right on target. He was a blue blood.

The door banged shut and he wheeled himself to the kitchen. Ben was warming his hands on the stove. "Cold got you, did it? There's fresh coffee and the stew's hot."

Ben turned his slight body. He was a little fellow, but strong and tenacious as alligators' teeth. "I'll just set a spell. There's some trouble in the corral with one of the mares. She's gone plumb loco." He wrapped his cold fingers around the hot cup of coffee. "Big John's with her now. Say, Jude, is there a chance she got ahold of some bad feed?"

Jude thought for a moment. "A big chance, I'd think. Leon let the fields go to seed. Kate had to buy hay from the neighbors. My God, you think the mare might be poisoned with locoweed?"

"I'll bet my life on it. We'll have to go through the stacks to find the bad one. What worries me is, did the other horses eat the same feed?"

"Burt used to tell about Scrap Iron Nickleson having locoweed on his place. Too lazy to clear it off. If Kate can remember which hay she got from him, that would be a good place to start." Jude looked out the window. "She should be driving in any time now. It'll be good to see Kate again and meet her son."

"She's young to have a six-year old. Are you sure he's hers?"

"She says so. He'd have been born the year Mrs. Martin died. I remember Burt taking her out of school. I never liked the way Burt treated her, but it wasn't my business. It's for sure he fed her good. I can't figure out who fathered the boy, though, they kept her real close to home."

"You don't suppose Leon ...?"

"No, Ben, it wasn't Leon." Jude's stomach churned, the idea of it was enough to make him ill. "Leon wasn't normal in that way. Even when he was assaulting those young girls he couldn't complete the act. Two out of nine. Norm says he could do it only if the girl was a fighter, or if there was imminent danger involved. The Gordon girl was for revenge, and she was only six. Knowing Max might catch him stimulated him enough to do it. The girl at the asylum, well, she fought like a wild cat, poor soul. He needed to show the others how powerful he was. Leon always loved an audience."

Ben swallowed the remains of his coffee. It tasted bitter in his mouth. "Well, boss, I'd better get to work. Do you need anything before I go?" Jude shook his head and Ben went back to the corrals.

The cold winter sun shone through the kitchen window. The warmth in the room made the sun seem friendly, as it shone its rays on the flowered wallpaper. Kate had set the table with her new china and candles adorned the middle of the table centered by a vase of dried cattails and twigs. Kate had tied a red ribbon around the make-shift centerpiece and was inordinately proud of the effect.

This was her first company dinner. Jude and Ben graced the table at both ends, Kate on one side and Mandy and Conner across from her. She'd wanted to ask Big John to stay. He'd worked so hard with the mare and she would enjoy him, but Christine had been cooler than usual to her and she decided to keep a low profile for a while. At least until John gave her a sign he was interested in her.

"If you're all done, I'll clear the table and get the cards. Bet I can beat you at Old Maid," Kate teased Jude.

She was amazed at the rollicking laughter and gentle teasing. This is what it's like to be a family; it's just so wonderful I could cry. They played Old Maid for an hour and by unspoken consent let the kids win the last three games. Kate sent them to be in the studio and said goodnight to her guests. She began the dishes, turning her back when Ben reached down to lift Jude. He carried him out to the truck. Kate knew it would shame him for her to see him carried like a baby.

She finished the dishes and looked in on the kids. A smile crossed her face when she saw they had crawled into her cot and were cuddled together, sleeping soundly.

The books were where she'd left them before her trip to Marshallville and she quietly picked them up and placed them on the kitchen table. It had been too long since her last study session. There were sixteen new words on her list and Kate shivered with excitement. She opened the dictionary. There it was. *Indigent.* She'd heard the word on a street in Marshallville, and, as was her custom, wrote it in her little book, so she could get acquainted with it later. First, she practiced speaking the word, with the right accent, then spelled it, and finally used it in three sentences. She followed Mrs. Lowell's advice to the letter.

Kate longed to see her. Nine years ago, the teacher had given her inspiration and made it possible for her to get an education. Now she wanted to give her the thanks she deserved. She hoped Mrs. Lowell would be pleased with her efforts. Eagerly she looked up the next word.

She drove Mandy to school the next morning and asked the new teacher where she might find Mrs. Lowell. Armed with her address, she decided to go in that afternoon and try to find her.

Conner motioned that he wanted to go to the barn and she nodded yes. He should be in school, but she didn't know what to do about it, since he couldn't talk. Maybe she could teach him at home. Determined to look at life more optimistically, she pushed the worry from her mind. There was plenty to do, and she'd better get to it. She decided to dress up for her visit to Ryan.

Emily Lowell wrapped the teapot in a thick towel and carefully placed it on the crate. Her packing was almost done. She had only to strip the bed and sweep the floor. This room was shabby, she hadn't noticed how shabby until her pictures and mementos were put away. Before she'd packed, the room was full of memories, full of her life. Such as it was. Now, old and useless, she couldn't afford even this.

The room she was moving to was on the top floor of the old hotel and a shudder of dismay passed over her as she pictured the small grainy room, the slit of a window, and the airless atmosphere. But that's what she deserved, going against her family's wishes and teaching school. There had been no choice for her. It was something she'd had to do, and nothing could have stopped her, but death.

Now the future stared at her and she was afraid. Her teacher's salary allowed her a bare existence, but while she was teaching she hadn't minded all that much. It was only now, with no job, and very little money that she realized how vulnerable she was. She'd been a fool. Somehow, she'd always thought she would teach to the end. That her job was secure. But no, they'd replaced her with a young man from the city. They'd put her on the shelf like an old relic. Well, so be it.

Kate knocked tentatively on the door. She was filled with dismay when she discovered her beloved teacher was living in these dismal quarters, but she was so excited at the possibility of seeing her again, she was smiling when the old lady opened the door.

"I'm sorry if I've interrupted you. I'm Kate. Kate Willow Martin and this is my son, Conner."

"Kate? Oh child. I'd know you anywhere. Those violet eyes have been in every sunrise I've seen. But what are you doing here?"

"I came to see how you are. And to thank you for teaching me." Kate looked beyond Mrs. Lowell and noticed the boxes and crates and the empty walls. She gazed at her benefactor's face and saw the rigidity of her muscles and the almost imperceptible tremors of her head.

"Your moving? I did come at a bad time, but since we're here, why don't I help you take these things to your new place and then would you have time to have dinner with us? I have so much to tell you."

Emily agreed after much struggling with herself. Kate ran down the stairs and moved the car to the front of the door. She insisted Mrs. Lowell take her light case and sit in the car, while she carried the things down. Her strong body did the work easily, and they were soon driving towards the main street of Ryan.

Emily pointed at the hotel and Kate saw the look of distaste cross her face. She's in trouble, Kate thought, and I mean to find out what's going on with her.

"On second thought, why don't we have lunch first? I've worked up an appetite." She didn't wait for an answer, but drove out of town to Barney's Café.

She listened quietly as Mrs. Lowell told her story. Conner sat still and listened intently. When she finished, he walked to her side; he took the worn hand and placed his own hand inside of it. Tears filled Kate's eyes as astonishment and pride in her son waltzed through her heart.

"I think Conner wants to keep you." An idea was forming in her head and she ate her sandwich while mulling it over. "Mrs. Lowell, I want you to come home with us. Don't say no," she countered the older woman's negative gesture. "Not until you've heard my idea."

Emily Lowell's posture became even more rigid. Her face settled into stern lines and angles, resembling a stone statue. The black felt hat hung precariously to one side, and the wilted looking daisies drooped down, as her head stretched upward.

Kate knew she was treading on dangerous ground. Her heart bled for the fine woman who had given her soul to her profession, pounding knowledge into those who cared little for it, and those who like herself, would be forever grateful.

"I need you. I have studied all these years, Mrs. Lowell, but there is still so much I need to learn. I've gone as far as I can on my own. If my dream of becoming a teacher is to happen, I must know enough to pass the test to get my high school diploma. You are the means to my goal."

The two women studied each other in the silence that followed. Kate could see she'd stoked up a spark of interest in the teacher, and she quickly took up her plea.

"Conner and I have the farm to ourselves right now. There's a spare room on the main floor. We could roll up our sleeves and have it ready for you by tonight. I'll pay you room and board, plus a wage, for your services." Kate crossed her fingers and sighed with relief when Mrs. Lowell nodded her head in agreement.

The winter wind blew cold as they fought their way to the Dodge. For once, Kate didn't notice the countryside, or look for deer and pheasants. Her real education was about to begin, and she was scared as hell. What if she wasn't as smart as she thought she was? When she'd compared herself to Leon or Pa, of course she was smart, but when she was with Angie and her friends, she felt like a yokel. Would Mrs. Lowell throw up her hands in disgust?

Ben was in the yard when she drove up to the house, and he carried the boxes in and moved the bed to the far corner of the room.

Kate gave Mrs. Lowell permission to raid the house and cellar and take what she wanted. The teacher found a table and two chairs and asked Ben to put them by the window. "We'll have our classes there," she said, "and I can use it for my tea when school is closed." In the cellar, she found bookcases and in the front room a small roll-top desk.

Kate ran to her studio and brought her a handful of pencils, an ink pen and a bottle of ink. And reams of paper. She asked Ben to carry all the books and worksheets Mrs. Lowell had given her over the years to the new classroom.

Next, she proudly opened a cupboard in the small hall and removed new sheets, two blankets, and a beautiful pink satin bedspread. There were matching pillowcases and new pillows. She'd bought them for Angie, as a surprise for when she came home, but it seemed right to put them on her teacher's bed. After she'd made the bed, she went to the door to go start dinner. She turned back to tell them she'd be in the kitchen and there was Mrs. Lowell bent over the bed, smoothing her hand over the spread with tender caresses. Quickly, she slipped out, and went to her bathroom and had a good cry.

Two weeks later, Mrs. Lowell did throw her hands up, but not in disgust as Kate had feared. "Kate, you know everything you need to pass a high school equivalency test. And more. You're better educated than most college students."

"But I don't feel smart. I can't hold my own with people in regular conversations."

"Hmm, you need practice. Keep up with current events, read the newspapers, and socialize. I'll hold some classes on how to listen, how to sit, what is expected of you in social circles. We'll act out situations until you feel at ease."

She beamed at Kate. "It will be like a real coming out. Oh, Kate, you've given me a new outlook on life. To think a child of eleven years could be so determined to be a teacher. I can't believe I was your inspiration."

Kate hid her smile, knowing Mrs. Lowell did believe it. It had been great to watch the cowed woman return to her former personality. They'd become great friends, too, except for the three hours a day in class, where she remained the earnest pupil, and Mrs. Lowell her stern mentor.

The days passed in harmony and for Kate they were the happiest days of her life. Conner was a constant source of delight, and Ben and Jude insisted on keeping him occupied while Kate was busy with her lessons. Ben had more free time now that she'd hire a couple of farm hands and one day he'd teased Emily until she'd gone ice fishing with him and Conner. She'd come home, triumphantly waving two trout in Kate's face.

Kate was surprised Jude and Emily didn't have more rapport between them, since they both had such a great love for literature. She'd expected Jude to enjoy long visits with the teacher, but that wasn't the case. He seemed almost resentful of her education.

Kate missed Mandy, but Angie insisted her daughter go back to the Clayton's until she and Noah returned home. The letter she'd received from her sister had been full of snide remarks and displeasure at Kate's unseemly conduct. Kate noticed that Angie didn't mention Conner by name in her letters, but she was sure Angie wouldn't be able to resist him once she was home.

Kate had finished decorating the upstairs. With Emily's help she'd turned the drab, ugly rooms into gracious living quarters. Angie would be warm and comfortable in her new rooms. As if on cue, the telephone rang. Noah said gaily, "roll out the red carpets, we'll be home Sunday."

"Kate, I know you'll understand it's time for me to move on." Emily spoke lightly and continued to dry the dishes, rubbing the gold stripe at the top of the cup with vigor.

"Move on! But Emily, you live here now. You're part of this family."

"I'm your teacher and your friend. I've come to love all of you very much, but it's time I take myself in hand and arrange a life for myself. I have a notion with the money I've earned here, I can rent a decent house and give classes in etiquette, and tutor on the side. I should be able to bring in enough to live quite comfortably."

"I won't let you. You're staying right here with us. I won't hear of it!" Kate surprised them both by bursting into tears.

"Oh, my dear." Emily took Kate's arm and let her to the table, pushing her down on a chair. She sat beside her and spoke determinedly. "Kate, I'll tell you the truth, though I hadn't intended to do so. I'm leaving because Angie and I would never get on. She'd no doubt kick me out before the week was up."

"But she wouldn't. I'll tell her how important you are to me. Angie isn't as bad as you think." But Kate's voice betrayed her own doubts, she wasn't sure Angie would treat Emily right. "You haven't seen her for years. She's changed."

"People like Angie don't change. She was a selfish, manipulative snob, and to tell the truth I never liked her. Most people didn't notice it, but I saw a lot of the same characteristics in Angie that I saw in Leon." Kate gasped, stunned at Emily's words.

"How can you say that? Why, Leon was and is insane according to Norm Larson anyway. And he is a doctor. Angie's perfectly rational."

"Leon's as sane as you or me. I'll never be convinced otherwise. As for Angie, she had the same cold thought process. If she wanted something, she got it. No matter who was hurt. I decided that both of them were lacking the thing that makes us human beings. Their souls."

"Like Pa." Kate's white face dawned with understanding.

The women continued to sit at the table, immobilized by the potent words hanging in the air. Finally, Emily cleared her throat.

"Kate, I am an outspoken old fool. The last thing I want to do is hurt you, but I had to speak my mind. I have a feeling for you, like a mother, maybe." She laid her hand over Kate's. "Please, watch out for yourself and Conner. Keep yourselves your top priority, and don't be angry at an old woman for butting into your family business."

It was as close to an apology as the indomitable teacher could come. She rose and went to her room to sort her belongings. Kate ran after her and put her arms around her. They stood embracing for long moments, then each went back to their duties.

Jude suggested that Kate call Mrs. Jolly and ask about an apartment. As luck would have it, there was an empty one-bedroom on the ground floor and there was a small parlor Mrs. Lowell could use for her classes.

Kate drove to town and looked at the apartment. The living room had large bow windows, and the whole place was freshly painted and cozy with clean rugs and curtains. The rent was more than Emily could afford, so Kate gave Mrs. Jolly one year's rent. Emily would be horrified, but Kate was determined to this time have her way. There would be no shabby hotel room for her friend.

CHAPTER

TEN

K ate prepared Angie's luncheon tray and started to carry it up the stairs, when Noah walked towards her, took the tray from her and said, "You look peaked. Sit down and rest a bit." She plopped onto the creaky rocker in the kitchen and sipped from a cup of tea. Christmas was just three weeks away and the mountain of work ahead of her seemed insurmountable. It seemed as if she was busy from early morning to late at night. Why was she doing it? Why did she take it as her sole responsibility? Jude said she was trying to apologize for living. That was an exaggeration, but he might be on the right track. She couldn't seem to stop taking care of everyone and everything.

Angie hadn't been too pleased when she realized Conner was living in the house with them. "Another scandal in the family, Kate?" she'd asked bitterly. Noah had been great about it, he and Conner had become good friends, but it was Jude that Conner trusted. He often slipped away to visit Jude and Kate understood his need. She did the same thing, more often then she thought was proper. Yet, there were times she felt herself apart, times when she saw herself as a broken doll and it was then she would run across the barnyard and talk to Jude. He always had time for her, and she had finally told him about Pa. Jude had held her as she sobbed into his lap forging a bond between them that grew stronger each day.

She longed for the days before Angie returned. She'd been a free spirit then, and those around her had valued her. Now she was the over-worked housekeeper, the glue that held them all together. The work itself didn't bother her as much as the way they thought of her. Like she was nothing.

The closeness she and Angie had shared was gone. Angie was a different person since Noah came home. Mean and spiteful, her mouth spewed complaints and derogatory gossip about their friends and neighbors. Kate couldn't understand it.

Norm said Angie was failing daily. Lord, I don't want her to die, I just want to like her again. What will happen to Mandy when her mother's gone? Noah meant well, but he wasn't very responsible. Noah had always been fun-loving and carefree, taking risks that usually left him penniless and remorseful.

The smell of fresh bread tantalized her stomach and Kate rose to remove the loaves from the oven. Childlike, she cut a thick slice off the end. Everyone like the ends and there's usually a mad flourish for the first slice. I'll get it this time, she thought with glee. I baked it and I'll eat it. Her laughter filled the kitchen, as she remembered reading 'The Little Red Hen' to Conner. She sounded just like that self-righteous, but very industrious, hen.

After eating the bread, she wiped her mouth on her apron. Her arm stuck out, long and thin, and she stared at it in shock. There hadn't been time to watch her diet, but she'd continued to stay away from the desserts. She strode into the hall and peered at herself in the full-length mirror. She was a tall woman, almost five foot seven, with long, coltish legs, and a slim, curvy figure. Who'd have thought it? But her hair looked bad. It hung below her waist in stringy clumps. Emily had shown her how to dress it, but there hadn't been any time lately, and her clothes were too large. Maybe Emily would go shopping with her and help her select the right fashions, but who would take care of Angie? Christine was able to spend a couple of hours a week visiting, but Kate couldn't bring herself to ask for her help. Christine was very cool to her. Kate was still easily intimidated, so she pretended not to notice. She just hated the fact that Christine's treatment of her made her feel guilty.

She still daydreamed of John, but he was so respectful of her she hadn't anything to feel guilty about.

Angie could hire a cook and housekeeper. She recalled how angry Angie had been when she heard Leon made Kate do the cooking and cleaning. It wasn't her money then, and it was easy for Angie to spend Leon's money. It was funny how Pa's inheritance had affected them all. Leon could afford to be crazy in luxury, Noah to buy the western suits and guitars he was so partial to, and Angie spent money on her cosmetics and new clothes, but resented buying for the house and especially the pantry. If Kate didn't supplement the groceries, they'd be on short rations. And I just go on acting like I owe it to them. The money she'd fought for had been a way out for her, but that was before Conner. He was worth it and she wouldn't let herself dwell on might-have-beens. She had to care for Angie until other arrangements could be made. "I'll get my teaching degree, there's still time," Kate assured herself, trying to ignore the doubt that lived deep within.

Kate was in a good mood again. The long rambling conversations she had with herself grounded her, helped her to focus on what was really important. The determination to make some changes was foremost in her mind as she prepared dinner for them.

The dinner she served that evening was a feast for the eyes and stomach. Kate had whipped the potatoes and made beef gravy. There were creamed carrots and peas, a large roast, and loaves of bread with butter and honey. Apple cobbler and cream finished off the meal. Smells of spice and vanilla wafted around them as they gathered at the table.

Angie turned to Kate, pushing her plate back. "Some of my friends are coming by tomorrow afternoon. Would you do up some of those little sandwiches, Kate? And, please, when you serve the tea, use the silver tea service. I was embarrassed last week when you brought up that old pot."

Shame flooded Kate's face, her happy feelings fell to the bottom of her stomach. Angie sounded so accusatory and condescending. Not a word of thanks for the delicious meal, no thought for all the work and time she had put into it. The unaccustomed anger rose in her hot and fierce.

"I'm sorry, Angie, I won't be here tomorrow. Conner and I are going to the city." She continued eating as if it were a common thing for her to do.

"To the city! Whatever for? Why, who will wait on my friends?" Angie's voice rose to a shriek.

"I suppose you will, Angie. They're your friends."

Conner and Mandy stopped eating, watching Kate with surprise and apprehension in their eyes. They'd never heard her talk back to Angie. Noah smiled to himself. He'd been waiting for Kate to take a stand, she'd put up with a lot from her sister, and he figured she'd fight back sooner or later.

Angie stared at Kate, wondering if she'd heard right and anger spread over her face as she realized she'd been very neatly rebuffed. Angie leaned forward, her posture threatening, warning Kate not to defy her.

"I heard from Leon yesterday. He's doing very well, getting better every day. I wouldn't be surprised if they didn't release him soon. I could put in a good word for him. I could bring him home."

Kate recognized the threat in Angie's announcement. Like Leon she was using whatever it took to keep Kate in her place. The familiar tentacle of fear wrapped around Kate, rendering her immobile. She tried to speak, but her throat closed-up and she struggled frantically to breathe. She saw her family through a veil of gray fog. She was vaguely aware of Conner pulling her arm and Noah rubbing her back, talking in soothing tones. As fast as it had come upon her the fear began to recede and she was able to breathe again. She gulped in air and leaned back in her chair waiting for the dizziness to pass.

Kate was struck dumb by the invisible yoke of fear that lived within her. It wasn't Angie's threat to bring Leon home that had affected her, it was the threatening stance her sister had taken, the evil power Kate sensed pouring at her from Angie's eyes. Emily had warned her and she was right.

She pushed herself up from the chair and took Conner's hand. "I'm tired and want to get an early start in the morning. After you do the dishes remember to fill the reservoir and bank the stove. It will make things much easier when you cook breakfast." She walked out with

Conner, a smile on her lips. They would go to Marshallville and stay in their own house. Suddenly she felt young and happy and very daring.

Angie went into a tizzy when Kate left the room. "What kind of an act was that? Talk about getting attention!"

"That's enough, just knock it off. Don't you realize the danger you put your sister in? Angie, you went too far. She couldn't catch her breath."

"Now you're on her side too. I don't notice you all that concerned over my illness. Besides, I let her live here free, the least she could do is help me out once in a while. How will I entertain with no help?"

"For crying out loud, do your friends have maids? You're the only one in these parts who can afford to think like that. Do you believe it's right to spend Mandy's money on frivolous things like servants?" Noah wondered sometimes how he was able to stand her. Selfish, high-toned bitch, then he remembered how ill she was and smiled at her kindly.

"Noah, you don't know what it's like. Kate is getting downright lazy. She hasn't brought my ironing to me and it's been at least a week since I told her to do it."

"She hasn't cleaned my tub," Mandy said, sounding so much like her mother that Noah looked at her sharply. "I told her to clean it yesterday."

"See what I mean? Even Mandy has to suffer because of her."

"Why don't you go to bed, dear? Mandy and I will do these dishes. Huh, Mandy? You want to help your old man?" Mandy giggled and started clearing the table.

"But Noah, Mandy shouldn't be doing dishes. Leave them for Kate, she can do them when she gets back. I never should have given her all that money."

Noah's heart beat furiously. He'd like to hit the stupid woman. Since Mandy inherited this damn farm, she'd been acting like a queen bee, giving herself airs and pretending her sister was her maid. Well, he'd make sure Mandy didn't take on those attitudes. Mandy was a naturally kind and generous kid and he'd help her stay that way. If it wasn't for Mandy he'd be long gone.

Kate and Conner slipped out of the house at 6 o'clock the following morning. She laughed as the rear end of the car fish-tailed on the ice ridden road. The wind had died down, and the early morning darkness gave them a safe, calm atmosphere to begin their three-hour trip.

Conner had fallen asleep and woke when she slowed down to drive through town. "Look, Conner, here's Marshallville. We made it, kid, aren't we something?" Conner smiled and nodded.

Kate sighed. If only he would talk. The charts she'd stolen from the asylum stated he was deaf and dumb. He'd been brought to the orphanage as a baby, by Burt Martin, distant relative. An agreement to send $200.00 per year was attached to the chart and signed in Pa's handwriting.

Kate had taken him to the clinic in Ryan and Norm had been perplexed by the charts diagnosis. When one of Norm's colleagues from Washington State visited him, he'd brought him out to test Conner and he, too, found no reason for his malady. She'd known from the start he could hear, and Jude said his comprehension was remarkable. So why didn't he speak?

Whatever the reason, she decided they were going to have a good time. Just the two of them, and he would have all her attention. She felt like she'd neglected him with all there was to do on the farm.

"Here is our new house." She pointed to the friendly white house sitting back from the tree lined street. The place was as pretty as a picture. The house and garage were painted white, both trimmed with black. A white picket fence surrounded the large yard and there were trees and shrubs placed strategically around the property. A thin layer of fresh snow covered everything. "Our own home, Conner. Do you remember the swing in the back yard?"

She parked the car in front of the garage. Conner helped with the suitcases and they walked silently to the front door. When she turned the key in the lock, there was a moment of hesitation. A subtle feeling that she'd made a mistake.

The house was absolutely perfect. There were two bedrooms with a bath in the middle, a small kitchen with a glassed-in dining area, and a large living room complete with all the furnishings. They ran through the house, opening closets and drawers, squealing with delight. Kate as much a child as Conner. They raced out to the backyard and she pushed

Conner on the swing. He grinned widely, his eyes shooting sparks of glee.

Janis had stocked the pantry with groceries and made up the beds. They stayed home all that day, enjoying each other and their new home. That evening they ate their dinner in the glass alcove and watched the sunset. Kate gazed at her son and her heart spilled over. He seemed different here, more open and confident. His little body wriggled with delight as he watched the pink and purple horizon. "The sun's going to bed," she told him, "and that's what we should do too."

Later, when she tucked him into his bed he hugged her tight and went to sleep holding her hand. Kate tucked the blankets around him, and tip-toed into the living room. She sank into the snug chair, and let her eyes wander about the room. It was lovely. Earth colors predominated the large living room. Dark green rugs splashed across hardwood floors. Touches of gold glinted from the furniture and mirror frames. The previous owners had loved his house, that was for sure.

Her mind insisted on returning to the scene with Angie. She'd tried to forget it, but now she decided to confront it head on. Angie's vindictiveness had shattered her, true, but her problem was with herself. The fear had come over her so fast, catching her unaware, like an enemy that lay in wait to spring on her in a moment of vulnerability.

Angie's threat to bring Leon home hadn't upset her, she'd known it was false bravado. No, it was fear of pain, that had to be it. When Angie leaned toward her, with that tough façade, the fear had started and when she'd seen the hate in her sister's eyes, it had rolled over her in full force. The hate reminded her... that was it. The eyes, Angie's and Leon's, were identical. She'd never realized it before, because Angie's eyes were always so bland or haughty, or smiling. But she'd forgotten herself, and let her viciousness shine through. Kate's shudder made a reverberating sound in her ears. She'd done enough soul searching for one day. Instead of going to her room, she climbed in with Conner and held him against her, praying he hadn't inherited the Martin curse.

Conner bounced all around the house the next morning. He checked the yard, the cupboards, and the drawers. He wants to make sure everything's the same, Kate thought, he doesn't trust, either. We're a lot alike, Conner and me.

"Let's get dressed and go buy you some toys. We'll get you a ball and yo-yo and you can pick out anything you want." What did boys want?

She lost him in the toy department. One minute he was by her side and the next minute he was gone. She looked around frantically. It was such a large store and she didn't really know where she was, how could she find him? Running up and down the aisles, calling his name, she missed the commotion, until she heard a shrill scream. She followed the sound and there he was, hanging on to a red wagon, his face white, and his violet eyes misty with tears. A red-haired girl was holding on to the other end, just as determined to have it. The girl's mother was prying Conner's fingers from the wagon and when she'd loosened them she gave his hands a resounding smack.

Kate sped to Conner's rescue, lifting him up into her arms. She turned to the angry woman and shouted, "This is my son. Don't think you can hit my son and get away with it." She bent down and took the handle of the wagon.

"We're buying this wagon, lady, and you get out of our way." She sat Conner in the wagon and pulled him to the counter, leaving the woman huffing, "I nevers," and the girl screaming shrilly.

When they'd loaded the purchases into the car they strolled down Main Street to look at the Christmas decorations. Kate and Conner got caught up in the magic of Christmas and ran delightedly from one store to the next, entranced with the lights and humming the carols that poured from the shops. Kate smiled shyly at the Santa Claus in the Rocky Mountain Emporium and they were both delighted when he lifted Conner on his lap and gave him a sack of candy. It was a new experience for them both. Two babes in the woods.

The drive home was restful, the evening still and full of promise. Kate glanced at Conner. He was sitting still for once and his great eyes spilled over with joy. Her heart contracted in pain, as she thought of the hard times ahead for him.

"It's days like today that make life worthwhile, Honey. Remember that when you have a bad day. We get through the painful moments if we remember the happiness." Conner gestured and put his hand over his heart.

"I'm not sure I can explain happiness. It must be that our souls are celebrating. It's a gift from God. We both had bad beginnings, but I think the joy is so much sweeter because of it, don't you?"

Kate parked the car in the garage and entered the house through the back door. They dropped the packages in the porch and removed their boots and coats. "Lay your coat across the clothes rack, Conner, we're going to Mass in the morning." Conner smiled and made the sign of the cross.

I should have realized he misses church, Kate mused silently, after all he was raised in one for six of his seven years. The farm and Angie had moved up to first place, somehow. Twenty years of enforced family servitude had ingrained a guilty sense of duty in her. It wasn't easy to break the habits of her lifetime.

Kate slept in Conner's bed again, and they lay close, warm and content. She was weary and almost asleep when Conner asked, "Are you really my mother? My real mother?"

"Yes," she answered and sat straight up and hollered, "You talked, oh, Conner, you can talk."

"Will you always be my mother?"

"Forever and ever, Conner." She wrapped her arms around her son and they slept.

Gus' soft-boiled egg was ready and Christine broke it into a bowl and added a slice of toast. She placed it beside the bed and said, "try to eat dear, I'm going out to help John with the chores. Oh, dear, that darn telephone always rings when I'm busy. I'll get it on the way out." She ran to the kitchen and answered it.

"Christine, come early today, will you? I need you to get things ready for the luncheon."

"I'm sorry, Angie, but Gus needs my help today. He's down with the flu, so I'll be busy in the barn,"

"But, Christine, I'm counting on you. Surely you can just run over and help me get a little lunch made up for the girls."

"It's impos…"

"I forgot to tell you. Kate ran off to Marshallville and left me with it all. I'm here all alone."

"Angie, your perfectly capable of making sandwiches. I really have to go, but I'll try to call you later."

"You sound as if those cows are more important to you than I am. Really, Christine, you can't be serious."

"You don't think so? Those cows are our bread and butter. Not everybody can afford to lie around all day. And you've got a new kitchen, how hard can it be? Why don't you hire someone to do your work? I have my own family to care for. I'm sure Kate would like a life of her own, too." Christine hung up with a bang.

Angie stared at the phone. How dare Christine hang up on her? "Blood will tell. That big, country bumpkin. Dumb sharecroppers that never had a penny to their name. She should be glad I let her hang around with mer."

She mentally crossed Christine off her list. Her feet thumped the floor as she paced, trying to think of someone who could help her. Jude! Quickly, she dialed the operator and gave her Jude's number. He answered and she said, "Jude, I need a teensy favor. Send Ben to me. That Kate took off and left me all alone and I'm expecting company in just a few hours. I need Ben to help me clean up and fix lunch."

"Sorry, Ben's out today."

"Out? Out where? This is important, Jude, call him and send him to me at once."

"Can't do that. He's out of the area getting some information for me."

Angie was astounded. Everybody had turned on her. Kate had set them all against her. She would call Rob tomorrow and see about getting all that money back.

She dragged herself into the kitchen and looked around helplessly. Noah and Mandy hadn't done a good job of cleaning up at all. She put the dishpan on the stove and lifted the lid of the reservoir. It was dry.

She looked in the cupboards and pantry. Kate hadn't prepared a thing for her luncheon or shopped for the little cans of delicacies Angie liked to serve her friends. She heard her sister's voice in her head, "Angie, you didn't give me your household money again this week. I've bought all the groceries for over a month." She should, thought Angie, living here with that orphan. Using Mandy's house like she owns it. If she thinks I believe that's Pa's boy, she's crazy.

Sobbing, she went to the telephone again and called her friends to cancel her luncheon. No one offered to help her. She wiped her eyes and slowly ascended the stairs. Her strength was about gone and she decided to stay in her warm room until Noah fixed the fires downstairs. God, she was lonely. She stood in the middle of her room, hating to go to bed again. Something cold and wet pushed at her leg. She jumped back, startled.

"Tippy! For lands sake, you gave me a fright." She sat on the rug and stroked his head. "I wonder what is it about you that we all love? I'd like to be loved like that." Without warning her sobs bubbled up and suddenly she was hugging the dog and weeping into his neck. "I'm so afraid, God help me, I'm afraid to die."

Noah knew he should go to the house and take care of Angie, but he hated to go in. She was either whining pathetically or using that hoity toity way of talking, running everybody into the ground.

Glancing over the house he noticed the smokeless chimneys. God, couldn't she even keep a fire going? He took his time getting into his coat. The old stove was hot and he'd spent some pleasant hours grooming the horses, and dreaming. Angie didn't like his dreams, they threatened her somehow.

She'd tried to change him from the start. He'd never been quite good enough for her, not enough spit and polish. It dawned on him that was another way of saying she was ashamed of him. His skin darkened.

He couldn't remember when he'd stopped loving her. A gradual loss of interest and one day he'd looked at her and felt nothing. He'd been so in love with her. He'd have died for her at one time. "That woman scares the life out of me," he admitted. "She's as cold and calculating as her old man ever was."

CHAPTER

ELEVEN

T he long winter days were a time of discovery for Kate and Conner. They spent their time learning about each other and enjoying the freedom their life in Marshallville afforded them. Kate had drawn some of Conner's past from him, but only small incidents. He seemed reluctant to speak of his former life and she didn't want to expose him to memories that would retard his progress.

He had two strikes against him right from the start. First, he was a Martin and second, he was illegitimate. Kate hated the thought that he was Burt Martin's son and Leon's half-brother, though try as she might she could see no resemblance to either of them. Not in looks or actions. Janis had asked her if she had trouble accepting him at times because of the way he was conceived, but Kate didn't think of him that way. The two incidents were, in her mind, totally separate. She looked upon him as a great gift, a reward for all the horror and pain she had lived with, one of the miracles Conner talked about.

Religion was foreign to Kate, except for what she'd read in her books, but Conner took it very seriously. At Mass he was solemn and immersed himself into the ceremony with devotion. He was too quiet after church to suit Kate, but she'd learned to leave him be until he was ready to resume his usual play and chatter.

She was teaching him to read and write and was amazed at the swiftness of his mind, but he was teaching her things too. Cursing came easily to her. She'd grown up hearing the expletives growling from Burt's throat. She smiled, recalling Conner's reaction when she'd hit her thumb with the hammer and let loose a 'God damn. Son-of-a-so-and-so.' Conner, eyes blazing, had informed her she was not to take God's name in vain, she would go to hell for sure. Well, she tried to remember and was thankful he trusted her enough to confide his beliefs to her.

Motherhood was scary and she felt so inadequate at times. Perhaps she would be more intuitive if Burt had not stolen him away from her. As it was, a lot of the time she simply raised him by instinct. She figured as long as they loved and respected each other things would work out.

Conner's confidence and willingness to learn new things amazed Kate. She knew his life had been hard and lonely, but he had grown strong and was full of purpose. He was a very determined and happy little boy. His happiness shone from his eyes and glowing face. He knew how to live his moments and be thankful for them. Perhaps she could emulate him and learn to trust life.

The ringing of the telephone interrupted her muses and she reluctantly arose and answered it. Mandy's voice came through, begging her to come home. "Things are just awful here, Aunt Kate. I don't know what to do. Mama can't get any good help and Daddy and I can't do anything to please her. Even if you don't stay, could you come home for a while and set things right? You know, hire some good help and train them?"

She promised Mandy she would do what she could and suggested she go to visit Jude for a while. "He'll be glad to see you and you'll feel better, too. We'll be there soon, honey. Everything will be fine, you'll see."

Damn Noah and Angie, so self-centered they couldn't see beyond their own noses. Well, she needed to go back anyway, get their things, and move out permanently. Poor Mandy, her heart ached for the sad little girl.

"Are you all packed, Conner?" They were getting ready for the trip home. Kate stacked their cases near the door and was gathering up her keys and purse when Conner squealed, "Mama, snow. It's snowing big." She went to the window to see Conner's snow. It was snowing big all right. Thank God they weren't on the road. The flakes were falling thick and heavy. Kate couldn't see across the street. In fact, she couldn't see the garage.

"Guess what, Conner? We're not going home. We're snowed in. We might have to spend Christmas here."

"Wheee!" Conner spun madly about the room, laughing and screaming. Kate yelled "Wheee!" and they danced around and jabbed playfully at each other.

"Mama, I don't know Christmas."

"I don't really know it either, son. We'll experience it together. Didn't you have Christmas at the Home?"

"Uh, uh. The sisters gave us more food, but they didn't have Santa and presents and things like they have uptown. We prayed extra hard and listened to the story of the Virgin Mary, Joseph, and the baby Jesus. Sister said if we prayed extra hard maybe God would give us a better Christmas, but He never did."

"You'll have it this year, Conner," she said with confidence. "And every year from now on." Giving him a kiss on his smooth cheek, she sent him to play while she called home. Noah answered her call. He expressed his disappointment at not seeing them for Christmas but was glad to know they were safe at their house. Mandy was downcast. Kate explained to the best of her ability, but felt she'd let her niece down. Angie was outraged at the delay. "I was counting on you. You can't do things like this. I've invited important people to eat dinner with us."

Something mean and dangerous fluttered in Kate's breast.

"Just what role did you have in mind for me, Angie?"

"Why I... I want you here as part of the family. I was going to ask if you'd wait on table, but of course..." Noah's voice cut in. "Just forget everything she said. You and Conner have a wonderful holiday. Wish Mandy and I were there."

Kate called Jude and learned that his mother was spending the holidays with him. He asked about Conner.

"That's one reason I phoned. Conner has an extra special gift for you, Jude. Hang on a second." Conner took the phone and yelled, "Merry Christmas, Jude. Merry Christmas, Ben." He jabbered away and Kate had a hard time getting the phone away from him. She explained how Conner had started talking out of the blue. "He hasn't shut up since." They hung up on a happy note and Kate was surprised how much she missed Jude and Ben. They're my family, she thought. She suddenly realized she hadn't told her own family Conner could talk.

"No matter how bad the weather is, the mail man manages to make his rounds." Kate grabbed her coat and ran out to the box. She was expecting an answer from Rob Holden about the property Burt had purchased in Marshallville, and the money in the Chicago bank. She'd sent him all the papers, including the insurance policy on Angie's mother. She took the pile of letters and raced back to the house. She stood straighter and a look of pride came into her eyes as she studied the enveloped. Miss Kate Sutton. She'd come a long way from picking up her only correspondence under a rock, to receiving mail at her own home. There were two letters for Conner, from Jude and Ben. She set them aside, to help him read later. She skimmed through the rest of the mail quickly, a letter from Norm, one from Mandy, and a thick envelope from Emily. These she lay aside also and opened the large envelope from Rob.

She felt a stab of disappointment when she saw it was typed by his secretary, informing her the land was not a part of the inheritance, but belonged to Conner Burtram Martin; he was to take possession when he reached the age of eighteen. Attorney Holden would send more information when the legalities were completed.

Kate was stunned. What kind of a man had Burt been? He'd denied his son by placing him in an orphan's home to live a lonely life without benefit of his Mother, and then given him a start after he reached adulthood. Did he have feelings for the boy, then? Tears stung her eyes, there's no use trying to understand him. He was a screwball. All the Martins were screwballs.

I'd like to change Conner's name to Sutton. Her anger at Burt rose in her, acid tasting bile erupting into her throat. She swallowed hard and continued reading. The insurance policy was invalid; the company had been out of business for years. The money in the Chicago bank was still being investigated. They would pass on the information as soon as it was received.

Her heart lifted when she noticed the note Rob had scrawled at the bottom of the last page. *'Life's always throwing us little surprises, isn't it? Hope this is a pleasant one. At least Burt tried to do the right thing for his son. Maybe this Conner will be a brother you can be proud of. Call me when you get back. We'll have coffee, or something. Merry Christmas, Rob.'* Brother! He thought Conner was her brother. But of course. NO one would think she was his mother. Not if they knew Pa was the father.

Her head spun. Everything was getting too complicated. Conner had to go to school, how would she enroll him? Pass him off as her brother? No, she wouldn't deny her son. She'd have to change his name, let them think she'd had a child out of wedlock. It was better than the truth. God, what a tangled web Burt had trapped them into.

The letter from Norm brought new worries. Leon was responding exceptionally well to his new treatment and surroundings. They were considering giving him a leave of absence so he could visit his family and farm. *'Don't be concerned, Kate. I showed the letter to Sheriff Henson and he got right on the telephone. He let them know in no uncertain terms, that Leon would be sitting behind bars the minute he crossed the Montana State Line, that he's wanted for murder and child assault and the only reason he's not in prison is because he's supposed to be crazy. That took the wind out their sails. I can tell you and they assured Henson that Leon would be kept under lock and key. I seem to be the bearer of bad news, more often then not, but I have to tell you also that Angie is failing fast. She's fighting it every step of the way, but I've done all I can do. I have suggested to Noah that it might be worth a try to go to Arizona with her, into the hot, dry climate. I guess that means we'll be seeing you around here again. I will be one that is glad of it. I miss you and hope we can see each other more often. You're like a quicksilver, Kate, but I plan to catch you some day. Love, Norm.'*

Restless, she paced around the front room. She glanced out the window and saw a farm truck pulling into her drive. Who in the world? The big fellow jumped down from the cab and Kate gave a glad cry and ran to the door.

"John, Oh, John, I'm so glad to see you. Come in, don't stand out there dawdling. Get in here where it's warm."

John Clayton smiled shyly. His eyes shining with friendliness and good humor. Just what I need, Kate thought, he's the medicine I've longed for, and didn't know it. She took his coat and hat and let him into the living room.

"Sit here by the fire, I'll get our coffee." She was half-way to the kitchen door when she suddenly spun around and said, "John, are you here because something bad has happened?"

"No, I'm here because I came to Marshallville to a Grange meeting. Gus gave me your address, on the sly, in case I wanted to look you up. I thought you'd like to know we have the horses under control again. Two of them, Little Lady and Wabash, ate the locoweed and they're dead, but none of the others were affected." It was a long speech for John, and she smiled her appreciation, as she swallowed her tears and ran to get the coffee.

Three hours flew by and John rose to leave. "I've enjoyed visiting with you so much, Kate Willow. It's lonely around the farm without your sweet smile." He reached over and gave a little hug. She like it and hugged him in return. They said goodnight and each noticed the wistful look on the other's face.

Sleep came easily to Kate, the happy feelings still with her when she closed her eyes, but sometime during the night her happiness turned to terror and she woke up shaking and cold with dread. Leon. She'd had the dream again, but the goose was larger than before, white and healthy, and this time it had almost caught her, had in fact grabbed a piece of her dress in it's beak, holding onto it while she strained to pull away. The dress tore and she ran to the cupboard and hid. The goose saw where she went. "Next time," he said, as he strutted away, "next time."

The blizzard continued through December 22, then the winds died down and she and Conner were able to get out for short spells. Kate couldn't help worrying about the livestock at home, though Big John had called her when he was safely back in Ryan, to let her know he'd made it and assured her he'd keep an eye on the animals, and the hired hands.

The bread dough was rising above the bowl edge and she punched it down loving the smell of the raw dough. Conner loved her friend bread and she'd surprise him tonight. He was with Janis' nephew Jeffrey today, they were going to a movie and then to eat at the café, before Janis brought him home. Restless, she picked up the Marshallville Daily News and stretched out on the sofa.

She was scanning the classifieds when she saw his name. Phillip Sutton, Accountant. Her father. Conner's grandfather. Could it be her Dad, or another man with the same name? Did she really want to know? Her thoughts became jumbled. There was no longing in her for a father. Her life with Pa had been such a betrayal. She was afraid of most men, tensing when they came close. Even on the street, if she noticed a man watching her, her stomach began churning and fear crawled all over her.

"I'm not the only one involved here," she reminded herself. "Conner has a right to know his grandfather. Lord knows, his family is small, and if Phillip Sutton is a decent man Conner will have a real grandfather.

She dressed warmly and went out to the garage for a shovel. Her mind calmed as she was worked. She cleared a wide path from the house to the mailbox. It had stopped snowing and the air was cold and still. The snow-covered roofs and mailboxes and large yards were untouched, gleaming whitely in the sun.

She breathed deeply in the clean air and walked around the house to the back yard, hating to ruin nature's masterpiece, but she'd better make a path from the door to the swing. Conner needed to get out each day. He was getting restless, hanging around inside.

He was a charming boy and she was enchanted by him. She could watch him for hours, marveling at his dexterity and grace. Whatever life brought her, it had to be good for him.

Retrieving the trash from the back porch, she waded through the snowbanks to the dilapidated garbage cans. The small "meow" startled her, and she jumped, and then laughed in delight as her eyes spotted the black and white kitten hunkered down between the two cans. She scooped him up and placed him inside her sheepskin. What a wonderful surprise for Conner.

Janis brought Conner home early in the afternoon and he and Jeffrey ran to the back yard to play. Kate and Janis sat in the alcove and sipped coffee, while Kate told her friend about Phillip Sutton's advertisement.

"You won't rest easy 'til you know. I'll stay here with the boys; you go and get a look at him. Just stay on the main roads, they're plowed clean."

"I have bread dough rising. Punch it down for me, later. There's a new addition to the family. A kitten. I put him in Conner's room."

"Don't fuss. We'll be fine. Now shoo."

Shaky and out of sorts, she drove slowly down the streets, looking for his address. It was in a part of town she'd never seen before. The atmosphere sent waves of shock through her. The street was littered with garbage and seedy looking men sprawled in the doorways and lined the alleys. Others, as unkempt, were shuffling around on the walkways, beating their arms against their bodies, trying to keep warm. Kate had known of these people, she read about them, but never had she pictured it like this. It was horrible, unbelievable. How could a city as grand as Marshallville let his happen in its midst?

The office was at the end of the street and Kate parked as close to it as possible. It's now or never, she thought. A bell tinkled as she pushed the door open. Her first impression upon entering the uninviting room was how cold it felt. She glanced at the stove and wondered why he hadn't built a fire. Maybe he's like Angie, she thought nastily, too good to dirty his hands. He wasn't there, and relieved, she turned to go.

A door in the back of the room opened at that moment and a raspy voice called out, "What is it?" Kate walked to the back and said, "I've come to see Phillip Sutton. Is he out today?"

"I'm Sutton." He shuffled out of the room, weak kneed and barely able to walk. "What can I do for you?"

Suddenly feeling weak herself, she went to the front of the room and plopped into a chair. She stared at him and he returned her look and gasped. He was looking at himself, looking into his own eyes. He stammered, "Who are you?" although he knew who she was. He'd dreaded this day for twenty years. Feared it and longed for it. Well, let her see the wreck he'd become, and she could decide if he was worth knowing or not.

Instead, she smiled and answered, "I am Kate Willow Sutton. I believe you're my father. Are you ill?" She took off her coat and wrapped it around his shoulders, talking all the while.

"I'll just get a fire built up. This cold isn't good for you." In a short time, the fire warmed the air and she looked around for water and a coffee pot. He gestured weakly towards the back room. She was glad to escape for a moment. She rested her head against the wall and willed her heart to slow down. His life was so different then she had pictured it. Never had she expected to see an old man, sick and in need.

The bare room she stood in told her he was alone and destitute. There were a few personal effects. A razor and shaving mug, a hairbrush, and a pair of small shears lay side by side on the washstand. Two pairs of trousers hung limply over a chair and two shirts were folded neatly on the chair seat. Ice had formed a soft crust over the water in a dented bucket. Alongside the pail lay two worn decks of playing cards. Not much to show for a man's life, but she shrugged and dipped water into the coffeepot and added the coffee grounds.

Carrying it to the office she set it on the stove and said brightly, "There, a cup of hot coffee will get our blood stirring."

Phillip continued to stare at her, his mouth open, his breathing labored. She was an angel, this daughter of his. A beautiful angel. He didn't deserve her, but he was happy she had come. He tried to smile at her, his lips wobbly, and said, "Thank you, daughter."

Kate poured his coffee and sank into the chair while he slurped it down. It struck her he was hungry. How could she cook here? There were no pots or utensils. There was only one thing to do and she didn't think twice about it.

"You must come home with me. My son and I have a house here. We live alone. Come spend Christmas with us. Conner will be happy to have a Grandpa. Please, do this for him."

He would have refused if she hadn't asked so kindly. She made it seem as if he were doing her a favor. What a grand girl.

Kate gathered his belongings and ran out to start the car. When she had him settled in the seat, she got the lap robe from the back and covered him with it. Soon they were on the road to her home. She drove cautiously, telling him she had just learned to drive, and this was her first time in the snow.

Kate ran into the house and explained things to Janis. They walked him to the house, one on each side, and soon had him warm and comfortable in the big chair by the fire. She heated some leftover chicken and noodles and took a tray into him. She'd added a few soda crackers and small bowl of fruit.

The women went into the kitchen while he ate. Janis thought Phillip needed a doctor. She would stop by her own on the way home and ask him to drop over. Kate thanked her and called the boys in. They said noisy good-byes, not ready yet to bid the day farewell.

Kate took Conner in to meet his Grandpa. He wasn't sure what a grandpa was for, but he liked Phillip and was soon telling him stories, repeating almost word for word the books Kate had read to him.

Dr. Beck came to the house late that afternoon. He put Phillip to bed and gave Kate instructions for his care. "He has pneumonia, a light case. Have him rest and stay indoors."

Kate asked Janis to spend Christmas day with them. "I'd love to, but every year I give away dinner to those who have no place to eat. My café is open all day. Even bums and derelicts deserve a Christmas dinner. That's really what Christmas is all about, isn't it?"

Kate was awed by the goodness in Janis. Why, she'd never thought of doing anything like that. "Janis, I'd like to help someone too. It's a wonderful idea. I didn't know people did things like that for others."

"Kate, you did it today when you brought that sick, old man home with you." Janis shook her head in wonder. Kate didn't realize how much she did for everyone. Janis had never met anyone like Kate and she was thankful to have her for a friend. "If you want to give to someone, what about those orphans you told me about?"

"Of course. How selfish of me to forget about those kids. I'll see about it right away. Thanks, Janis."

"Dad, will you keep an eye on Conner for a little while? I'll make it as fast as I can. At his nod, she told Conner to be good and help Grandpa.

She hoped the new administration had made things nicer for the kids, but when she stepped into the familiar hall, her cheerfulness began to seep away. It was the same dingy, hopeless place. The kind of place that sucked the joy right out of a person.

The children's ward was empty. Kate decided they must have moved the kids to a warmer room. She went back into the hall and walked by the open ward. She glanced in and stopped, stunned. Betty. What was she doing there? "Betty, hello. Can I talk to you?" The girl turned wild, red eyes in her direction and then recognizing her sidled to the door. "Why are you in this place?" Kate asked, motioning towards the bedlam.

"I'm the only one left. The others were 'dopted. I'm not 'doptable."

"Betty, you're not crazy, are you?"

"Oh, no, ma'am. I'm just damaged goods. No one would want me."

"I want you. I'm taking you out of here. Come." Kate took her hand and led her out the back door. "My car's out front. We'll have to go around the building so bend low, we don't want to be seen."

Betty gaped at her. "You're stealing me? You can't do that. You'll get in big trouble."

"Betty, you just told me you weren't adoptable. You're in an insane asylum. Do you want to live here for the rest of your life?"

"No, ma'am, let's go."

Kate deposited Betty into the back seat of her Dodge and told her to lie still and stay out of sight. She drove to Main Street, trying to figure out a way to get Betty's chart. She parked in front of a general merchandise store and the camera in the window gave her an idea. Quickly she ran in and bought it. The clerk loaded it and showed her how to snap a picture.

"We're going back to the asylum," Kate said, "I have an idea how to get your chart." Kate was remembering the deranged patient in the last cell, next to Leon. His name had been chalked on the iron cross bar and the name Cyril Bench had stuck with her. She patted Betty's hand. "Don't poke your head up while we're parked there. What is your last name?"

"It's Stanton. A name they gave me at St. Peters."

Kate wasn't nearly as confident as she was acting. Her knowledge of the world was limited, but she'd seen Angie overcome the odds by acting like she was somebody and flashing money in the faces of her opponents. She decided to act like Angie. She knocked on the office door and sailed in.

"Mr. Brown" she said, "I'm Kate Sutton. "She held out her hand. He reached across the desk and shook it, trying to place the Sutton name. He looked her over carefully. Better be careful, he didn't want to lose his job like the last superintendent.

"I'm sorry to take up your time, but I'm in a terrible fix and you can help me if you will."

"What kind of problem do you have my dear?" He smiled encouragingly.

"It's like this, Mr. Brown. I have a relative here, a Mr. Cyril Bench. I have to prove to Daddy that he's here and will be here forever. Now Daddy's on his deathbed. He is mad at my mother for some unknown reason and wants to leave his estate to Cyril." She groped for her handkerchief and wiped her eyes.

"What do you want me to do?" Mr. Brown was completely bewildered.

"Oh, not that much, just go down to the dungeons and take his picture for me. If I can prove he's here, then my Daddy won't leave my Mama destitute. Could you do that for me, please?" She cocked her head to the side and looked at him through half lowered lashes, ala Angie. At the same time, she opened her purse and drew out a wad of money. "I'll pay you well, if you do it personally. I'd rather not see Cyril myself. He frightens me so."

"Take his picture, huh? Let me get his chart."

"He's in the last cell. The one with the double locks on the door. Just go to that cell and take his picture. You don't even have to talk to him." She reached into her bag and withdrew the camera. "It's loaded, all you have to do is aim and push this button."

As soon as he left the room, she shut the door and opened the cupboard. She hoped they hadn't moved Betty's chart, but the drawer was empty. She opened the drawer Leon's file had been in and searched. Sanford, Seeley, Stall, Stanford. Betty Stanford. She crammed it into her bag and went back to the chair. When Mr. Brown returned, she thanked him nicely, putting fifty dollars on his desk and fled from the building.

"Betty, you can sit up now, you're a free girl. We're going to buy you some nice clothes on our way home. Conner will be so happy to see you."

Kate watched the salesclerks in the Emporium and chose a young redhead that acted a bit giddy and lively. "I want you to outfit my sister, five outfits for school, two good Sunday dresses, underwear, shoes, socks, the works."

"Yes, how old is your sister?"

"I'm fourteen," Betty said. "I was fourteen on December second."

"Small for your age. Do you want to save what she's wearing?"

"No, toss the things away. Please do a good job with her. She's been through so much and it would be better if you took her to a dressing room and brought the clothes to her there. I'll shop around while your getting her fixed up." Kate bought Betty a locket, a watch, and a pin for her coat. Darn, she'd forgotten to tell the clerk Betty needed a coat.

She need not have worried. The happy clerk had added a coat, a jacket, boots, mittens, hats, sweaters, and even a shiny blue lunch box to the list. The stock boy carried their purchases to the car and the two well-dressed girls went in search of a beauty parlor.

The mud colored hair became brighter and brighter. Kate watched, fascinated by the changing color and when at the last rinsing, she saw the lustrous chestnut colored hair, she gave a loud whoop. "You're the same color as Ginger Spice," she said. "What gorgeous hair. Cut it," she ordered the operator. "It's natural curly, cut it so it curls all over her head. Something like Shirley Temple's."

The girl created magic with her scissors. Betty's tears flowed when she saw herself in the mirror. "Is that really me?" She peered over her shoulder, sure someone else was behind her. Kate looked the girl over carefully.

She saw a piquant, pixie face with a scattering of freckles across her nose. The chestnut curls bounced around her head and framed the little face, setting off her odd hazel and gold eyes. She was dressed in a pale-yellow pinafore, with a blue shirt under it with a blue and yellow belt around her narrow waist. Smart boots peeped out under the dress, and all in all, she was pretty as a picture. Kate smiled her pleasure. They raced to the car and headed home, anxious to get settled.

"I'm tired as an old hen at roosting time," Betty announced as she plopped into the car seat. "I ain't never had my head scrubbed like that. I thought that gurl's scrub my scalp clean off." Betty's remarks hit Kate's funny bone and she laughed and laughed. Soon Betty was laughing with her. Kate had to park the car until she could get herself under control again. She reached over and ruffled Betty's new curls. "I have a feeling you are going to be a handful," she teased.

TWELVE

They sat in silence, by the big window in the kitchen. Half-heartedly playing a game of checkers. Mandy's eyes were red from crying, and she sniffed occasionally. With an abrupt motion, she threw her red checker to the side.

"What's wrong with me visiting Jude?"

"I don't mind, Mandy, but your Mother thinks it's not nice for you to go there. Dr. Larson said to keep things calm for her and I just don't know where to draw the line."

"Jude is my friend, Daddy. He doesn't deserve to be treated mean. Mama should be good to Jude. He's good to us."

Noah knew Mandy was right. She's got more sense then either her Mother or me, he thought, wishing he didn't have to be in the middle of these squabbles. He wasn't cut out for this kind of thing. A man should have some peace in his own home. He thought wistfully of the eager red head he'd met at Barneys. The telephone rang, and he answered it gratefully.

It's Aunt Kate, he mouthed silently, a big grin lighting up his face. Mandy smiled at him, glad to see him happy for a change. He said, "I'll be there in the morning. Get your brood ready and I'll have you here by noon."

"We've got work to do, Puss. Kate's coming home. Mandy, your Aunt Kate just stole another orphan from the asylum. She has her real dad with her too. I'm going after them in the morning. What will Angie say when Kate comes home with two orphans, an old man and a kitten?"

The thought of Angie's reaction wiped the smile from his face. "There'll be a to-do here that'll shake the whole country." Grinning, he shook his head. "That Kate, she's really something."

Noah looked up the stairs and wondered if Angie was sleeping. He'd like to take Mandy and go tell Jude and Ben about this. Hell, why not? Why let one little bitty woman run his life? "Put on your coat, we'll go see Jude together."

Jude laughed at Kate's ingenuity, but he had some concerns regarding Angie. "Find someone else to help Kate. It's important that Angie doesn't know that strangers are living in Burt's house. You need to take Angie and start on that trip Norm suggested."

"Hell, man, I haven't told Angie we're taking a trip yet."

Ben walked over to Noah and patted him on the back. "Your wife's a sick woman, Noah. She has to be your priority. I doubt if she'll make it through the winter." He looked at Noah sadly. "She knows, friend. She's scared as hell. All her screaming fits are her way of denying her death. Try to understand and do everything you can to make her last days memorable and happy. Remember, when she's gone you still have to live with yourself."

A radiant Angie and a quiet, tender Noah drove away early the next morning. They would board the train in Marshallville. Noah had hired a private car so Angie could ride in comfort. Angie was sure the hot dry climate would do wonders for her.

Kate and Ben stuffed the cars with children, gifts, quilts, baskets of snacks, and suitcases. Phillip rode in the back seat of Kate's car with the boxed kitten and Betty. Conner asked to ride with Ben.

A longing for the farm swept over Kate. She missed the space and the animals, and the quite beauty of the countryside.

Images of her last day of shopping came to her mind. The crowded stores, the angry people shoving and jostling each other. The sidewalks teeming with unhappy citizens. She hadn't known there was so much despair out there, hadn't thought about other folks having such a share of misery. As much as she hated to admit it, because of Burt Martin, her family hadn't known what it was like to be hungry; none of them had suffered the degradation of poverty.

Kate didn't feel guilty for taking Conner and Betty from the asylum, but she couldn't stop the niggling fear that someone might be looking for Betty. She was so stupid, giving her own name to Brown. Leaving a trail of clues, and especially talking about it on the telephone. There were six other families on the party line. There were some who loved to gossip, especially Prissy Green.

"Betty, what do you say to using another name? In case they do look for you."

"Can I choose? I know just the name I should have." At the enquiry in Kate's eyes, she rushed on.

"I'd like to be named Elnora, Elnora Claire Kingsley."

"Wow. That's a name fit for a princess. From now on we'll call you Elnora."

"Ellie is pretty too. We could nickname you Ellie." Phillip was enjoying the easy banter between the two women.

"Ellie. Yes, I think I like that. You can call me Ellie, Mr. Sutton."

Three weeks passed in a flurry of activity. Kate enrolled Ellie and Conner in school, and so far they were enjoying the new life she'd chosen for them. Ellie had invented a whole new background for herself, claiming to be the daughter of rich adventurers, and a friend of the Martins. No one questioned her stories, but Kate cautioned her to talk of her past only when she had to. Arousing peoples' interest could lead to trouble.

Ellie was still awed by the amount of food Kate put on the table, and when she was preparing their meals Ellie would peek around the corner of the door, afraid they might have eaten everything up. The art of surviving was strong in Ellie, though, and she couldn't quite trust anyone.

Kate derived so much pleasure from the kids; she had to pinch herself sometimes to be sure she wasn't dreaming. She'd only known a few moments of happiness at a time, and not very often, and now she realized what glory it represented. She'd seen the metamorphous of two little faces, changing from fear to eagerness. Two broken hearts mending a little day by day. She'd watched hope bury despair and confidence overpower helplessness. There was a part of herself in each child, their achievements like her own. She tried to help them fill the empty holes in their hearts and minds.

Conner and Ellie bubbled over with life, busy and noisy, demanding attention and taking up much of Kate's time. Mandy, well, sometimes she forgot the girl was there. Mandy had taken to staying in her room, coming down only for dinner, to go to the barnyard and mingle with the animals. She kept Tippy with her, and Kate heard her talking to him at odd hours of the day and night. She's missing her folks, Kate thought. I need to spend more time with her. Mandy's image flashed into her mind. At breakfast this morning she'd smiled at her niece, noticing for the first time how wan she looked. Dark circles framed the bottom of her eyes and she was deathly still, moving her arms in stiff, jerky motions. She hadn't looked at anyone and left the table as soon as she'd eaten. Kate decided to talk to Jude, he might have noticed something. Mandy visited with him daily, usually stopping in on her way home from school.

"Mandy isn't that much different from Conner and Ellie. She's having a hard time accepting the absence of Noah and Angie. Jude, I don't know how to help her. She's sullen and resents Ellie. What can I do?"

"I'm not the one to advise you, Kate, but if it were me, I'd find a real home for Ellie. She needs parents, a home she can call her own. You're doing a good job with her, but she's only six years younger than you. She's living in Mandy's house and that must stick in her craw. And has the thought crossed your mind that she might be the one with resentments? No, I wouldn't want to tell you what to do, but I'd remember Mandy is family."

The shock of Jude's answer kept her speechless for a while. She'd expected sympathy for herself and Ellie. Jude made it sound as if Ellie were the problem.

"I'll get home and think on what you've said. Thanks Jude, I need to look at this from Mandy's eyes, too." She strolled along the path, deep in thought. Mandy. She'd always been so quiet and good. Now she was given to tantrums and bursting into tears over nothing. I'm all she has right now, and I've been so busy trying to make like the good guy to Conner and Ellie, I haven't really watched out for her needs. We live here on her place, but she's become almost unimportant to us all.

She slipped in the back door, quiet so she wouldn't disturb the kids at their lessons. She'd left them sitting around the table doing their homework. About to peek around the door, she stopped, shaken, as Ellie's voice broke the silence.

"I told you I'd get Conner out of the way. You're not safe just 'cause he's here. I've got him wrapped around my little finger, and if I tell him to jump in the river, he'd do it, he's just a silly little boy. You're a silly girl too, your folks don't want you, they left you high and dry. No one wants you, Mandy. Not Kate or Jude. They just feel sorry for you and they're stuck with you."

Kate held her hand over her mouth, disbelief making her immobile. My God, what was Ellie saying?

"I want your room. You have to change with me. Your room is much nicer than that old thing Kate gave me. I wouldn't be caught dead in it if I had a choice. Just 'cause I'm an orphan I get stuck with the bad stuff."

"It's my Mama's room. I won't give it up." Mandy spoke softly, but with a stubborn timber in her voice.

"Oh, you'll give it to me, alright, or I might hurt Conner. You'd get the blame. Everyone knows how I just love that little kid."

Kate bounded into the kitchen to hush Ellie up and was shocked to see the girl twisting Mandy's arm.

"Damn you, get your hands off of her. You manipulating ingrate." She smacked Ellie a good one on her rump and sent her sprawling towards the door. "Get up to your room and stay there. I can't stand the sight of you. Move!"

She wrapped her arms around her frightened niece and carried her to the chair. She sat down and dropped Mandy onto her lap and rocked her, whispering apologies and promises. Conner came in and said tearfully, "I couldn't find the robin's eggs Ellie told me to get. The nests are empty." Noticing Mandy, he ran to her. "Are you sick, Mandy?" He reached into his pocket and withdrew a red agate. "Here, you can hold this, it'll make you feel better."

Kate explained to Conner that the robins wouldn't be laying eggs until spring, then sent him to visit Jude. Kate continued rocking until Mandy fell asleep. She carried her to the study and placed her on the bed. "Why, she's not as heavy as Conner, she's such a little thing for a seven-year-old. And she looks so sweet and very vulnerable in her slumber."

Her eyes traveled over Mandy' face. She resembled Noah but had Angie's nose and determined chin. Her straight black hair hung loose to her shoulders, skimming the sides of her high cheekbones. She needs some loving care, and I need to see what's in front of my eyes for a change. Carefully, she covered her with a quilt and left her to sleep.

The window was open by the desk and she went to close it, then decided to sit down and go through the mail while Mandy slept. There was a pile of letters from the Merritt Mental Health Clinic, unopened. Funny, why hadn't Angie read them? Because she didn't see them, Kate answered herself. Noah had hid them.

She tore one open and sat back, startled. Leon had written this letter. She tore open all the others, ten in all and they were all from Leon. Her hands shook as she held one up to read it. It was nothing, just a how are you, I am fine letter. She looked at the others. They were written in the same vein. Why? It must be part of his treatment. Write home and let the folks know how well you are doing.

The letter became alive in her hand and she tore it up and threw it into the trash. The others followed. He mustn't impinge on our family. I won't let him. Nothing of him can be in this house. She remembered his threats to Mandy and her blood turned cold. Frantically, she pulled the scraps of paper from the trash, and smoothed them out on the desktop. Yes, here and here, and again, he'd written "give my love to Mandy." "How's my Mandy?" "Tell Mandy her uncle thinks of her often." Kate took the scraps and tossed them in the fire. If Leon were only so easy to get rid of.

Ellie threw the last of her clothes into the new trunk and ran downstairs. She had agreed to live with the Pasternacks on a trial basis. If they were compatible, she would become their adopted daughter. 'Course we'll be compatible, she told herself complacently. I can mother up to anyone for private rooms of my own and no brats to share it with. It sounded like heaven to her. She could see herself entertaining her friends in her sitting room her friends being the cream of the crop, naturally. The Paternacks were one of the richest families in Carey County and she heard their house was like a castle. I'll fit right in; I was born to be grand.

She danced down the stairs and tickled Conner and teased Mandy, until the room was filled with laughter. Kate and Phillip smiled at her, enjoying the ease with which she'd accepted the new arrangements. Kate was relieved to learn Ellie hadn't formed any real attachments for her or the kids. But she wondered why she hadn't? Maybe the ability to form real relationships would come for her in time.

The car came for her and they all said their good-byes. They stood on the porch and waved until she was out of sight. Phillip suggested a card game and Conner ran to get the deck of cards. Kate made popcorn and Mandy set up the table. Tippy rested his head on Kate's shoe and they spent a pleasant evening, the Suttons and the Martins and although nothing extra-ordinary occurred, each one would look back on this evening with yearning, for the peace and love that wrapped them together in close harmony would be a long time coming again.

Hundreds of miles away from the Martin farm, the Merrit Clinic crouched on the snow encrusted flat land; long and low, it cast a cheery façade out upon the cold winter's afternoon. The benevolent bricks offered warmth to its residents, the large windows, a sense of freedom.

In room 206, Leon Martin finished his meal and set the plate aside. In his mind, was a picture of his sisters feasting on steak and fried potatoes. Eating Martin beef in his kitchen. A smile crossed his face as he acted out in his mind the plans he had for them. They would pay for sending him away. Slowly and painfully, they would pay. He'd played his cards right and his plans were complete. Soon, he would be on his way home. Home to pay his debts.

THIRTEEN

K ate sobbed softly. Noah stood over her, stroking her hair. "I couldn't bring her home, Kate, that damn disease destroyed her beauty and she made me promise to bury her in Arizona. I think it was best, this way you and Mandy can remember her as she was."

Kate shifted and looked up at her brother-in-law. His face was haggard, drawn, and fine lines showed on his forehead and alongside his mouth. He's suffered greatly, Kate realized, as she squeezed his hand.

"It's just such a shock, Noah. I guess I believed she would get better in a warmer climate. And I felt guilty for thinking of her so unkindly. I wasn't a good sister to her, and I hated her sometimes. I was impatient and didn't understand her."

"We all felt that way, Kate. We have to forgive ourselves and go on. I'm worried about Mandy. She felt that way, too, and she's so young; can she understand enough to forgive herself? She loved Angie so much, but I'm afraid she'll remember the times she hated her. God, what a mess." Noah's ragged smile told Kate how much he dreaded telling Mandy her mother was dead.

"I can't believe this has really happened. And yet, I'm glad it's over." Hesitantly, he added, "She died believing I loved her. I gave her that, at least." He picked up his Stetson and suitcase and slowly climbed the stairs. "I'm going to lay down for a bit. I want to see Mandy as soon as she gets home."

Kate washed the dishes, talking to herself, trying to calm down before Mandy and Conner came home from school. Noah was right, she would have to forgive herself, but could she? For the first time in her life, she was on the wrong side. She was the one who had acted badly.

Every event in her life had happened because of someone else's actions. But this time it had been her own smallness, her selfishness, that caused her to resent Angie. Her face reddened as she realized she had wanted Angie to feel guilty for her victimization by Pa and Leon. Angie. So fragile and helpless. Yet, she had the courage to stand up for Leon, frightened of him as she was.

I'll tell Mandy that, she whispered to herself. "Your mother was a woman of rare courage," I'll say, "and that's the truth." Angie had stood up to John Duggin, and she'd found the courage to bring Mandy here, so sick and weak she had to crawl. Suddenly she bent over the sink, retching and gasping with sobs.

Then, going to the back porch, she put on her sheepskin and her work boots and went out to the barn. After an hour's hard work, she felt strong again and able to carry this new burden. "I'd better go in and get ready for the kids. Mandy will need me."

She wondered how Noah would handle things with his little girl. But she shoved the worry aside. Mandy and Noah were family, just as she and Conner were, however, he told her, it would be alright. Noah and Mandy had a rare rapport between them, a sixth sense of each other's feelings and thoughts.

Kate was back to square one, it was her own feelings she had to live with. She would start by reading the letters Angie had written her from Arizona and remembering the good times they'd had. Comforted by her ideas, she pushed her grief deep down and covered it.

Her heart heavy, Kate packed Mandy's things in the boxes and suitcases Noah had brought to her. Noah and Mandy were leaving her. They were going to Noah's folks and didn't know when they'd be back. She had argued with him, stating that Mandy should be raised on her own property, but Noah had been adamant.

"She needs to learn about her people. She's half Gros Ventre, but except for a short visit with my mother, she's had no connection with us. Mandy will never know herself if I keep her away from our people. Haven't you noticed, Kate? Mandy is more Indian than Angie liked. This is right for her. She must learn our culture, our traditions." His hands reached to Kate in mute appeal.

"Now that her mother is gone, she will have the chance to live among our people. After she learns our ways I will send her to you for her education. She has to live in both worlds. That's a hard thing to do."

"Has it been hard for you, Noah?" Kate hadn't realized the problems Noah faced living in the white world.

"It's been really tough at times. Even though I was lucky enough to get a good education, I'm still considered a lazy Indian by so many of you and if I get a little tipsy, then I'm a drunken Indian. I can't buy any booze in the taverns. We Indians have to get it under-cover. We're not allowed the same privileges as you white folks. They don't see me as a man, a human being that loves, cries and wants the same things as every American."

Noah knew he'd made himself too visible by daring to marry a white girl. He'd been so crazy about Angie he'd have risked his life to be with her. But except for Mandy, it hadn't been worth it.

As soon as the newness wore off, Angie had found herself unable to cope with his heritage. She was ashamed of loving an Indian and not strong enough to hold her head up in times of trouble.

"There's a lot of prejudice where we're concerned. You'll see it yourself now that you're out in the middle of things. That isolated life you lived kept you from learning a lot of bad stuff. You don't seem to have any preconceived notions about people. That's a big part of your charm."

He smiled apologetically. "I love you, Kate; you've had more than your share of bad times and I admire how you're putting yourself together, but well, haven't you ever wanted to get away? Is Conner going to think this is all there is?"

"Wanted to get away? That was my dream for years." Kate threw the last box across the room where it banged against the wall. "But every time I thought I could go, something stopped me. Pa and Leon trapped me here. There was Conner. I had to make a normal home for him, didn't I? She grabbed a pillow from the bed and tossed it in the direction of the box. "Then with Angie so ill, I had to care for her and this place, and who would have taken care of Mandy? I'm the only one left, Noah. Leon is locked away. Pa, Ma, and Angie dead. What can I do? How can I get away?"

Pounding the top of the dresser, she looked at him wildly. "It's easy for you to tell me what I should do, but I notice you're the first one out the door. Why don't you stay and run things and I'll show you how fast I can leave." Kate sagged onto the bed, spent, her breath shaky and loud.

"Kate, you don't need to run things here. You don't need the money from the farm. Forget it for a few years. Close things up and go. Gus would take over the land and animals. He could put Mandy's share in the trust and make a profit for himself too. Whatever you decide let me know. I'll agree to anything you want. But please, for your sake, and Conner's, do open your life to new experiences. Have you ever wanted to do anything besides farm?"

"Yes, I . . . I've always wanted to teach. I had a teacher I loved very much. She said I was bright, that I could do anything I wanted if I had a good education. I wanted to be like her, to teach, but more than that, to give kids hope, and praise, kids like me that don't think they are much." She sat on the edge of the bed, looking into space, lost in her memories. Then she jerked herself back to the present.

"Pa took me out of school soon after, but her kind encouragement gave me strength to live through the nightmare that became my life. It doesn't sound like much, but it was like a promise, something to cling to. I think I would have died without her words."

Noah held her close, tears in his eyes. "You get out of here, honey. Do it for her if you can't do it for yourself. But do it."

They left on Saturday morning, and Kate, Conner, Jude and Ben gathered in the yard to say their goodbyes. "Go with God, Mandy," Kate whispered.

"Nurse Reed says you want to see me."

"Yes, I have some bad news for you, Mr. Martin. Please, sit down." Dr. Merrit motioned to a chair and picked up a newspaper from his desk. "You have a sister named Angela Marie Senecah living in Ryan?"

Leon nodded and took the paper the doctor handed to him. "I'm surprised your family didn't notify you. Your sister has died, Leon. Her husband took her to Arizona for treatment and she died there."

Leon buried his head in his arms. Angie dead! What a blessing. Now, to put on a good show and play the bereaved brother. He couldn't contain the jumping of his legs and tried to press them down with his legs, but Dr. Merrit saw the body gone amok and ordered medication for him.

Tears streamed down Leon's cheeks and he was remembering Angie as a young girl, comforting him after Pa's whippings. Angie sewing the tear in his pocket so Pa wouldn't find out he'd been crawling the fence. And the sweet smiles she gave him at school when the kids teased him.

"Please, Dr. Merrit, could I be alone for a while? I need to get my bearings. A shock, a terrible shock. Oh, Angie, my sweet Angie." Leon sobbed pathetically and Dr. Merrit shoved his hanky at him. "I'll just go have a cup of coffee. You pull yourself together."

The door to the medication room was ajar and Leon hurried through it, his heart hammering, his eyes darting over the shelves searching for the bottles of pills that calmed his body and helped his mind stay focused. His eyes grew wide when he spied them immediately and he took three of the bottles and wrapped them in a handkerchief. He stuffed them in his pocket and returned to his chair.

When the doctor comes back, I'll ask him to let me call home. They hadn't answered his letters, but now that Angie was gone, he'd have Kate in his pocket. The fat cow. A picture came before him, Kate, at the asylum, slimmer than he remembered. And pretty. She'd been wearing nice clothes and her hair was done up fancy, like a lady. He'd soon take the fanciness out of her.

He'd hated her passionately since he'd seen her with Pa. Kate belonged to him. He remembered Ma telling him so when she was born. "Leon" she'd said, "this is your new sister. I had her just for you, so you'd have someone all your own. Now you'll never be alone again."

Leon's request for a leave of absence was refused. Dr. Merrit reminded him he was under court order. "You'll be arrested and put in jail if we release you. No, it's better for you to say here, where it's safe." He felt Leon's disappointment and decided to be more lenient with the man. After all, he'd been a model patient so far and never caused any trouble and he was having a hard time with his sister's death.

"Tell you what I'll do. You're a farmer, how about taking over my chores in the evening? Not much to do really. Just feed the goats and chickens and gather the eggs. Not too exciting, I admit, but it would get you out in the air and give you something to do."

Leon showed the expected gratitude and Dr. Merrit went home, happy he'd suckered Leon into caring for those confounded chickens.

Leon struck pay dirt the first night he did the chores. After he'd gathered the eggs he looked around the hen house and saw a hack saw hanging on the wall. It fit under his coat. In another corner he picked up a whisk broom. This he hid in his coat pocket.

Outside the hen house a wrecker bar leaned against the wall. Leaving it for later he went behind the shed and forced open the door of a small lean-to. A workbench had been haphazardly braced against the wall and Leon drew in a deep breath as he saw the array of tools. He fit a long screwdriver into his back pocket and a claw hammer inside his belt. There was a small knife but not what he needed. What he wanted was the machete from the kitchen. The cook was chopping meat with it when Leon had strolled by and he'd hungered for it then. Yes, he'd figure a way to get it.

He stepped silently out of the shed and closed the door, jamming it so it stuck. His footprints were all around it, damn, that would give him away for sure. A noise startled him, and he jumped, then he laughed as he saw it was just the old Billy goat butting his head against the shed. That gave him an idea and he ran around the building and chased the goats around to the back. He laughed as they scampered around, trying to butt the scarf he waved at them. The snow soon became full of little hoof prints and Leon went back to the clinic satisfied.

He'd done a good day's work. He was in charge again and then he remembered the wrecking bar. He'd forgotten it. His boot kicked at the snow angrily. Well, better not go back tonight. It would wait until tomorrow.

It became a common sight to see Leon escorting the more confused patients on walks in the hall, or to the dining room. Soon he was sweeping the hallways and helping out in the kitchen. The tired nurses neglected to report his helpfulness. Any help was better than none, and he was a pleasant man. Why not let him do a few things that made him happy?

Leon had a difficult time keeping this elation in control. Sometimes he wanted to kick up his heels and dance and holler. His escape was just around the corner.

When he'd been checked into the clinic, they'd make him take the medication, and he'd fought them. Then he realized he had good control of his body when he took it. His mind became clear and he could think, but best of all, he could talk. Like Kate talked and Ma. Hell, he could talk as good as Dr. Merrit if he wanted to. As long as he had the pills, his escape would be fool proof.

Ben had innocently filled Norm in on Kates' exciting escapades at the asylum. A law-abiding man, Norm could not begin to understand Kate's actions, but he was also afraid for her. He high tailed it to the big house to confront her.

"What in the blazes were you thinking of?" Norm slammed his fist on the table.

"I . . . I didn't think. I only knew I had to get my son out of that hellhole and the same with Ellie. When I saw what they'd done to her, I had to take her out of there." Kate began to cry, then blinked back her tears and turned on him furiously. "I'd do it again, someone has to stand up for them. Conner's my son; I have a right to him and Ellie needed help. What would become of her if I had turned away?"

"You are out of control, Kate. You should be working out your own problems."

"This is my way of healing myself. For the first time in my life, I have goals, commitments instead of dreams. I love waking up in the mornings. My days are full, spent with people I love and that love me. How can you say that is wrong? How does that make me out of control?"

"Kate, Kate." Norm shook his head helplessly. "I'd like to explain your actions to you if you'll sit down and listen. Please?"

She wanted to walk out of the room. It was hard for her to like Norm despite all his helpfulness and he obviously wanted a closer friendship with her. She would let him talk and hopefully he would leave her alone. She sat down and motioned for him to begin.

"When I said you were out of control, I mean you haven't been free from your bondage long enough to know how to limit yourself. You're running like a car that's idling too fast. Your need to experience life is robbing you of common sense."

"I have lived, more than you know. I studied with Emily Lowell and I've read three years of Ryan's Daily News to catch up on the ..."

"Your emotional growth is stunted, dear. A mature woman wouldn't steal her child from the State. She would go through the proper channels. She wouldn't buy a house in secret and run away for a month and a mature woman certainly wouldn't walk out of an insane asylum with a girl classified as a mental patient." He paused to see her reaction.

She was staring at him, wide eyed, listening to his words with rapt attention. "You also brought home a man who claims to be your father. You didn't check up on him, did you Kate? You just took his word for it. Don't you see, you're so obsessed with filling your life with people, you're, you're not using any sense. You let circumstances run away with you." Putting his hands on her shoulders, he gave a gentle squeeze. "Your first priority should be to deal with your past. You can't effectively help anyone until you know yourself. You are, in many ways, still a child yourself.

Contempt bolted from her eyes as she continued to stare at him. Why, he didn't know her at all. He was reciting a bunch of claptrap he'd read in a book. I'd like to sock him in the kisser, she fumed silently. He'd spoken to her as if she were stupid and with such condescension.

Kate rose from her chair and stood tall. She smiled at him. "Maybe I'm just a horse of a different color and maybe you aren't as smart as you'd like me to believe." She walked to the door and opened it. "I thank you for your analysis. Now please leave."

Norm wanted to cry as he scooted out the door. She'd misunderstood him. He only wanted to help her. He loved her and wanted to protect her. His face reddened as her parting words beat like a drum in his head. Groaning, he knew she felt betrayed. He'd overstepped the boundary of their friendship. God, she'd looked so beautiful standing there, so regal and proud. Her flinty purple eyes flashed before him and he cringed as he remembered the loathing that lurked in their depths. Instead of going home, he decided to visit Jude again. He needed a friend.

Kate needed a friend too, and she was about to call Emily, when the telephone rang. She answered it eagerly. "Hello." There was air in the line and she could hear someone breathing. She said it again. "Hello, is anyone there?"

"Kate, I heard Angie died. Just like I planned." His voice was whispery and rasped on her nerves. "Angie told me you had a telephone. She told me a lot of things about you." The whisper changed to the voice she was used to. High and mean. "You get off your high horse, girl, you ain't no lady. I'll tell 'em about you, Kate. You're ruined." He was quiet again and Kate stood there, petrified, aware of the wail that screamed through her mind.

"Get Mandy ready for me, she belongs to me now. You're all through, Kate, you're finished. Mandy is going to take care of me from now on." He hung up. His high-pitched cackle echoing in Kate's ear.

She called Sheriff Henson and repeated the call from Leon word for word. He assured her Leon was still locked up but would check it out and get back to her.

She wanted to talk to someone. John had gone back east to represent the family at a funeral, and she missed him. She decided to call Christine and see about mending their relationship. Neighbors were important if Leon were to break-out she would need all the help she could get. Thank God Mandy was safe.

If Angie had reported their daily goings on to Leon, he might have a vendetta against the Clayton's too. To Leon, almost everyone was an enemy. He'd told her many times, "When I hate someone, I hate 'em all the way through," and he'd make a slashing motion across his throat.

Christine answered on the first ring and listened quietly while Kate told her what was happening. She finished by saying, "I don't know whether to take him seriously or not. I hate to start a scare in our community, but I know from experience if he sets his mind on something he focuses on it until it happens."

Christine was supportive and when Kate hung up the fear and anxiety had lessened considerably.

The house needed reinforcement and she needed to tell Jude about Leon's threats. "Dad, I have to go to Jude's for a few minutes, do you want to come with me?" He came out shoving his arms into his coat and they strolled along the path, enjoying the feel of the cool wind blowing on their faces.

"It smells like spring," Phillip commented, "I was always partial to spring."

"I'm so glad you're here with me, Dad, it's really a pleasure to know you."

"Now, don't go getting mushy, daughter. To tell the truth I regret the years we missed. I find myself thinking of your mother a lot since I've been here. One of the loveliest women I ever met."

Kate couldn't say a word. Ma lovely? My goodness. Her thoughts were interrupted when Ben poked his head around the corner.

"I'm just getting a load of firewood, go on in. We were hoping someone would stop in this afternoon."

"You go in Dad, I'll help Ben."

They watched Phillip until he entered the house and then Kate began to speak. When she asked about sealing the windows, he nodded. "We need to get right on it. I'll make that old house so tight a lizard couldn't slip in. Kate, I hope to God this ends soon. You and Jude are in danger from that nut as long as he lives. For two cents I'd plug him right between the eyes."

"Let's start tomorrow, Ben. You look it over and I'll pick up what you need in town. I'll sleep a lot better when the doors and windows are Leon proof." But she knew, deep in her bones, nothing would stop him.

Phillip stayed on to finish the card game he and Jude were engrossed in and Kate started for her house. Joy surged through her when she saw the Clayton's truck and she ran to the road to meet it.

"Just want to take a gander at those colts," John said.

Kate put her hand on her chest. Her heart was flip flopping and her eyes were glued to his comedy face.

She struggled to break through the shyness that attacked her. After what seemed life forever, she managed to say, "Good, stop at the house and have coffee with me." Then she turned and ran up the path, feeling as giddy as a schoolgirl.

The sense of being alone, since Mandy and Noah had moved on, the fear Leon was behind every tree and building she looked at, all evaporated. She was whole again. Was she sweet on Big John? Yes, damn it, she was. Since he'd hugged her and she hadn't felt the usual revulsion, she'd ached for him.

Christine might be polite enough to me and love Conner, but she'd drop us in a second if she knew how I feel about Gus' brother. Here she was making something out of nothing. John treated her like a sister and that's probably how he felt about her. She was being whimsical again.

She got busy making coffee and setting out the oatmeal cookies she'd baked yesterday. Then, unable to help herself, she went to the window and peeped out, to get another look at him.

But it was Phillip she saw standing at the edge of the yard. His eyes were turned towards the main road. The sun shone full on his face and she let out a gasp of dismay as she recognized the dissatisfaction and longing written on it. Was Dad not happy here, then? She continued to scrutinize him, until his face settled into its usual benign expression. He walked into the kitchen and kissed Kate on the cheek, "I'm going to rest awhile."

Phillip rubbed his thumbs and fingers together. The tingle ran clear up to his shoulders. He removed the deck of cards from his pocket and caressed them. Yes, he was hot, the old electric charge was back and all of a sudden he hated the farm, longed for the city and the bar rooms.

Filled with euphoria he saw himself winning game after game. The stacks of money piled high in front of him. His cronies open-mouthed with admiration, as he played on, tempting providence, a winner at last, and forever.

He opened the closet door and was gratified with the large assortment of clothes Katie had bought him. He checked the suits, shirts, trousers, and ties for spots. All clean and ready to wear. Katie was a dutiful daughter. The drawer was brimming over with underwear, pajamas, and socks. On a hook inside the closet door hung belts, garters, and suspenders. Looking down at the floor he smiled as the new cowboy boots, laying in the box. Beside them, like soldiers standing at attention, were slippers, work shoes, and his pride and joy, a shiny pair of patent leather loafers.

The new watch gleamed elegantly on his arm. He admired the rings and chose two, slipping them over his well-manicured fingernails.

He frowned when he counted the money in his wallet. Only three hundred dollars. There was more where this came from, Katie had plenty. Be careful, he warned himself silently, I don't want her to suspect I'm bailing out. Women were a controlling lot, quick to give, but wanting your heart and soul in return. She'd already been asking too many favors of him. "Dad, could you teach Conner to read a compass?" "Go ask Grandpa, he'll help you, I'm sure."

She didn't consider him in her requests; everything was for the little prince. He'd never like kids and was tired of his Grandpa role. She should have left Conner in the asylum where he could learn his place. He thought of Katie's son with distaste. Any baby born from that kind of union had to be bad. Yet, she doted on him, exaggerating his small triumphs, acting as if he were the next president. Yes, it would be good to get away from here; he'd had about all he could take of domesticity.

A strange twinge pricked at his heart at the thought of leaving Katie. She'd been so good to him, saving him from the grave, but that's what children were supposed to do for their parents, wasn't it?

Sleigh bells rang in the air and he watched from his window as Katie and Big John climbed into the horse-drawn sleigh. They must be going to pick up Conner. The house was empty, and he decided to use the free time to vamoose. It was fate, a sign he was making the right decision.

He carried his belongings to the Dodge and disgruntled, wondered why she hadn't bought him a new car. His hints went right over her head. The three hundred dollars was nagging at him again. He went back into the house. The study door was open and he stepped softly through the doorway. This room was off limits to everyone but Katie.

She laughingly told them it was her sanctuary; it was also where she kept her farm books and business records.

Phillip opened some desk drawers, but quicky closed them. He wasn't interested in the workings of the farm. He stood undecided in the middle of the floor. Then he noticed her pocketbook under the desk. Swiftly, he picked it up and rifled through it. There was a folder in it with four hundred dollars.

Whooping loudly, he transferred it to his wallet. It was as he bent down to return the bag where he'd found it that he noticed the metal file box. It was locked but he picked it with one of Katie's hairpins and had it open in a jiffy. His breath caught in ragged gasps. Money. Lots and lots of sweet money. Katie had started a fundraiser for orphans and this must be the take. So much! He couldn't believe people would give so much to a bunch of no names.

Within minutes, Phillip was driving away. "That bit of fun I had twenty years ago paid off. I'm a rich man. Watch out world, Phillip Sutton is back at the tables." He drove swiftly away from the farm.

"Katie won't begrudge me this money. She's naïve and not too bright where people are concerned. The gods are smiling on me again. With the luck I've had lately, I'll clean up. I'll pay Katie back," he decided magnanimously, and the last traces of guilt evaporated.

He drove unerringly to Katie's house on Vine Street. Reaching under the dash, he removed the key she had taped there. The perfect place for him, and he proceeded to move in. He'd get settle today, stock the kitchen and call on his old friends. By tomorrow night the place would be alive with his poker-playing friends and the best whiskey money could buy. He chuckled as he felt the electricity in his fingers; he was on a roll. God, it was good be alive.

FOURTEEN

L eon leaned against the sink in the kitchen, watching the circles form as the water churned down the drain. The machete hid among the soapsuds. His plans included stealing the machete and escaping from the institution tonight.

Rivulets of cold sweat trailed over his face as he kept an eye out for the cook. The guy was onto him; he'd been watching him for the last three days. He'd surprised Leon by telling him to finish the dishes. Then he'd left to run an errand.

Leon plunged his hand into the hot suds and groped for the machete. The moment this hand curled around the handle he knew it belonged there. Power surged through his body. His muscles tightened and his mouth settled into a straight, stern line. He raised the machete out of the water and wiped it off reverently.

A chill ran up his arms and he jerked around. The cook was staring at him with narrowed eyes and a mean grin. "Thought I didn't know what you were up to, didn't you?" Before he could swing his arm around and grab Leon, the machete sped forward and separated the fold in his neck.

Surprise and horror swept across his face. His mouth gaped open, but his attempt to scream created no sound. He sagged to the floor, spurting blood over Leon's shoes and pants legs.

Leon dragged him into the pantry. He grabbed a stack of towels from the shelf and used them to pack the wound. He then locked the pantry door. That should keep the blood from running under the door. Working against time, he scrubbed the floor and put the dishes on the shelves. The cook shouldn't be discovered until morning.

The hall was empty, and he made it back to his room without being seen. Quickly he hid the machete under his mattress, changed pants, and made himself comfortable in a chair.

It was six-thirty, Friday, the seventeenth of February 1938. Holding his tongue between his teeth, he wrote the date in his notebook. His entry read, "Enemy came from behind, surprise attack; enemy eliminated." The notebook went into his back pocket, the pencil in his shirt. He was ready, where was the damn nurse?

"Oh, Mr. Martin, I'm sorry to be so late. We've lost Harry and everyone's been out looking for him. Have you seen him since your walk?"

"I remember seeing him in the community room just before dinner. He was sitting in that brown rocker by the heater."

"I hope we find him soon. We're all behind on our work as it is. Dr. Merrit's a stickler for promptness. Organization and promptness, that's his motto. Doesn't take into consideration that some of the people he brings in here are of a different mindset."

"Just forget about my back rub. You go on to your work. I have to do some chores for the Doc, and when I'm finished, I'll just crawl in bed. I'll see you tomorrow. I'm kind of tired anyway, had a lot of work in the kitchen tonight. Oh, and tell that new desk attendant I'll be going out for a bit, will you?"

"I sure will and thanks. That will help out a lot. Gosh, I hope we find that old geezer, nothing like this has happened here before."

Old cow, she could have found six people by the time she quit flapping her lips. Now to get out. He spread open his winter coat and shoved the machete into the lining. His winter cap and gloves went into the pockets. Two bottles of the pills went into his pack, the third into his pants' pocket. He decided to cover his pillows and make it look as if he were asleep but changed his mind. If they found the bed empty they'd assume he was around somewhere.

He walked down the hall and out the front door, nodding to the chart nurse, then went directly to the chicken coop in case they were watching him.

Stepping lightly over the snow packed path, he veered around to the tool shed. Be quiet, he reminded himself. You don't want to get those hens cackling. He managed to open the door to the shed a little at a time without too much squeaking.

He hoisted his bundle onto his back. The coiled rope went around his shoulders and he slithered off into the night. He figured he'd be home in short order.

He walked backwards, teasing the goats with carrots he'd swiped from the kitchen. Three of them ran after him, destroying most of the footprints he made. Luck was with him as it had started to snow so any footprints left behind would be covered. At the edge of the cliff, he paused to make sure he was in the right spot.

Cautiously, he placed first one foot and then the other over the edge. Climb down about two feet, he told himself, and wipe your tracks again. He used the machete to cut a tall shrub from the wall of the cliff and swept above his head where he'd left his prints. Now for the hard part.

He turned around and looked below. He figured it was about thirty feet to the bottom. Plenty deep and dangerous. He made his way slowly toward a protrusion in the gully and crawled onto it, testing its strength. Good. He folded the rope in half and wound it around the protrusion. He swung out on the rope and let himself drop.

I hard yank on the rope and it coiled at his feet. His landing was perfect. Too far and he might have smothered from the snow. He'd landed at the base of the bluff and would have to walk along it until he came to the path that met the main road.

Laughter swelled from his throat as he thought of the clinic, just above him, and the commotion the nurses would make when they found the dead man. Working his way along the bank bottom was tricky. He leaned into the cliff and steadied himself with one hand on the bank.

Darkness enveloped him before he'd gone a mile. He shrugged off his pack and took out the lantern and can of kerosene. He'd wrapped the lantern in straw and a piece of wool, and it hadn't a crack in it. After he poured in the fuel and lit it, he could see good enough to go on.

He wound his way, slowly but steadily along the cliff. He'd taken only two of the pills and still felt calm. At midnight he stopped, ate, and drank some the sweet cocoa. He'd figured it would take ten hours to walk the cliff. By seven o'clock he should be at the crossroads. The delivery truck would be heading for the clinic. The driver would stop for him, that was a forgone conclusion; no one would pass a guy by in this freezing weather.

He almost missed the path that slanted upwards to the road. He'd tied a yellow rag on a scrubby pine close to the ground, but the wind had blown snow around the base of the tree and almost covered the makeshift flag.

Leon gloated when he drew out Pa's watch from his pocket. He had forty-five minutes to reach the road. His body clamored for rest, but the need to complete this difficult piece of his journey egged him on. If the wind hadn't sabotaged him there'd be a dug-out in the snow for him to hide in. Yes sir, he'd made his plans and followed them through, step by step. Up to the time he took over the delivery truck. From then on he'd have to improvise.

The cave he'd dug in the snow was open and he gratefully sank into it. Chilblains attacked his legs and they felt tight and swollen. His face was numb, and his feet were blistered, but he'd made it. Once he had the truck, he could take care of those problems. The cave was snug, and his loose-jointed body curved down until he was hidden from the wind. Cold beef sandwiches and cold cocoa revived his energy.

The quiet of the morning surprised him. The breakfast crew usually reported to work at six a.m., and he'd expected some chaos from the clinic by now. Maybe they figured the cook had gone on a bender or most likely, they thought he was there, cooking their morning meal. If that was the case, he'd have another hour before the murder was discovered.

As sweet as it was, killing the cook hadn't been in his plans. The guy had surprised him, and he'd done what he had to do. His body warmed as he recalled the exquisite feeling that poured over him when he sank the blade into the cook's soft meat. The best feeling he'd had in his whole life.

His hand reached inside his coat and he fingered the knife. This is what he'd use to get rid of his enemies. He was so caught up in the wonder of what was to come, he almost didn't hear the grinding sound of the delivery truck. Unwinding his body, he climbed out of the snow cave and ran to the road.

Hal was in a hurry. This delivery job had been shoved off on him at the last minute and he was in a foul mood anyway. His wife was a basket-case and his only son was failing in school. He'd planned on taking his paycheck and getting drunk, forgetful drunk. Then they'd sloughed this job off on him. Well, the clinic was just ahead, he'd unload the medication and sundries, and get the hell back to town.

The glare of the snow hurt his eyes and he cussed again, wondering how anyone in their right mind would live in this god-forsaken expanse of white nothingness. "Course where I'm going, they're not in their right minds," and he burst out laughing, tickled that he had unintentionally made a joke.

There was somebody walking up ahead, he slowed down, and came to a stop at the guy's side, wondering what kind of fool would be walking on a lonely road like this. "Better jump in. You'll freeze your ass off out there."

"Yeah, thanks, brother." Leon scrambled into the truck and squatted on the floor. There was only one seat, for the driver.

"You can sit on one of the boxes in back." Hal was abrupt, wishing he'd left the guy to make his own way. He hated small talk, and this guy didn't look any too bright.

He looked sideways at him and his words caught in this throat. He watched the machete flash towards him, felt red-hot pain in his throat, and darkness poured over him like black ink. His body arched forward onto the steering wheel. Hal's troubles were over.

Leon pulled the driver off into the empty space where he'd been squatting and clambered behind the wheel. He had to get away quick. If they'd found the cook's body, the Sheriff would be on the road. He turned the truck around and sped ahead looking for a place to dump the stiff.

Fifteen miles later he found what he was looking for. A farmer had broken a path to his haystacks and Leon turned off and followed it. He stopped by the stack and got out. He'd leave the sucker here; the haystack was as good a hiding place as any.

The dead eyes stared at him, wide and horrified. Leon couldn't bring up any emotion for the man. Only when he wielded the knife did he feel anything. Once they were dead, he was indifferent to them. He wished he could conjure up the ecstasy he experienced when using the knife.

He buried Hal deep in the haystack and washed the blood from the truck with snow. The farmer might wonder about the blood but would think a cow got caught in the barbed wire. Luck was with him, he was a winner, and he'd get the son-of-a-bitches that set him up. One at a time.

Sheriff Henson slammed the receiver down on the telephone. That queer asshole at the clinic let Leon escape and waited a week to tell him. Someone had to let Kate and Jude know. He'd send Norm, or someone close to the family. First, he had to talk to the law in Minneapolis. He got the operator on the line and waited for her to ring back.

He usually loved his job, but this kind of thing took the soup right out of him. He hated dealing with the families. He should have arrested that piece of filth in the first place, but he'd listened to Norm, and got caught up in trapping that repulsive piece of humanity.

"He out-maneuvered us, too. Acted crazy and got sent to that luxury hotel for cuckoos. I won't make that mistake again. This time he's going in the slammer."

The phone rang and he jumped at it, lifting the receiver and shouting, "Sheriff Henson, here." His face turned white as he listened to the officer two states away. Murder! And on the lam. No one had seen hide nor hair of him.

"Roberta, emergency. Call the deputies and have them report to me. See if you can find Dr. Larson and tell him to get a hold of Rob and come to the office."

He searched frantically for the map. He spread it out on his desk and found the area where the clinic was reported to be. Their terrain was flat, Prairie land, seventy miles from the city. A few small towns scattered along the road.

The snow would still be on the ground in that part of the country, but no tracks were found. How the hell did he get away? Or did he? Maybe he'd done them all a favor and froze to death, but like Kate, he had a feeling Leon was out there somewhere, fulfilling his destiny. A murder at the clinic and that cockroach that owned the place didn't let him know. He'd bet his boots that Kate or Jude hadn't heard from him either.

Kate had never felt so alone since she'd been cooped up here with Leon. They were gone, Angie, Noah, Mandy, Ellie, and Phillip. An oppressive atmosphere had hung over the place lately, a feeling of doom that made her restless and jumpy.

Nothing had come of her feelings for John and she dismissed them as foolishness. He'd hugged her again when he said good-bye, but he hadn't done anything to make her think she was anything but a good friend. So be it.

Jude and Ben were still here and Tippy. She was a lucky woman and she'd better remember to be grateful for this good life. Conner was confused by all the comings and goings of people he learned to love only to lose them in an instant.

Phillip's disappearing act had hurt him terribly. Kate wasn't able to think of Phillip Sutton without her heart pounding in her ears. Fathers were certainly not the best things God ever created. Not fathers for Kate, anyway. The trouble with her, she loved too easily.

Phillip had been different from anyone else in her life and she'd grown to admire his fastidious habits. His tall, slender body always so well groomed, his graciousness full of old-world charm. A perfect gentleman, she'd thought.

He read fluently and wrote a beautiful hand. When she introduced him to her friends, she was surprised to hear the pride in her voice when she said, "my Dad" and he'd left her. Stolen her money and car and high-tailed it out of here like a snake in the grass.

Depression settled upon her like a heavy weight until she couldn't stand herself for another minute. In desperation she decided to go to Marshallville and visit Janis and buy spring wardrobes for herself and Conner. The house there needed to be opened up for a while, anyway, and they just as well might try to enjoy themselves. Conner was so far ahead in school she knew taking him out for a while wouldn't be a problem.

Ben offered to overlook the hired hands and keep an eye on the place. Sheriff Henson had returned her call two days ago, telling her to relax, Leon was still in custody at the Merrit Clinic. She had no worries and lots of money and freedom. But somehow no matter how hard she talked to herself, her spirits didn't lift. *It's as if there's something waiting to do me in.* Fear came over her easily these days and she was uncomfortable walking in the woods, uneasy and jumpy in her familiar surroundings.

Pa's shotgun was loaded and stood at the head of her bed when she slept at night. There was a loaded pistol in the desk drawer. The others had decided Leon was simply tormenting her again and tried to convince her he was hot air blowing in the wind. She stopped airing her concerns about him, but she could feel him near her, in the way her stomach churned, the constant nausea, and she knew he was closing in. Someday he would stand at the door and, like he'd said, she'd be a goner.

Marshallville rose before them and Kate's heart quickened. She was happy to be here. It made her feel anonymous and her body relaxed. Conner looked around with wide-eyed interest. "Let's get to our own house, Mom. I can't wait to see it again. Didn't we have fun there?"

"We did and we will again." She tousled his hair and leaned against her, content.

By the time she drove to Vine Street, Conner was asleep. Her house was just ahead and she drove slowly, to see what changes might have taken place in the neighborhood. Then she noticed the cars were parked around her house. Five of them and someone had parked on the lawn. Confused she stopped in the middle of the street and got out to look. Her Dodge was sitting in front of the garage.

Phillip! He was using her house. Hurt cut her like a knife and she climbed awkwardly into the car. He was so sure of her he hadn't even hidden himself. Dumb Kate. Good sweet Kate. A father's blessing, he liked to say. She'd show him what a blessing she was.

She sped to Janis' house, explained things to her and left Conner with her. Then she headed for the police station and reported finding her stolen car and trespassers in her home. She followed the police to the house and when they opened the door, she walked in.

Smoke hung heavy in the room, covering the occupants like a shroud. A sour odor wafted around Kate and she leaned against the wall to steady herself. The place was like a pigs' stye, whiskey bottles and ashtrays on every surface.

Her eyes grew accustomed to the dimness and she was able to see Phillip. He sat at a table studying his cards. Three men were at the table with him, and a large pile of money dominated the middle. Phillip was scowling, red eyed and teary. A large stain blotted the front of his shirt. Scorn for him rose in her as she watched his eyes shift from man to man. Like Leon, she thought, shifty eyed and sneaky.

Kate pointed to Phillip. "Arrest that man. Arrest all of them. They're trespassing on my property and that one", she gestured to Phillip, "stole my car and the key to my house."

Phillip gaped at her, unable to believe what was happening. He had been about to win back some of his money and anger at the interruption caused him to shout at her. "You bitch! I could have paid you back. You lost me the game. Damn you, damn you."

The men were in jail within thirty minutes. Kate followed them to the station. At the last minute she told them about the money Phillip had stolen from her. He didn't try to deny it. He knew his luck had run out. He was done for; the same one that had lifted him up had knocked him back down. Well, life's a gamble. You win some and you lose some.

The little house sparkled and looked like home again. Two days of cleaning had restored it and the women smiled at each other, glad to be done. Janis had been a trooper, helping Kate in her spare time. "Janis, you've been a God-send. How can I thank you?"

"I loved doing it. You can thank me by moving here permanently."

"Maybe soon. When school is out. We have to head home, much as I hate to. I don't like leaving the house empty." She was thinking of Leon's threats, but didn't want to worry Janis and hadn't told her about Leon's call.

They hugged good-bye and Kate and Conner loaded the car and locked up the house. It had been a trying vacation and Kate was still hurt from Phillip's behavior, but guessed that was part of growing up.

She was learning to accept some things as inevitable; she sort of understood that her dad was two people. That he couldn't control himself when the gambling fever came over him. If he'd been honest with her, she might have been able to tolerate.

In the future she would be more careful with her favors. People would have to prove themselves to her before she gave them her heart. There were a lot of Burts in the world, in one form or another.

Conner was quiet on the drive home. He'd been quiet a lot lately and Kate knew he was growing, too. Trying to figure out where he fit in his world must be very difficult for a little boy.

When they reached the farm, she was surprised to see Ben waiting on the road. He'd see her car turn in at the gate and ran out to flag her down.

"Just thought I'd go up to the house with you, missed you two something awful." After she parked the car, he helped her in and unloaded the luggage. Conner ran off to look for Boots, the kitten who had become a cat too soon, now the mother of four kittens.

"What's wrong, Ben?" Kate asked quietly.

"Sheriff Henson asked me to talk to you. There's some bad news about Leon."

"The Sheriff called me just before I went to Marshallville."

"He told me and feels really bad about that. They lied to him. He learned two days ago that Leon has escaped. The thing is, Dr. Merrit didn't report it for a week. Which means Leon has been on the loose for about ten days now."

"My God. They haven't caught him? Why not?" Kate looked around wildly, as if expecting Leon to materialize in front of her.

"There are no clues. No footprints in the snow. No one reported any hitchhikers. Nothing. It's like he flew out of there. The only thing they found out of the ordinary was a delivery truck that broke down close to the Minnesota North Dakota border. They're checking it out now and Henson hasn't heard anything on it yet. The Minneapolis police don't think it pertains to Leon. Evidently the driver was having problems at home and since he's missing, he might have decided to bail out."

"I should have left Conner with Janis. What will I do?"

"We all have to leave here. You and Conner can stay with Emily. Jude and I are going to visit his mother. The Sheriff wants us out of here before dark."

Kate nodded helplessly. "Let's take the suitcases to the car again. I'll have to take Tippy with me. Maybe I should call Christine. Are they home yet?"

"Yes, and you don't have to call them. It's all arranged. They'll take the cat and kittens and we've already moved GingerSpice and McTavish to their place. The others are out to pasture, along with the cattle. He won't bother them if they're not in the corrals. Kate don't worry about the animals. They'll do fine, I promise. The weather has warmed up considerably and we're not likely to have another cold spell right now." He patted her on the shoulder feeling awkward and ineffectual.

"Oh, Ben, when will it end? Where will it end?" He gathered her in his arms, and she laid her head on his shoulders and wept.

Ben hadn't been able to tell her about the man Leon had killed. The Sheriff would have to do it. His instincts told him she needed to know, to better protect herself and her son, but for some danged reason the words just wouldn't come.

"Let's get Conner in here and you two hit the road. Jude and I will be right behind you. Stay put with Emily and you'll be safe. Leon doesn't know about her or Conner, things have changed mightily since he left here so he's at a disadvantage."

He was babbling like a fool and he kicked himself mentally for talking about everything but what she needed to know.

Emily helped them get situated in their rooms and took Conner for a walk. He's happy here, Kate thought. Emily was like a grandmother to him. She decided to go back to the farm and leave Conner with Emily.

She took the car and visited Sheriff Henson. "You're holding out on me. I know Ben was evasive. Now tell me what you know. ALL of it." She listened silently as he spoke.

Her body froze, her emotions numbed, as she listened to the grim tale of a monster, a clever monster who ingratiated himself to the nurses, became indispensable to the doctor and patients. Finally, committing murder and disappearing into thin air.

"Yes, that's the Leon I know. The one I tried to tell you about. He's doing what he does best. You'll never catch him, but he'll come back to the farm and when he does it will be a fight to the finish. You'll have to kill him to stop him."

Desolation lay over the land. The hard winter had taken its toll and the farms and fields appeared neglected and sad. Kate saw the clouds were swollen and dark, threatening rain. She came to the mailbox and turned in, detouring off the main lane to a path that meandered to the corrals and the barn. She parked her car inside and closed, then locked the back door. Tippy followed her out of the barn and they checked every door and window on the out-buildings. She ran to the house afraid he was watching, hiding in the woods, ready to grab her. Once she was inside with Tippy, she bolted the door and sank to the floor, weak with fear.

Emily and Conner thought she was going to Marshallville. She'd told the Sheriff and Norm the same story. "I'm on my own now," she said to Tippy. "Whatever happens, happens," She was tired of being afraid, tired of always being on guard. No matter how it ended it would be a relief to have it over with.

Which personality would her brother be wearing when he walked into his home? The diabolical murderer? The pathetic victim, sodden with tears? Or the crazy monkey, slobbering and dancing all over the place? Would he have murder in his heart? She was sure of it. Unlike the others, she knew how his mind worked. She'd witnessed his torture of the chickens and other animals. Felt his fists and boots on her flesh. The thoughts of him chilled her body. She built a fire in the fireplace and warmed herself, then went into the kitchen and rechecked the doors and windows.

She made coffee and sandwiches and took them into the study. She looked around to make sure everything was ready. The shotgun stood against the desk. The pistol was loaded and waiting in the drawer of the bedside table. Kate sat next to the window, folded her hands in her lap and waited.

FIFTEEN

"**M**arch, march, march." He repeated the words over and over as he forced one foot in front of the other. To stop would be his death warrant. The glacial wind bit at his face, pushing him backwards. A freak snowstorm wasn't in his plans. How had everything gotten so messed up?

He'd been driving along, making good time until the truck quit him fifteen miles from the North Dakota border. He would have been home in a couple of days. Now here he was, on foot, braving the freezing elements, alone, cold, and hungry. Tired. God he was tired. It wasn't' supposed to be like this, but he'd make it or his name wasn't Leon Martin.

He decided to change course and turned so the wind was at his back. It didn't really matter which direction he went and there was bound to be shelter somewhere along the way. All of a sudden he was falling headlong into a drift, his left leg trapped in a hole. He plunged his hands into the snow and tugged on his leg. A sharp pain sliced through it and when he brought the leg up he saw blood and a tear in his pants. He lay there, stunned, unable to comprehend. Fear enveloped him. He searched under the snow again and found the remnants of a fence post. The nails poked through it, the ends long and sharp.

Relief swept over him. He'd heard tales of rattlers hibernating in postholes and thought at first he'd been bitten by one. "This damned snow makes a person's mind short circuit."

Saliva was thick in the mouth and he reached for his pills and then remembered they were lost, along with his pack. Two days ago hunger had forced him to stop at a Mom and Pop grocery store to get some victuals. The radio was on and the old man had his ear close to it, his back to the door. Leon dropped his pack and opened it so he could get at his money.

The old man turned up the volume on the radio and Leon heard himself being described over the air. The newscaster said he was armed and dangerous and anyone seeing him should contact the Sheriff's department immediately. He'd grabbed a loaf of bread and high tailed it out of there, forgetting his pack.

He'd driven non-stop until the truck quit on him. Without the pills he couldn't concentrate. He was forgetting a lot of things lately. When he'd left the truck, it slipped his mind that the machete was hidden under the seat.

A picture formed in his mind. He was sitting at the table in his house, eating bacon and eggs. Mandy was prancing around, making him comfortable, pouring his coffee. He reached out and pinched her arm and she smiled at him. Not like Kate, the crybaby. Always sniveling and begging him not to hurt her.

Engrossed in his mental wanderings he didn't notice the wall until he banged into it. At first he was stunned by the sheer coincidence of it. Then he took heart from the fact. It was a good omen.

The air smelled of smoke and a pale, yellow glow showed through a crack he knew must be a window. He figured he'd been trudging through the storm for about six hours. His mind was cloudy, and he couldn't decide if he should walk in or not. Finally, the pain in his leg and his hunger decided for him.

Making his way around to the other side, he noticed the peeling tar paper and rough window frames. He stole to the door and pushed it open.

An old woman was standing by the stove, warming her hands. He leaped across the floor, wincing from the pain in his leg. He grappled with her for a few moments, overpowering her. The feel of her nauseated him, she was as stiff and unyielding as a block of ice.

His eyes darted around the room. A roll of heavy twine lay coiled among an assortment of tools, in a corner by the cupboard. He dragged her into a small bedroom, picking up the twine as they went by and threw her on a chair. Carefully, he tied her to it. First her hands, then her legs. He went back to the kitchen to warm up and get some grub in his belly.

There was a bucket of cow pies standing against the wall and he tossed some in the stove and opened the oven door. Next, he dragged an overstuffed chair in front of the stove and sat in it. His leg hurt like hell. Gently, he pulled his pants leg up and examined the wound. Oh my God! It was full of pus. A circle of red was spreading around it, the tainted skin glossy and tight.

He hopped out of the chair and grabbed a bucket to fill it with snow. It took a lot of snow to make a bucket full of water, but finally it was done and the water hot. Gingerly he placed his foot in the water and felt relief when it covered his wound. He fell asleep, hoping Ma's remedy for infection would work for him.

There were some old towels next to the washstand and he used them to draw out the infection all the next day. The sore was better and didn't hurt so much now that it had drained. He'd slept a lot and eaten some of the sour beans sitting on the table. It wasn't a palace but a hell of a lot better than the frozen prairie.

On the third day his mind cleared, and he remembered the woman. There hadn't been a peep out of her. The bedroom door creaked as he pushed it open.

He limped into the room and their eyes met. She was sitting as he'd left her; her back ramrod straight, her chin pointing up. He hadn't gagged her, yet she'd remained quiet. Anger filled him as he recognized the mockery leaping at him from her eyes.

He leaned forward and shorted, "Hey, you old hag. Can't you talk?"

Not a muscle or nerve moved. She continued to sit motionless, her eyes filled with scorn. She spooked him and he jumped back, cursing at her. "You ignorant old bat. Don't you have sense enough to be scared?"

A hideous grin split her face and she spat at him. Furious, he boxed her ears screaming, "You mind your manners. I'm libel to shut you up for good." There was no response. He backed up to the bed and sat down on it. Leon studied her. He'd never run across anyone like her. Intimidation was his game, and he was used to people fearing him. The old bat's looks were enough to make him want to run.

She looked like hell with long stringy hair as gray as her face and a nose you could use as a fishhook. It was her eyes that spooked him. Big, like a Jersey cow's, but full of smoldering messages. He lowered his eyes and swept them over her bony frame.

He sneered at her mud, colored dress, her dirty apron, and the men's oxfords on her skinny feet. Her fingernails were long and pointed and stuck out from behind the chair.

He decided to try another tactic. "Are you hungry? I could fix you some grub." Her hate filled eyes grew darker and colder. Leon didn't like this at all. He felt threatened somehow, nervous. He left the room quickly and leaned against the wall, waiting for his shakes to calm down.

He could have killed her by now, but without the machete he didn't have the nerve. There were no knives in the place that would do the job. He decided to leave her for now and check the outdoors.

A dilapidated sheep shed stood about a hundred yards from the house and he went to check it out. From the looks of it, it might fall over any minutes, but he was bored, so went on in. A hushed, "Oh", poofed from his mouth as he stared at the gleaming pickup. He figured it was five or six years old. It had a new coat of black paint on it. It was his for the taking. His only problem was to get to the main road. The snow was so deep. He might have to shovel a path from the house.

First, he had to find out where the highway was. A shovel and an axe were propped in a corner of the sheep shed. He was able to shovel a path to the house before his leg began to hurt so bad he had to go back in and soak it. Hot water was no problem now that he had an axe to use. He would chop some of the timber in the shed and keep the fire going good and hot.

The old woman fascinated him, He knew he should just kill her and get it over with, but he was afraid to go near her.

There was nothing of importance in the shack. In fact, he'd bet his bottom dollar nobody lived here. The woman must have been looking for shelter and happened by, like he did. There was hardly any food, only two plates and one skillet. The drawer in the table held two forks and a spoon, and dog-eared deck of cards. He banged his fist on the table. Something was wrong here. He could feel it. Agitated now, he continued to search the small room. Finally, in desperation he went back to the bedroom. He'd make the old woman talk, or his name wasn't Leon Martin.

They looked at each other for a long moment. Sweat broke out on Leon's face and his armpits itched. Saliva dropped from his mouth and his body began twitching, bouncing up and down, causing the woman to part her lips and smile gruesomely.

"Hag! Ugly bitch!" His fear of her caused his voice to rise to a squeaky soprano and he turned red from embarrassment. His eyes fell from her face and fastened on her dress. He was out of control. He needed his pills.

They had told him at the clinic to fix his mind on something and concentrate only on that object; this would quiet his mind, they said, and he'd found it worked sometimes. He stared at her dress, counting the buttons on the lace collar. His eyes moved down to her thick waist and he studied the buckle on the velvety belt.

He felt as if he'd been kicked in the stomach. It couldn't be. He raised his eyes to hers, stunned and unbalanced. How could she have changed her clothes? She was tied to the chair. It was impossible. He was mistaken, these must be the clothes she had on when he tied her up, but the mud, colored dress flashed into his mind's eye and dirty apron and the cracked men's oxfords. He forced himself to look at her feet. A strangled sound forced its way past his lips. Her long feet were encased in a pair of snug fitting leather boots, as red as blood.

Her chin jerked up and her eyes dared him. As explosion went off in his head and he lunged at her, grabbing for her throat. Her hands flashed in his face, slicing it apart from top to bottom. She raked her nails over his face again and again, until Leon had squeezed the last breath from her body.

He left her slumped in the chair and ran out of doors into the snow. Falling on his belly he plunged his burning face into the cold slush. He saw the pink streaks on the snow where his face had bled.

He ran back into the house and over to the small looking glass. Long pieces of skin were hanging loose on his face. Blood coated the scratched and seeped a pinking fluid that ran along the crevices she had carved into his skin. The sight revolted him, and he angrily went to the old lady to make sure she was dead. He'd like to kill her again, but she was dead all right. She'd fallen on the floor. Her hands reached towards him and he could see skin and blood under the sharp nails. He laughed when he saw some of her nails had broken. In a moment of futile frustration, he raised his leg and kicked her ribs. The crunch of her bones put a satisfied grin on his torn face.

The highway was a scant two miles from the shack, and he had a path shoveled before nightfall. He drove the truck to the main road and turned left. He was on his way home.

As the hours passed, he began to relax and started planning his strategy for getting rid of Kate and replacing her with Mandy.

He stopped only for gas and to buy bread, cheese, and a jug of milk. It was hard to eat, his mouth was cut up so bad, that old bitch had sliced him up good. He'd won, though, she could never scorn him again.

His next payback was Duggin. In time he would get his revenge on them all. He played their names over in his mind. Duggin. Norm. Holden, Sheriff, Kate. The Claytons. And Jude.

He drove until he was twenty miles from the Carey County line. A warehouse loomed ahead of him and he parked behind it. He needed a little shuteye. Tomorrow he'd sleep in HIS own bed, on HIS farm. He'd eat at HIS own table. He'd never leave the farm again.

Sheriff Henson was walking to his car when an officer came up to him and identified himself.

"I'm Sheriff Green from Brewster County, North Dakota. New evidence has come in on Leon Martin. For starters he's wanted in North Dakota and Minnesota on murder charges."

"I knew about the murder at the clinic. What about the other one?"

"There's two others. One is the deliveryman. He was stashed in a haystack in Minnesota, about twenty-five miles from the clinic. Leon slit the poor sucker's throat, ear to ear. In North Dakota we found an old woman strangled to death in an abandoned shack. She'd hidden a letter inside her dress. She wrote about a crazy guy breaking in and imprisoning her in the bedroom. Gave a good description of him. There was a lot of blood and skin under her nails, so she put up a good fight. Martin must be a holy mess."

"He's also damned dangerous. That makes five people he's killed. I've got to find him before he chalks up another one. Anything else Sheriff Green?"

"Look for a 1930 Ford pickup, with a new paint job. Black. This Widow Mallor and her sons were car thieves. She confessed it all in the letter. Guess she knew her time was up."

Sheriff Henson went back into his office and looked at the map. Brewster County. If Leon drove straight through, he could be here any time. Green wasn't sure of the exact time of the murder, but they'd found the body day before yesterday. Hell, Leon could be here now. There was a feeling in his gut that so matter what he did Leon would win this round, too. Kate's words pounded in his brain nothing would stop him.

Leon dreamed he and Kate were in a barren field. Kate picked up a fence post and using it like a bat and Leon as the ball, she batted him across the field. He landed under the tractor Pa was using to till the ground. Just as the razor sharp disks ran over his left leg, Pa changed into Jude. Leon screamed in terror and pain and looked for Kate to help him. He reached for her, but she dissolved and the old woman from the shack flew around him, shooting arrows from her eyes. His screams woke him, and he lay across the truck seat, disoriented and sick. His leg throbbed, relentless in its attack. He opened the door to get out and stretch, but the leg hurt so bad he couldn't move it. He sniffed the air, wondering if there was a dead animal in the truck. Putrid fumes wafted around him and he gagged.

As the light of dawn entered the cab, he forced himself to look at his leg. It was swollen, the pant leg tight around it. Groping for the hem of his pant leg he tried to tear the fabric apart, but the slightest pressure set off rivulets of pain and throbbing. Deeply frightened now, he desperately searched around the floor of the cab for a tool of some kind to cut his trousers. His fingers came in contact with a file and he sighed in relief. He used the ridged surface to cut through the pants along the upper thigh and pulled the fabric down, easing it away from the rotting flesh.

Horror filled him as he stared at the puncture wound. It had enlarged at least three times its usual size. The skin around the sore was surrounded by a bluish, purple border. The yellow center pulsed as if something held prisoner were straining to escape. It was alive, breathing, and Leon cringed under his fear. "Kate. I'll go to Kate. She'll know what to do."

He drove erratically, one hand on the throttle, using his right foot to operate the brakes and clutch. A steady stream of tears ran over his raw face. Chills attacked his body, alternating with a feverish heat. God, he was scared. "Ma, Ma, help your boy. I'm in trouble, Ma, your boy's in trouble."

It seemed to Kate that Leon would never arrive. Frightened of him as she was, the waiting was torture. Her nerves stretched as tight as a new clothes' line wire, every noise causing her to jump and her heart to beat furiously.

Desperately, she picked up a book and began reading. Then she put it down again. She felt unreal and went into the kitchen to look at herself in the mirror. Her great eyes stared back at her, almost black in their intensity. Her white face stood out in contrast, framed by tendrils of black hair. Her face seemed thin and tired. For the first time in her life, she saw a resemblance to her Ma. Strangely enough, seeing Ma in her face gave her the boost she needed. "If I can be as strong as my mother, I'll be fine.

Tippy's growling alerted her and she ran to the window in the study, picking up the shotgun as she passed it. The black truck weaved its way up the drive to the house. When it stopped in front of the house, she had the shotgun pointed at the driver. He was lying back against the seat. She'd wait.

Fifteen minutes later Leon opened the door. He fell from the cab and his screams sent waves of horror through her. This wasn't going the way she'd planned. She'd had herself all built up to shoot him when he walked through the door. Now, it seemed as if he couldn't walk at all. Was he playing a game? "He'll see. I'm not as naïve as I used to be. I won't fall for his tricks this time."

He began crawling towards the house, screaming her name. "Kate. Kate." She watched him closely, noticing how he used his arms and right leg to propel himself forward. As he came closer, she knew he wasn't acting. He was a mess, his face cut to ribbons, his left leg useless.

She placed the shotgun behind the studio door and went to the telephone. "Operator, this is an emergency. At the Martin farm. Please, contact Sheriff Henson and Dr. Larson. Tell them Leon has come home." Then hesitantly, filled with dread, she walked through the front door to help her brother.

The bright sun was warm on her face and she thought irrelevantly, "It's six months since Angie came home. Spring is just around the corner." She wished fervently this winter were over. So many dreadful events, so many exposed secrets and so much love and hate bouncing around. Now she had to contend with this. Leon. Death. The smell of death was all around her. Confused, she glanced around.

Leon was stretched out on the ground and her eyes lit on his bare leg. She screamed. The swollen leg seemed to be visibly palpitating. She backed away covering her mouth and nose with her hand. The stench emanating from his wound was unbearable.

Leon turned his head towards her. "Kate, get me Kate."

"I'm here, Leon. I am Kate."

"Ma . . . Ma told me to come to you. She said you'd help me. Help me, Kate."

"Yes," she whispered. "Yes, I'll help you."

"I can't see. Oh, Kate. I've had an awful time of it." He began sobbing with short gasping breaths.

"How did you get so messed up?"

"Fell, nail went into my leg. Old woman scratched me."

Kate couldn't make sense out of what he said. She let him ramble on and went in to get some supplies.

She covered him where he lay and placed a pillow under his head. She knelt beside him, unaware that the ground was dampening her dress. Tentatively, she placed her hand on his brow and jerked back. His hot skin sent a tingling through her cold palm. He began jabbering and interrupted himself with a great scream as he thrashed his body about, tossing off the blanket. His right foot kicked the bad leg and pus erupted like a small volcano. The rotten smell hung thick in the air.

Kate arose with the idea of getting some towels and water. She stepped back and he reached out and grasped her leg. He jerked hard and she fell backwards, crying out. Desperately, she kicked at him and his hand slipped down, grabbing her boot. She searched for something to hit him with, but there wasn't even a stick close by. So much for neatness. She raised her left leg and brought the boot down on Leon's wrist. He yelled, letting go and she jumped up and raced into the house, locking the door behind her.

The stench from Leon's wound was in her nostrils and she gagged. Running into the study she picked up the gun and looked out the window. She didn't see him at first, then she realized he'd rolled closer to the house. He was rolling his body towards the door screaming intermittently, high sharp screams. He lied, she thought, he can see. As though he could hear her thoughts, he laughed, a sound so evil and inhuman Kate lost the last traces of the compassion that had welled up in her heart. She opened the window and pointed the gun at him.

He rolled closer and closer, seeming to get stronger and more determined with each roll. When he reached the bottom of the steps he lay back and rested. He transcended the pai, he was Leon Martin, on a mission. A soldier, fulfilling his destiny.

Kate's finger tensed on the trigger. She was sick at heart at the waste of Leon and at the total lack of human dignity that surrounded him. She remembered the State Asylum and the hoards of wasted humanity existing within its wall. Wouldn't it be a kindness if they could die, or better yet not be born at all? No, life is too precious, she decided. It is not up to us to decide our fates. I must not rationalize my actions in order to kill Leon.

A picture of Pa entered her mind. Pa with a gun. One of his horses had been a fence crawler and gotten cut by barbed wire. Infection had set in. Pa nursed that horse day and night by putting hot wet towels on the wound until one day he'd come in and loaded a rifle. A few minutes later they'd heard the gunshot.

Now Leon had an infected leg and he's crazy to boot. Her mind reasoned, "If I have to kill him, I'll be doing him a favor." But she knew the real favor would be to herself.

He was on the second step. Two more steps and he'd be at the door. She had no idea how he'd get in. She only knew without a doubt that a locked door wouldn't stop him.

She was about to pull the trigger when three cars pulled up on the lawn. Suddenly weak, she dropped the gun and sank to her knees. It was over, but was it ever really over? Would she forget she had almost killed her half-brother? She stood up and walked to the door.

"Bring him in," she said. "Put him in here on the cot." Leon was sobbing hopelessly, all the fight gone out of him. They laid him on the cot and believing he was harmless, Norm went back to his car to get his medical bag. Rob and Sheriff Henson went into the kitchen to call in a report and put water on to boil. Kate and Leon were alone. Leon spoke first. "You were going to kill me, Kate."

"Yes. Better you than me."

"Do it. Do it now, before they come back. Take me out of my misery. Use the pillow, like I did with Ma."

She stared at him, dazed. So, he had killed Ma. Tears welled up. Ma shouldn't have had to die like that.

"C'mon, damn you, do it."

"I ... I couldn't, not like this. You're not a danger to me now."

Leon eyed her coldly. He reached behind his head and pulled out the pillow. He placed it over his face. She watched him trying to smother himself and forgetting her fear, she went to him to remove the pillow. Leon continued to press his hands down against the pillow until she felt herself doing the job for him. She kept pressing until her arms grew tired. As his breath became less he struggled against her but she continued to press down, with a sense of inevitability. All of a sudden Leon arched and shoved his arms up against her. She landed on the floor clutching the pillow.

Leon turned to the side of the bed and opened the table drawer. Kate watched in horror as he grabbed the pistol. She couldn't move and closed her eyes waiting for the bullet to enter her body. Leon would finally kill her as he'd promised, but she wouldn't leave this world as a coward, but as a woman with value; as a woman who had a right to live and had pride in herself.

She opened her eyes and straightened her body. She lifted her chin and looked at him. Kate was calm. If her fate was decided, she would go out with as much grace as possible.

Leon looked at her for long moments. He smiled and slowly raised the pistol. For moments only he pointed the gun at Kate's head. With shaking hands, he put the pistol against his own head and pulled the trigger.

Sheriff Henson and Norm found her there, rocking back and forth on the faded blue rug with her face buried into a pillow. Leon Martin was sprawled half off the bed, lying there stone cold dead.

Jude slapped the book closed. Steinbeck would have to wait. His mother had been pecky all morning and he and Ben felt more and more like intruders.

The cramped, dingy room closed in on him. He detested the smells of Marcie's cooking. The pile of dirty clothes lay like a shrine in the corner of the living room. Marcie added to it every morning. He wondered how high it would have to get before she washed it.

Against his will he heard himself shout, "Mom! Why haven't you moved to a decent place? You can't enjoy living like this. I give you plenty of money to live good."

Marcie turned her lips down and refused to answer him. He yelled at Ben, "Get our things, we're leaving. A man can't get an honest answer around here. I'd rather take my chances with Leon. At least we'll have some clean air to breath and comfortable beds to sleep in."

Marcie squirmed on the broken settee, fluttering her hands in the air. "Wait, Jude, I gotta tell you something."

"So you can talk, can you? Well, say what's on your mind. Ben and I want to get started."

She didn't know how to say it, she'd been mulling it over in her mind for three days now. Finally, she swallowed and said, "It's about, uh . . . I got to tell you 'bout the beginnings."

"My beginnings?" Jude echoed stupidly.

"About your Daddy. He owes us and we should get what we got coming Jude. You're Burt Martin's son."

Jude froze, unable to speak for a moment. Rage as black as night descended over him.

"You're crazy. What are you trying to pull? Don't work your cons on me, Mom. It don't wash."

"Why did you run to hide out in those woods when you left home?"

"Right." She nodded her uncombed head. "I was meetin' Burt there. When we were fishin' I'd go to him. We met there for months. He use'ta come to our place before you were born and for a while after. He didn't want anyone to know he was your dad. For some reason I never figured out, he was scared of being noticed."

Jude wheeled his chair around so he was facing her, close enough to grab her arm. "I don't believe a word you're saying. You're a greedy old woman, trying to get a free ride."

"I know whose son you are, Jude."

"Really, Mother? I seem to remember you were a very busy woman in those days."

"I know, I know, but when I was seeing Burt, he was the only one. I had a decent place to live and after you were born, he took care of us for a while. Remember when I took you to the circus?"

Jude nodded and she added, "Burt was supporting us then. We had it pretty good. If I hadn't been so young . . ."

"My name is Bainville. I'm no corn cropper's son."

Goosebumps erupted on Marcie's arms. She hadn't thought for a minute Jude would take it like this. "You're his son," she shouted, unwilling to see her dreams die. "We should be livin' in the big house. You deserve a share of that farm and a part of all that money. You're the oldest son. He should've pervaded better for you. That's why I haven't moved. I'm thinkin' we'll be takin' our rightful place at Martin's Little Kingdom."

Jude raked his eyes over her. She'd grown soft and plump. Her undergroomed body and hair repelled him. She had the morals of an alley cat and now that her youth was long past, she looked sleazy and common. For the first time in his life he actively hated his mother.

"Get that pipe dream out of your head. That place belongs to Mandy, as does the big house and money. I have what he gave me. He was my friend."

His harsh voice caused Marcie to shrink into her skin. Desperately, she wondered how she could convince him without showing him the papers that proved Burt was his dad, but also that Burt had damaged him. She didn't think Jude could handle that. She tried once more to convince him. "Burt didn't tell me you were living in the shack. He quit meeting me. I thought it was because I'd gotten married, but I know now he didn't want me to know he had you." She snorted, "Free labor is what he got. A penny pincher from the word go. He used you, used us both. We deserve to share some of what he left behind."

Jude motioned for Ben to wheel him out. Marcie jumped up and shoved some papers under his blanket. "This'll prove I'm not lyin'." Jude didn't acknowledge the papers and ignored Marcie. Stung, she screamed at him. "It's Burt fault you have them fits. His fault! You'll see. Them papers says it all."

Jude and Ben were silent on the drive home. Ben left Jude alone. He could see Marcie had upset him something awful. Jude was a fanciful fella, talked about being descended from nobility. He really believed it, too. He'd been a sight to behold when Marcie sprung the news that he was Burt's spawn. Poor guy, he had so many strikes against him, it was a damn shame that mother of his had to knock him off his pedestal. For the life of him, he couldn't see what difference it made. He was set up comfortable and had more than most.

Ben reached over and patted Jude on the shoulder. "Buck up, now. You've heard worse on your life. A man's folks don't determine what he is. Your life won't change because two people got it on in the woods."

Jude remained silent so Ben decided he'd better leave it alone. These sensitive types were a pain sometimes. They drove the rest of the way immersed in their own thoughts.

SIXTEEN

Leon was buried two days after his death. They laid him in the ground beside Ma. There were three graves on the small hilltop now and a marker remembering Angie.

Kate, Jude, and Ben listened to the drone of the preacher as he talked of Leon's life and dedicated his soul to God. It had been Kate's wish to have a closed burial.

"Leon is beside his mother again. He'd have liked that." Kate said. "His reign of terror is over."

They went to their own homes afterwards, Jude declining Kate's invitation to visit for a while. A stab of disappointment pierced Kate. She needed someone to talk to. Jude had been acting strange and aloof since his return.

Leon's death raced through her mind again. She'd almost killed him. Not out of mercy, but because once he'd pressed her hands down on the pillow, a feeling of certainty had come over her. Something so strange she couldn't describe it. As if she were born to live that moment. As if by killing Leon she would be fulfilling her destiny.

Leon himself had kept her from becoming a murderess. But why? Had he at last felt something for her besides hate? Had he regretted his mean treatment of her? Had he simply wanted to escape punishment?

The truth would never be known. It was just one more mystery to add to the craze deeds of the Martins.

Leon was no more. He'd joined the rest of the Martins. Except for Conner and Mandy, they were all gone, but she was left with the dregs. She had to carry on in spite of the fears, the negative emotions they had instilled in her. She didn't have to fight the Martins anymore. She had to fight the ingrained memories, the fear of failure, the inability to stand up for herself. To walk alone in the world and put forth a façade of confidence and strength caused her to shake with trepidation.

The following morning Kate opened her eyes, feeling restless, and out of sorts. She took Conner to school and went home wishing she could stop and see Jude. He was so silent and taciturn lately, she felt uncomfortable around him.

She could go to Ryan and do some shopping. Suddenly, the idea of dressing up appealed to her and she decided to make a day of it. She'd been thinking of having Rob make a will, so Conner would be protected if anything happened to her. Eagerly, she dressed and by the time she drove into town her mood had lightened considerably.

Rob was ushering out his first clients of the day when Kate came in. He drew in a sharp breath, taken aback by her beauty and grace. She moved toward him, smiling. He shook her hand, hoping she couldn't hear the loud drumming of his heart. He couldn't keep his eyes off of her. The pink silk suit fitted her willowy figure to perfection, the short jacket nipped in at the waist and the skirt skimmed her hips and fell to soft folds at the hem. The pink color brought a soft blush to her cheeks and the contrast with her dark hair and purple eyes, just about brought him to his knees.

He forced himself to act business-like and they discussed the will. Kate reached over to sign it and their hands accidentally touched. She felt a tremor go through her body.

"Thanks, Rob. I'd better get along."

"Wait, Kate. Would you consider meeting me for lunch?"

"Yes, I'd like that."

"The Steak Place okay? In forty-five minutes?"

She nodded, smiled, and ran out the door, almost waltzing in her delight.

It took all of ten minutes for them to get over their self-consciousness and they spent the next hour trading small talk and joking. Rob was charmed by her. He loved the way she laughed with that breathless catch in her voice, and he was surprised to find her so intelligent. He remembered her as she'd been when he first met her; overweight, frightened and cowed. Now she was a woman to reckon with.

"Kate, I'd like to see you again. Could we take in a movie this weekend?"

"I don't go out at night. I have Conner to care for."

"You're raising your little brother?" Rob hadn't known Conner was at the farm. He searched his mind, trying to remember the deed. Yes, Burt had deeded that Marshallville property to Conner.

"Conner is my son. I assumed everyone knew about Conner."

"It doesn't matter, but I really hadn't heard he was your boy." He took her hand and held it gently. "I guess you were married during the time everyone thought you were away at school."

Kate was at a loss. How could she tell him? It was such a dirty story. How could she tell a nice guy like him about the muck she'd lived in? He'd never understand people like them. Shame washed over her, and she sat motionless, unable to answer him. She felt dirty, untouchable.

Pulling her hand free, she blurted, "I'm sorry, I have to go. Thank you for a nice time." She bolted from the café and was driving away in her car before he realized what had happened.

Terror chased her all the way home. Old fears and memories took over her mind and she was unaware of the beauty of the small, well cared for farms along the narrow road. She felt cheated when she realized she'd driven all the way without looking at her favorite places. After she parked and got out of the car, she kicked the car tire and stomped into the house, wiping tears from her cheeks.

"I'm not going to answer that damn phone." She let it ring six times then angrily picked up the receiver. "Yes?"

"Miss Sutton? This is Alma Pasternak. We're the ones who took Ellie to live with us."

"I'm happy to hear from you. How is Ellie?"

"We need to talk. Things aren't what we expected. We'll be there in an hour if you can see your way clear."

Kate worried as she changed into her housedress and let her hair down. Ellie. What could be wrong? She was a good kid, just needed to get used to home life. Maybe the Pasternak's were too old to put up with her exuberance. It was a stroke of luck for Ellie when the Pasternak's wanted her. It was rare for an older child to be offered a home, except for unpaid labor.

They brought Ellie with them and she walked in front, carrying her battered suitcase. She walks like she'd going to meet the hangman, Kate thought, and she looks guilty.

Kate flew to the door and met Ellie just as she started to climb the steps. Kate wrapped her arms around her and whispered, "Don't worry, whatever is wrong, we'll fix it."

She led the way to the living room and when they were seated, she told Ellie to go upstairs and lie down. "You look peaked; I'll call you when you're needed."

Mrs. Pasternak sat stiffly, her back straight and her lips tight. "She should look peaked, after what she's been up to."

"Ellie is a good girl," Kate answered her. "What can she have done that has you so upset?"

"What's she done? I'll tell you what she's done. She'd had dealings with a man, that's what." She sat there, glowering at Kate. The spitting image of an old crow, Kate thought nasilty.

"What man is bothering her?"

"Oh, no one we know. She was in her condition when we took her. The doctor says she's five months along. We certainly can't keep her now and shame on you for pawning her off on decent folks. Come, Carl." She gathered up her scarf and gloves and the two of them marched out of the room and out the door.

Kate didn't try to stop them. She was stunned. Ellie pregnant. Only fourteen and pregnant. Like me, oh God, how had it happened? Who had done it? She knew she had to talk to the girl and suddenly she was afraid to hear the story. It would be an ugly story, she was sure. She was tired of ugly.

Ellie was sitting in the hall, sobbing. Kate coaxed her into her room, and they sat on the bed. Kate was floundering. She was out of her element. The words Ellie needed to hear were stopped up within her. Finally, she decided to be blunt. She'd been rocking Ellie to and fro, letting her cry out her disappointment. Now she moved back and looking into Ellie's eyes she asked, "Did you have a boyfriend before you came to live with me?"

"No, I never had one."

"Ellie, you know how a girl gets pregnant, don't you?"

"Yes, I know, but I didn't do that. Someone did it to me. Oh, Kate. He attacked me. I couldn't stop him."

Kate gasped. "You better tell me about it. You'll feel better if you share your nightmare."

"How do you know it's a nightmare?"

"I'll tell you someday, Ellie, but now we have to take care of you. I need to know what happened so we can make some decisions. This is your life we're talking about. If someone forced you, you're innocent of any sin. It's not your fault, Ellie, you got that?"

Ellie nodded her head and composed herself. She whispered, "It happened at the asylum. The nurse told me to carry the kids' dirty clothes to the laundry. I was coming back to the rooms and I was just by the crazy ones' open ward when this guy jumped on my back. He knocked me down and started pinching my legs and hitting me."

Ellie crossed her legs tightly and put her head in her hands. "Then he started crowing and he was spitting on my neck and it was running round to the front of me and … then he did it. It was awful; it hurt so bad and all the loonies were screaming, and some tried to pull him off me, but he wouldn't get off."

She drew a long, shaky breath and continued her tale. "I was so scared. I couldn't get up at first and then this nurse, she kicked me on the leg, and she said if I'd stayed where I belonged it wouldn't have happened. Oh, Kate, they blamed me. Said I was damaged goods, and no one would adopt me. They put me in the regulars. If you hadn't come … Now I've lost my home and I'm having some crazy's baby." Ellie lay back, exhausted, and Kate managed to stay with her until she fell asleep.

Ellie's words threw Kate into a tailspin. She stumbled down the stairs into the study and went to Pa's desk. The shaking began in her legs and crept over her slowly, until her body trembled like a leaf in the wind. She cried weakly and sagged onto the sofa.

The enormity of Leon's depravity sickened her. He's dead, but his seed is upstairs in that little girl's belly. He lives on and through that seed there'll be more Leon and more, until he lives to the end of times.

Sleep finally claimed her, but she couldn't escape Leon, even there. In her dream she bought pillows, dozens of them. The wind carried her over the fields and rivers, and she landed in front of a long low building. Carrying her pillows, she went in and started to count the baskets that lined the room. Hundreds of them, and each one held a baby that resembled Leon. Each baby had the green reptilian eyes and as she bent over them in turn, the eyes bored small holes into her heart and each hole filled with ice. Carefully and quietly she pressed a pillow over each face, but there was no end to them. She knew Leon had won, that she would spend all her days here. This was to be her life's work. In the background Leon's diabolical laughter echoed through the air.

Her screams woke her, and hysterical laughter erupted from her throat. She teetered to the telephone and shrieked at the operator to ring Norm. Leon had beaten her in death as he couldn't in life. Sagging to the floor she lay motionless, her body still, and her mind a black hole. Norm found her there, cold, and unaware. Gently, he picked her up and carried her to the bed.

Kate drifted in and out of consciousness for five days. She was aware of gentle hands bathing her, smoothing her hair, spooning food into her mouth. She lay inert, unwilling to face reality.

The sun streamed over her bed, warming her face. She remembered Conner and forced herself to open her eyes and sit up. Noises from the kitchen drifted into the room. She noticed a woman sitting in the rocking chair, by the window. The woman smiled and said, "I'm Elizabeth. Dr. Larson asked me to sit with you." She swung Kate's legs over the side of the bed. "Easy now. You've been out of it for five days. You'll be a bit weak at first."

"What's wrong with me?"

"Nothing, dear, that a little rest won't fix. Dr. Larson said you'd had a great shock. If affects some people like this."

"Who's in the kitchen?"

"Your girl, Ellie, and a cute little scamp who tells me his name is Conner."

Kate looked her over carefully. She'd never seen her before. "Who are you?"

"I'm a woman like you. Someone who has gone through hell and I'm here to help you if you'll let me." She stretched her long legs and moved to the foot of the bed.

"Some women have a hard time of it. I had a husband who used me as a punching bag. Can you believe I stayed with him for sixteen years before I finally got up the courage to leave? I got that courage from a woman in my neighborhood. She helped me and I've made it my work to help other women."

She shrugged her shoulders and raised her hands in a futile gesture. "Lord knows there are no resources for the likes of us. Women and children don't really count in our society, you know. We have to support each other. I can help you if you'll let me."

Kate began talking to Elizabeth that very day. It was a bitterly, hard task and she cried often during their sessions. "If it weren't for Conner, I would not do this," she told Elizabeth. "I know I have to be a whole person and free from the past to give him a normal upbringing, but God, it hurts."

"Someday you'll realize you're doing it for you, too, Kate."

After an especially painful session with Elizabeth, Kate turned on the radio. "The Battle Hymn of the Republic" was playing, and she sang along. Soon she realized she was singing her own words and she grabbed a pencil to jot them down.

As she read over what she had written, she found herself crying again, but with relief. The poem was her first acceptance of the despicable acts of Burt Martin and the first step in ridding herself of the denial. It was also a reaching out to help others who had suffered as she had, as Ellie had. Strength filled her as shame lifted its shadow from her mind.

Silently she handed the poem to Elizabeth, who said, "It's what I've been waiting for, a breakthrough for you. May I read it aloud?" Kate nodded. "It's to the tune of 'The Battle Hymn of the Republic'." Shyness overcame her as Elizabeth settled herself in the rocker and smoothed the paper out.

Kate walked over to the window and kept her back turned while Elizabeth read her poem aloud. This is what they call putting one's self on the line, she told herself, but as she listened to the words she had written from the depths of her mortification, she felt at peace with herself.

Elizabeth's soft monotone filled the room. She began to sing the words and Kate joined in. Their tears ran, their voices cracked, but they finished the song.

> *Mine eyes have seen the terror of the coming of the fist,*
> *Mine ears have heard the cracking of the broken nose and wrist,*
> *Mine teeth have felt the pressure of the hands that never missed,*
> *But my soul is pure and strong.*
> *Glory, Glory, I have spoken, Glory, Glory, I'm not broken,*
> *These words I carry as a token,*
> *May these truths help right the wrong.*

> *Mine eyes have seen the terror of the coming of the strap,*
> *Mine Lord was cold and hungry and surviving in the trap,*
> *Mine heart is scarred and ragged, like lines on an old map,*
> *But my soul is pure and strong.*
> *Glory, Glory, I have spoken, Glory, Glory, I'm not broken,*
> *These words I carry as a token,*
> *May these truths help right the wrong.*

> *Mine eyes have seen the horror of the coming of the lust,*
> *Mine body has been punctured with incestuous, brutal thrust,*
> *Mine mind is shattered pieces and I never more will trust,*
> *But my soul is pure and strong.*
> *Glory, Glory, I have spoken, Glory, Glory, I'm not broken,*
> *These words I carry as a token,*
> *May these truths help right the wrong.*

"Fantastic!" Elizabeth said. "You'll heal now. It won't happen very quickly but you will eventually put your hurtful experiences in their proper place. They belong in the past, to be brought out only when they will help you or someone else. Just keep that attitude. You are a winner, Kate. I'm so proud to know you."

Kate finally understood what Elizabeth had been saying. She'd just begun to realize the magnitude of the betrayal in her life.

Always she'd blamed Pa and Leon for her pain, but the deeper hurt came from her Ma. She'd had no love, no nurturing or protection from the person who should have loved her more than anyone, and she'd grown, her Ma's total rejection of her, along with the abuse from Pa and Leon, and formed a non-person. There wasn't any Kate.

As a child, Kate knew she was unlovable. She took the fact for granted. She didn't expect anyone to like her. She'd had a few friends at school, but Leon scared them away. When Mrs. Lowell had taken her hand and smiled at her, she'd treasured that moment above all others, and her studies and reading kept her sane. "I was used unjustly by them all, but the fact is, they're dead, and I'm still here. I mean to leave my mark in this world and Conner will be proud of his Mama."

There was still the problem of Ellie. She was at a loss for a solution. She walked into the kitchen and found Ellie and Elizabeth drinking coffee at the table with their heads together, talking in low tones. Kate felt a twinge of jealousy.

"Am I interrupting?"

Ellie jumped in, her rosy cheeks taking on a darker hue. She nervously waved her hands and shook her head. "I need to tell you something, Kate."

"We need to talk about Ellie's future," Elizabeth interjected.

Kate smiled. "Do you need to be so nervous about a talk?"

"To be honest with you, I feel like I've overstepped my bounds. You see, I want to adopt Ellie. She's exactly what I've wanted in a daughter. We get along famously, and she shares my feelings."

Kate leaned against the door jam. More damn surprises.

"This isn't something I can just say yes to. Another couple said the same thing and look how that turned out. I like you Elizabeth, but

Ellie is my responsibility. A decision like this takes a lot of thought and I won't have her hurt again."

"But Kate, I want to live with Elizabeth. I know it's the right thing for me."

"It's not just you and her. There's the baby. Have you also decided what to do about that?" She hadn't meant to scream at Ellie and reached out her hand to apologize. Ellie flashed her an angry glare and ran from the room.

The two women eyed each other. Elizabeth spoke first.

"I'm going to help Ellie care for the baby."

"No!" Kate shouted. "No. This isn't a matter of Ellie having a baby. It's a matter of her having Leon Martin's baby. It might not be right. There could be bad days ahead with this child."

The blood drained from her face and she staggered towards a chair. Elizabeth helped her into it and stood behind her with her arms around Kate's neck. A cup of hot coffee was on the table. Kate reached for it and took a big swallow, relishing the burning as it slid down her throat.

"I'm over-reaching again, but I'm so afraid for her to have this baby. She doesn't want it, surely?" Kate licked her dry lips and sipped at her coffee.

"No, she doesn't want it. She hates it and the man who did this to her. She's still a child. I want to give her the kind of life her parents should have given her."

Kate was silent, thinking. "Tell me, is there a way to get rid of the baby?"

"You mean abort it? No legal way. Shoot, that would be the answer, though. I wonder ..."

"It's a crime to make that little girl have an insane man's child. The Martin family is touched by some kind of madness. I lucked out with Conner, but Leon was criminally insane. Burt thrived on sadistic behavior and Angie was unstable. The chances that this baby will be born normal is a slim one."

Elizabeth felt that she should point out the illegality of what Kate proposed. Kate believed in justice and hadn't yet learned that the right thing was not always the legal thing. She used her inborn sense of right and wrong. Well, Elizabeth sighed, give her a few more years and she'll be like the rest of us. Afraid to step over the line. It was a sad thought, as part of Kate's charm was her impulsiveness.

"Do you think Dr. Larson could help us? He could give us some advice anyway."

Kate shook her head. "He's in love with the Hippocratic oath. No, we have to go farther away from home."

"I'm going to town and talk to him. He's a compassionate man, Kate. You don't appreciate him enough." With a wave of her hand, she ran out the door.

Kate rubbed the large square of bacon rind across the top of the cook stove, watching the dull surface turn bright and new looking. If only we could clean ourselves up as easily, she thought, taking pleasure in her mundane task. A noise behind her caused her to turn around. Ellie stood in the doorway staring mutinously at her, a suitcase beside her and box under her arm. "Why Ellie, what's up? I thought you were resting."

"I can't stay here. You said this was Leon Martin's baby. I heard you talking to Elizabeth." She glared accusingly at Kate. "You knew all the time it was your crazy brother that did this to me. You lied to me. I thought you were my friend."

"I didn't know until you told me what happened to you. I knew he'd attacked a young girl at the asylum, but the nurse told me she was ten years old. I just didn't connect it to you."

The forlorn face of the girl shattered her, and she reached her arms out to her. "I'm so sorry, Ellie, I'd give anything if it hadn't happened. Please, put your things away. We'll work this out."

"I won't. I have some pride left. Us orphan kids might not be much, but we're worth more than this."

Kate looked at her sharply. The straight shoulders and lifted chin showed strength and determination. How had this abandoned kid acquire so much pride in herself? Kate envied her and admired her too, she admitted to herself. If I had that much natural pride, my life would be easier.

"I understand how you feel, but please wait for Elizabeth. She'll be terribly hurt if you walk out on her. She's gone to see Norm about the baby to see if there's a way to end the pregnancy."

186

Her eyes shooting daggers at Kate, she said, "I'll be in my room, then. Please tell Elizabeth I want to leave as soon as possible."

"I could cut my tongue out. What a stupid mistake. Ellie is devastated. Can you change her mind, Elizabeth?"

"I think it would be best if I take her home with me. No, don't argue. You are at your limit, Kate. You don't need this added stress. Norman is making arrangements with a doctor in St. Louis to end the pregnancy. I'll travel with Ellie and then she can move in with me. I'm going to try to adopt her legally. It's what we both want."

Norm sat quietly, listening to the two women. He knew Kate felt left out as he and Elizabeth had made the arrangements without her. He tried to soften the sting. "Kate, we both want you to rest. Do things with Conner and live easy for a while. I'd like to see you continue your education. Get out of here and do what you want. Fulfill your dreams and I'll always be here for you."

He rose and went to the window and looked out at the moving clouds and big sky. "Ellie will get over her hurt. She's just so afraid of this pregnancy she's lashing out at you. Don't take it to heart. None of this is your fault. You warned us about Leon. None of us listened to you. Me, most of all."

He turned and faced her, trying not to let his love for her show. He turned to putty when he was around her and unlike the others, he'd fallen in love with her before the lost weight. He should tell her that sometime. It might give him an advantage."

Elizabeth hugged Kate. "I'm going up to get Ellie. We'll go straight out to the car. I love you, Kate. Take good care of yourself." And she was gone. Like the good fairy, she'd done her good deeds and disappeared.

Norm said goodbye and Kate sat alone, waiting for Conner. She began to enjoy the silence and the privacy. There'd been little enough of it lately. She rummaged around in the pantry and soon the kitchen was full of the smell of cinnamon and she hummed as she baked cookies and made cocoa for Conner.

The next three weeks passed quietly. Kate continued to improve, and her nervousness eased. She worked out of doors each day, preparing for the ensuing spring. The sun dyed her cheeks with a healthy hue and energy replaced the dullness and lethargy that had invaded her body.

Time was flying by and she hadn't made any plans for the summer. She looked at the calendar. March 16, 1938. School would be out soon. She and Conner would go away. Something nagged at her and then she remembered Phillip. He would be going to court soon, charged with theft. Suddenly, she ran to the telephone and called the police station in Marshallville.

"When is Phillip Sutton's case due to appear in court? One week from tomorrow? No, I've changed my mind. I want to drop the charges. A mistake. Yes. I was wrong. Please release him. Thank you, officer."

Next, she called the Superintendent of Schools. She could take her test for a high school diploma next Friday. She made the appointment, shivering with excitement and fear. Could she really do it? It had been a dream for so long, but always out of reach. Now could she make it a reality? Tomorrow she would visit Emily and go over her lessons again.

She made arrangements for Conner to stay with Ben and Jude. Kate was saddened to see the gloom and disillusionment that hung over their cozy home. Jude seemed to become more depressed each day, and nothing she did or said had any effect on him. Ben was silent about Jude. Just told her not to worry that it was something Jude had to work out for himself.

Jude's eyes lit up when she told him about her test. "That's good, you show them, Kate. Show those Martins you're not one of them." He spoke with a bitter tinge to his voice, leaving Kate more confused than ever.

SEVENTEEN

riday dawned, mild and sunny, promising a warm spring day. Kate scrutinized her clothes. What would be suitable for taking a test? She finally chose a soft blue blouse and a dark gray skirt and jacket. At the last moment she strung her mother's cameo pin on a velvet ribbon and tied it around her neck.

Conner ran off to Jude's and she began her long drive to Marshallville. The drive was so relaxing she had to force herself to stay in contact with the present. After so many years of living in her fantasies, it was a struggle sometimes to stay centered in the real world. Now that she knew she could control her thoughts, she felt stronger and she worked diligently at keeping her mind where she wanted it to be.

Emily had written down the directions to the school and she went around the city instead of her usual route. The long winding lane that led to the schools left her breathless with delight. New homes were built on large parcels of land, most of them brick, with shutters and large glassed-in sun porches. The yards boasted a diversity of trees and rock gardens and Kate envisioned the birds and butterflies, the flowers that would soon be in bloom and the lovely green lawns. She'd like to raise Conner in a place like one of these. As if on cue, the last house had a for sale sign in the large front window. She noticed there were two chimneys and the roof sloped gently over the long rooms. It was a lovely house. A house that love built, Kate imagined. So warm and welcoming.

She picked up speed and drove on and soon forgot the yearning she'd had to buy another place. Nervousness settled over her again as the school appeared before her. "Please, Conner's God, help me pass this test."

She parked in front of the school building with fifteen minutes to spare. The large room she was directed to smelled of wax and chalk dust. There were three other women and one man taking the test with her. One woman looked to be in her forties. Kate smiled at her and felt her own courage grow. She was happy the woman was finally getting her diploma and wondered what had postponed it for so long.

They were given two hour and forty-five minutes to complete the test. Kate finished just a hair before the deadline. She gave her booklet to the instructor and waited in the back of the room. He began correcting her answers and she watched him breathlessly. If she had failed the test she could come back on another Friday, yet it seemed as if her life were on the line. What would she do if she failed? It mattered so much. She still couldn't believe she'd actually gone ahead and taken the test. Her dream of becoming a teacher had grown strong again, but she couldn't trust life enough to believe she would really be one someday.

Her hands grew clammy and her heart pumped furiously as the instructor walked over to her. He smiled and handed her a temporary diploma. "Congratulations. You're now a high school graduate. You will receive your official diploma in about three weeks." He shook her hand and she managed to thank him. Clasping the paper to her heart she walked outside and ran to her car. There she screamed and shouted and finally looked at her diploma. A feeling of pride, fierce and primitive, swept over her. Her dream was in her hands.

Suddenly, it wasn't enough that she knew, she wanted to share her happiness with others. Steering Angie's LaSalle towards the city center she decided to check out her house on the way to the café. She drove slowly, savoring her latest accomplishment.

It was like she could hold out her hands and grab anything she wanted. Life was finally on her side, and the fear was waning, the dream had become rare, coming in spurts, and fading away. Soon, please God, it would be no more. A grin split her face as she said aloud, "Yes, Mr. Honker, I do believe your goose is just about cooked."

As she steered the car into her driveway, she saw Janis sitting on the front steps. "Janis, what a surprise. I was on my way to see you. I passed the test, Janis. I've got my diploma." She waved the paper in the air, laughing exultantly. Janis ran over and hugged her. "Kate, that's wonderful. I'm so proud of you." They did a short version of the Charleston and sat on the steps, breathless and laughing.

"So, what are you doing here? Trouble?"

"I'm afraid your house has become a haven for the homeless, Kate. First your Dad and now me. I've been staying here. I was evicted, with no place to go. I wanted to call and ask you, but I felt so ashamed."

"Of course, you can stay here, but can we go in? I need a drink of water. My throat feels like sandpaper." She went through the door and stopped in wonder. "It's beautiful, Janis. You've redecorated and made it into a real house." She poured herself a glass of water and said, "Let's sit here and talk. Tell me what's happened to you."

Janis drew a deep breath. "I rented the house I lived in from my brother-in-law, Peter. He had me to understand that whatever work I did on the house would be like a down payment when I could afford to buy it. I fixed the house up, repaired everything, and last summer I painted the outside. It really looks beautiful, Kate, but Peter started acting like I wasn't doing enough. He began to be dissatisfied with everything I did." Janis grabbed a loose strand of hair and pinned back on top of her head.

"I put in a new front lawn last fall and it's starting to come in now. Susie, my sister, says I'm imagining it. That I'm the one who's changed. She said I should be grateful I had the house as long as I did, that they could have gotten lots more rent for it from someone else."

Janis was silent, trying to get her emotions under control. "It shouldn't matter so much, I guess, but I love the place, it's my home. I made it what it is. Then there's the café. Someone complained and the State closed me down. Said the sanitation was under code. All of a sudden, I was homeless and unemployed. I almost moved in with my sister and Peter, but oh, how I dreaded the thought. I had the key to your house and thought you might not mind.

Kate was aghast at her friend's misfortunes. "It's for sure Peter wants to cash in on your hard work. The house is worth so much more now that you've fixed it up and he could be the one that reported you to the State. Had he been in the café shortly before the inspectors came?"

"Let me think. Yes he came for coffee about three days before. He came into the kitchen and said he'd check things over for me. Kate, you think he did it, don't you? Why would he want to ruin me?"

"So you couldn't pay your rent and he could evict you. I have a feeling he's got plans for that house you renovated."

Kate was silent, running ideas through her mind. Janis looked so woebegone. If only Kate could think of something to bring back the vitality and energy that was Janis' persona. She noticed Janis' cinnamon eyes were dull and her face pale and drawn. Her red hair was pushed into a careless bun, but the saddest thing of all was her lack of vitality. It was Janis' energy that made her so attractive. The girls were quiet as they sat by the window, comfortable with the silence while they strove to come up with a solution to the Janis' misfortune.

When Kate spoke there was an excited gleam in her eyes. "Janis, you don't really care about getting the café back, do you? I mean if there were a better way for you to earn a living?"

Janis shook her head. "No, not at all. It was all I had money for, but I didn't make a good profit at it. Why Kate, do you know something I don't?"

She told her about the house and property that had so impressed her. Kate's eyes glowed, the color changing to soft lavender with flashed of blue and back to violet.

"Janis, why not look it over?" They ran out to the car and drove out to the house. Kate almost swooned when she discovered there were twenty acres behind the house and a creek running through the property. "It's wonderful. Do you like it, Janis?"

"Well, of course. But Kate I can't go in with you on this. I'm broke remember?"

"You don't have to. You have to run the business."

"What business? Stop teasing me, you fiend."

"I'm opening an interior decorating shop. I'll fill it with fabrics and lace and all the things you need to decorate peoples' homes. You make a list and I'll furnish the supplies. You'll have your own rooms and I'll move in when things are settled on the farm. Conner and I will live here someday, Janis, after school is out. What do you say?"

"But Kate, I don't know about doing other folk's homes. I've had no experience."

"You just did mine and a finer job I've yet to see. You're a natural, Janis. You'll be a great success. Business is picking up now, people have more money. They'll want to rejuvenate their homes after their struggle to get through the hard times. I noticed new homes are going up all over the area. Give it a try." Janis agreed, scared to death, but as excited as she'd ever been in her life.

An hour later they'd bought the house and grounds. The papers were drawn up making herself and Janis legal owners. Kate opened a bank account for Janis to use at her own discretion. They each got a set of keys and Kate drove Janis back to Vine Street where she would get her own car and move into the new house the next day. They hugged good-bye and Kate promised to return as soon as possible.

When Kate had told Janis her decorating of the house was the finest she had ever seen it was a true statement, but it was also the only place she had seen. Visiting wasn't something she had started yet, so her only reference was her own home and the hotel she and Angie had stayed in. Janis would be a success, she just knew it. She crossed her fingers for luck.

Next, she went to Phillip's office, on the slight chance he had gone back to it after being released from jail. He was sitting at his desk, despondent, but clean and presentable. "Hello, Dad." He jumped up and hugged her.

"Kate, you're a sight for these old eyes. Thanks, daughter, for my release." He blew his nose and asked her if she could sit awhile.

"I'm in a hurry, but I've come to give you this. You can take possession after tomorrow. "She handed him a check and the deed to the little house on Vine Street. "Everything you find there is yours, including the Dodge. It's in the garage." She gave him the key to it and said, "I'll keep in touch with you, Dad. I'd like you to have a place in Conner's life."

"Daughter, I wish I could do something for you. I don't deserve your goodness." His voice broke and Kate put her hand on his sleeve.

"Dad, I'm not as wonderful as you think. I did a terrible thing; in fact, I've done some things lately that would make me look pretty bad, if they were known. I learned through them that we do all make mistakes. Who am I to judge you? Besides, you and Conner and I are family. I … I'd like to show you something. Walk me to my car, will you?" Phillip took her arm and when they reached the car, she took out her diploma and handed it to him.

Pure pleasure lit up his face. "Why Kate, what a wonderful thing you have done. I'm proud of you, daughter." He hugged her tightly and Kate drove away with a new kind of happiness in her heart.

Her Dad's pride in her accomplishments added a new dimension to her emerging personality. She felt softer, more acceptable. The future looked exciting, her goals seemed possible and suddenly she was anxious to get started. A vision of her standing in front of a class of students came into her mind, and she laughed aloud as she realized she was talking, standing, and using the same gestures as her beloved teacher, Emily Lowell.

CHAPTER

EIGHTEEN

R ob and Norm met by chance at the Eatery. They took a table
together and ordered roast beef sandwiches with horseradish and
mustard. Rob had the pretty waitress dimpling at him in no time.
"You have a way with the ladies."

"I strike out sometimes. In fact, I've wanted to talk to you about
Kate Sutton. You know I investigated Burt Martin's background and
thought I knew the family inside and out. What's with her, anyway?"

"Why do you want to know?" Norm's voice boomed in the quiet
room.

"We had a lunch date, and everything was going just fine, then all
of a sudden she bolted out of there and drove off. Didn't explain or call
me. Is she touched in the head like the rest of them?"

Norm wanted to strangle the cocky bastard. "What were you talking
about?"

"Nothing important. Oh, I think she was going on about her kid
and I asked her about her marriage. That's when she took off."

Norm took a large bite of his sandwich and spent some time
chewing, so he could think. Rob and Kate. Fear swept through him
at the thought of Kate being with another man. Especially Rob. The
typical ladies' man, he'd gotten quite a reputation in the short time

he'd been in Ryan. A good attorney, he'd give him that, but not good for his Kate.

"You go easy on Kate. She's not used to dating. She's had a hard life and needs time to know herself. She'd not for you, Rob."

Rob was intrigued. He'd been going to forget her, but Norm had added mystery to his latent interest. What was her story? It was a sure bet he wouldn't find out from old sober sides. He decided to needle his friend. "You sound as if you have an interest in her. Are you dating her?"

"No, I'm not dating her. I'm her doctor." Norm stood up, threw a silver dollar on the table and mumbling an excuse about seeing a patient, hastily left the café.

Rob mulled over their conversation. The good doctor took himself too seriously sometimes. It wasn't Norm's business what Kate did in her private life. She deserved a good time, didn't she? He had a couple of hours to kill and decided to drive out to her farm and see if he could get a foot in the door.

Kate and Tippy were coming out of the woods when Rob drove into the yard. She was glad to see him and called out," Hello, wait up." They walked to the house exchanging pleasantries.

"I've been in Marshallville. Just got home yesterday. I apologize for my rude behavior that day at the Steak House."

A pot of beans and ham simmered on the back of the stove and she stirred the pot, wondering why Rob was here. She wasn't used to visits from people she hardly knew' maybe she shouldn't have invited him in. He seemed so cocky and sure of himself.

Rob joined her at the stove. "Mmm, smells good," He sniffed appreciatively. His arms wrapped around her waist and he pulled her to him. "You smell good too." He was muzzling her ear when she slapped him with the wooden spoon.

"You let go of me." Frantically, she hit him again, aiming for his head. He dropped her and in startled voice said, "Hey, what's the matter? Just having a little fun. No need to get so huffy." He licked the spot on his arm where some bean juice had burned him.

"You better go. You're no gentleman. I really was glad to see you again, Rob, but you take too much for granted. I don't want you to come here again."

She went to the door and opened it, waiting for him to leave. Instead, he walked to the door and kicked it shut. "Don't put on that pure act with me. You've had a kid. You're no virgin.

Kate gaped at him, unable to speak. He took her silence for acquiescence and closed in on her, reaching out and squeezing her breast. Fear made her legs weak and she started to sink to the floor. Images of Leon flashed through her mind and she was once again helpless and frightened.

For a moment only, did she sink into the past. Her diploma waved like a red flag in her mind and suddenly she was fighting, scratching, and kicking with all her might. Rob backed away and she followed him, kicking him hard on his shin. He swore and tried to shove her away, but she grabbed onto his shirt and balling her hand into a fist, socked him square in the eye. She was getting ready to sock him again when someone lifted her from behind and walked away with her.

She screamed, kicking, and flailing, her arms and legs going every which way. A big arm came around her and trapped both of her arms against her body. Then a voice boomed, "Get out of here, you son of a bitch." Norm! Kate quieted down and watched Rob run from the house.

"Are you all right, Kate? Did he hurt you?"

"No, I'm fine. Oh Norm, I just went crazy. What's the matter with me?" She cried bitterly, knowing she had reacted too intensely to the situation.

"You did what any self-respecting woman would do. I'm proud of you, Kate."

She smiled at him shyly. "It was partly my own fault. I was too friendly. I thought he was my friend and though I was surprised to see him, I invited him in." She chewed on her lower lip, a thoughtful look in her eyes. "Norm, thank you. I have some news for you. She went to the desk and drew out her diploma. Handing it to him she said, "and thanks for this. You were the one who kept after me to finish school."

Norm smiled and then laughing loudly, he picked her up and swung her around. "Aren't you the tricky one? Kate, you're an enigma." He swung her around again before depositing her on the sofa.

"I'm going to see Jude before I leave. He's got something stuck in his craw and it worries me. Do you know what could be wrong, Kate?"

She shook her head. "He's been acting kind of aloof lately. Like he doesn't want to be bothered. He's still really warm to Conner, but I'm afraid he's giving me the cold shoulder."

"Odd. Me too. As far as I can figure, he's been like this since he went to visit his mother. Do you think we hurt his feelings when we sent him away?"

"No, he was as happy as a child to take a vacation, but you're right. Something must have happened on that trip."

"Well, I'll check on him. Bye, Kate. Be good now."

She watched him stroll down the path and hoped he could get to the bottom of Jude's unusual behavior.

Kate placed the last plate in the cupboard and glanced out the window. Ben was running towards the house, propelling his legs as if he were in a race. She met him at the door. "is Jude sick?"

"No, Kate, but he's gone plum loco. He fired me and is moving to the Poor Farm. He's made up his mind and nothing I say makes a danged bit o'difference.

"What's he thinking of?" Grabbing her jacket, she ran out the door. "Hurry, Ben, we must stop him. The Poor Farm! Something terrible must have happened to cause him to act like this."

A faded brown car clanked into the driveway and Kate raced towards it. "Jude, please don't do this. Whatever is wrong I'll make it up to you. I'm sorry if any of us hurt you."

"No, no." Jude spoke gently. "You mustn't take any blame on yourself. This is my decision and has nothing to do with you. It's what I want." He reached into his coat pocket and pulled out some papers.

"This is the deed to the property. I've turned it over to you. I don't want anything of Burt Martin's and hang on to this." He placed a small gold key in her palm. She was staring at it stupidly when he nodded to the driver to go on, and they drove off in a cloud of exhaust, leaving Kate stunned and bewildered.

Ben helped her into the house and sat her on a chair. She sprang up and he pushed her down again. "You stay put now. I'll tell you what this is all about, but first I want to call Norm. On second thought make us a pot of your good coffee."

Ben related all that had transpired during their visit with Jude's mother. "And that's it. I haven't seen the papers Marcie shoved at Jude, but they're suppose to prove that Burt is his dad, and that it's Burt's fault that Jude has them fits."

"My God! Doesn't it ever stop? I swear, Ben, that man didn't have a soul. He was a devil, every bit as much as Leon. He exploited Jude, his own son. Used him like a work horse." She wiped her eyes and poured coffee in the mugs.

"Jude worked twelve, fourteen hours a day, from the time he was twelve years old. We weren't allowed to talk to him. Oh, Ben, when I think how grateful Jude was to live in that old shack and how he stood by Burt through everything. Jude must be very bitter and disillusioned."

Suddenly, she ran to the telephone and dialed the operator.

"I want to call the County Poor Farm. Yes, that's what I said. Oh, I hadn't thought of that." Kate hung up with a bang. Red stained her cheeks as she told Ben, "Fiona got a good laugh at my expense. She said if they could afford telephones out there it wouldn't be a poor farm. She called them freeloaders; can you imagine?" Kate kicked the wooden stool, sending it spinning across the room.

"Here now, you calm down. We'll drive out there tomorrow and see if we can talk some sense into him. Now, I'm going to see if I can find them papers Marcie gave Jude."

The two cars wound their way slowly over the rough trail that would end at the county farm. The deep ruts in the makeshift road caused the passengers to bounce and fall against each other. Gus and Christine were riding with Ben and Kate. They followed Norm and his nurse, Betsey. Kate sat mute, looking with disbelief at the rolling plains, the tumbleweeds, and scruffy grasses. The barren acres appeared to be unfriendly and sinister. The howling wind sent chills up her back. Large boulders dominated much of the ground.

"Rattlesnake heaven," Gus said. "This is close to the badlands and lots of coyotes and foxes live here too. There were a few families that settled out here and raised sheep. Some of the biggest and best sheep ranches in Montana are still here, but not everyone can live with the wind, the dust, and the loneliness. Some woman was hauled into Ryan a few years back. Guess she went plumb out of her mind."

"I don't understand why Jude would need to move to the Poor Farm. He has money and his own house." Christine looked askance at Kate but got a shake of the head for an answer.

"These pest houses were built for the most destitute, the most forsaken of people. Some are so ravaged by drink they can't take care of themselves; others are infirmed. Most think of it as a place to die." Gus was silent for awhile thinking of the thing Jude had done.

"You know, Jude had to pay a two dollar a month fee to get in here. I just can't figure out why, if he wanted to live in a pest house, he chose this one. It has been mainly forgotten by the county commissioners."

Gus had served on the Board of County Commissioners for three years. His knowledge of the Poor Farms came from his hands-on experience during that time.

"Most Poor Farms are in a heck of a lot better condition. There's one in Yellowstone County that has indoor plumbing and electricity, and it sits on about 60 acres of good land. The folks there raise hogs and plant gardens. They also have a hospital on the premises and a good cook. One of the commissioners and myself visited the place. It sits on the east bench of Billings and overlooks the Yellowstone River."

No response was forthcoming, so Gus gave it up. He'd hoped to take their minds off Jude for a while, but it seemed nothing could do that. They were all horrified and bewildered by Jude's actions. They'd all come to depend on him for a good joke, a warm greeting, the sense of goodness that permeated from him.

Silence reigned in the car as Gus drove through the dust and over the never-ending ruts, the wind continuing to keen and moan. Kate wanted to cover her ears.

How could Jude stand this? He was used to the soft winds slipping through the branches of the tall willows and cottonwoods. He would listen for the owls and the rushing water of the creek. This would be pure hell for someone whose ultimate enjoyment came from the beautiful gifts of nature.

Even in the winter, during a blizzard, there were the deer come to feed, the birds to eat the treats Jude made for them. He kept holes chopped in the ice so all the wild ones had water.

"Do you think his spells are getting so bad, he wants to hide it from us?" Christine, like Kate, was trying to figure out why Jude would go to such extremes.

"That isn't the reason," Ben said. "He's here because of Burt Martin. That's all I can say on the subject, but don't you folks go blaming yourselves. You gave Jude the most happiness he's ever known." Ben clamped his mouth shut and refused to talk about it further.

Kate shivered and was relieved to hear Ben announce they were turning into the farm. "Jude can't live here. He'd die without his forest. It means more than anything to him."

The six friends huddled together, silently assessing the ramshackle buildings. The sagging barn bowed out on the sides, its roof caved in and boards missing from the door. The other outbuildings were in the same neglected condition. Three milk cows stood in the dilapidated corral, their ribs poking up under loose hide. A few chickens pecked half-heartedly at the bare ground.

Slowly they walked to the house, leaning into the keening wind. What had Jude felt when he'd seen this place?

"This used to be a farm, the house a regular house." Norm told them a story of the farmer who had lived here for twenty years and raised a family that consisted of a doctor, an attorney, and a jailbird. He sold the place after his wife died.

The wind blew the hat off his head and Norm chased it around the yard. When it was settled back on his rusty colored hair, he continued the story.

"The new owner lived here for five months and high tailed it back east where he came from. Before he left, he gave the place to the town of Ryan. They turned it over to the County Commissioners. The county built the addition when they decided to turn it into a home for the indigent. They moved some overseer on it, and, for the most part, forgot about it."

The addition, built shotgun style, was attached to the rear. Its unpainted wood stood out in sharp contrast to the original, with its blistered sides shedding great patches of gray paint. Here, too, the windows were cracked and grimy and the whole scene blended in with the gray day.

They moved as one to the broken steps and Gus pounded on the door. It opened under his onslaught and they filled in grimacing at the putrid odors of unwashed bodies and haphazard housekeeping.

A woman stood by the stove plopping spoons of thin oatmeal into bowls and handed them to a line of the most bedraggled people Kate had ever seen. She was surprised there were so many families here and older men and children who seemed to belong to nobody. The kids were the workers, pouring milk, and doling out the syrup to pour over the mush. A boy and girl about ten years old were wrestling with the water pump that stuck up from the cupboard, trying to fill buckets then emptying the water into a tub on the stove.

Norm stepped forward. "We need to see Jude Bainville, please."

The woman said, shyly, "I don't know that name. You'll have to ask Mrs. Pomley. She gets up after we finish here."

"He's new, came in yesterday. We'll just look for him."

Norm went ahead and they followed him into the next room where people were sitting at tables eating. Kate noticed a family of four bowing their heads in prayer. The misery of the place seeped into her bones and she was afraid to see Jude, afraid that even in such a short time, the colors and atmosphere might be permanently stamped on him.

They walked single file into the shotgun addition. There were no doors between the rooms though some enterprising dwellers had hung fabric to simulate privacy.

Christine wrinkled her nose, "What's that smell?"

"That's urine," Betsey answered. "I noticed they have outhouses here. I imagine some of the kids use pots at night."

Kate was overwhelmed by the poverty. Her family had lived close to the bone and she'd yearned for a softer bed, new clothes and prettier shoes, but she'd had more than most of the kids here and the Martin family took cleanliness for granted. She had never equated lack of money with filth. She'd never seen or smelled such complete squalor. Pride in her Ma welled up in her as she remembered how Ma was always cleaning, polishing, and picking up around the house. It was due to Ma that they'd had their baths and a clean house to live in.

"If Jude thinks for one minute we're going to leave him here, he's in for a fight." Kate searched the area. Where was he, anyway? They must be close to the end of the house. It was a weird feeling walking through all these rooms and a nervous giggle escaped her lips as she pretended not to notice the listless bodies that sat dejectedly on the beds or were making attempts to clean themselves.

Norm heard the commotion before they entered the ninth cubicle. He motioned for everyone to stop and went into the room alone. His heart sank when he saw the jumping bed and heard the guttural sounds. Jude was in the throes of a grand mal seizure. A young girl stood beside the bed trying to obey the orders from a brutish fellow in a yellow-checkered jacket.

"I'm Dr. Larson. How long has he been like this?"

"Off and on all night, since about ten o'clock."

Norm shoved the man aside and motioned for Ben. They managed to roll Jude on his side, knowing nothing really helped, but they felt better doing something.

"We need clean sheets. His bed is wet."

"Only one set every other week. Them's the rules." The man spat in the corner, eyeing them defiantly.

Norm rolled the bottom sheet and Ben slipped it off the bed. They managed to slide the top sheet under Jude. Norm questioned the man.

"Has he had any medical help?" The man stared at them stupidly. "Did you get him a doctor?"

"No, Miz Pomley, she don't hold with that. Says to keep him quiet and sent this one to help." He bobbed his head at the younger girl.

"Do you know what set him off?" He spoke gently to her, her white face showed strain and he could see she'd been crying. He guessed her age at about sixteen.

"He was trying to get to bed. He fell from his chair and hit his head on the bed leg. That's what he told me." She pointed at the man. "He was supposed to take care of him. He's Mrs. Pomley's son."

The man glared at her, raising this arm to strike, but Norm stepped up to him and wrapped the urine-soaked sheet over his face. "Get out of here and round up some sheets and blankets for my patient. I'm a doctor and I'll report you and your mother to the board of health. Get." They all smiled as the bullish man clawed at the wet sheet and ran from the room.

"Jude's not slowing down, Norm." Ben was as scared as he'd ever been in his life. "I've helped him through a few of these, but this is different. It's like he's having one after another. How much can he take?"

Norm placed his hand on Ben's shoulder. "Not much more, Ben. It's hard on the heart. If the seizures don't stop, he'll die."

Kate, Betsey, Augusta, and Christine bunched themselves together, filling the doorway and spilling over into the room. They were horrified at the scene that was playing out before them, but unable to pull their eyes away.

Norm turned to his friends and sorrowfully shook his head. "The seizures are getting stronger. I don't think he'll come out of it this time."

Jude died at one o'clock in the afternoon.

He left behind a filled gunnysack tied together at the top with a frayed shoestring.

Jude's funeral was held in the Lutheran church in Ryan. It was a heart-warming service and Kate was overwhelmed by the number of people in attendance. Had Jude been aware he was so well thought of?

They laid him to rest in the town cemetery. Kate wanted to bury him in his beloved forest, but it was on Martin land, so she'd found a plot that overlooked the river and was shaded by two large pine trees. She told him good-bye with an ache in her heart. He'd been her first real friend.

Jude had brought something fine to the community. She couldn't define it, but it was goodness, a purity of thought that lingered long after you'd been with him. He would not be soon forgotten.

The tulips were popping out of the ground and Kate scratched the dirt around their roots, glad spring was near. April second. Time was flying and school would be out soon. She had to get busy and make arrangements for the farm and get her and Conner moved. She spied him coming down the lane and went to meet him.

His tears wet his lips when she kissed him hello. His face was scratched, and his shirt torn. She picked him up and carried him into the house and rocked him while he cried. "Tell me what's wrong, honey."

"Mom, did we send Jude to the Poor Farm?"

"Why no, Conner, it was his own decision. We went out there to try to bring him home." Her heart hammered in fear. "Who told you such a thing?"

"The kids at school. They say he was a Martin, and that all Martins are crazy, and that your brother did nasty things to little girls." He sobbed loudly and Kate held him close, her throat tight, while the fear seeped through her and she saw her family through the eyes of the community.

"Mama, the kids won't play with me."

Kate didn't know how to answer him. He was too young to understand his heritage and knowing wouldn't help in school, anyway. She continued to rock him, feeling useless and incompetent.

After he'd gone to bed and was asleep, she called Janis. It was she who suggested Conner come to stay with her. Kate agreed it would be the best thing for him; she didn't want him to run away from his problems, but he was so little, and she must protect him. The evil the Martins had visited upon this land would obscure the truth for years to come.

NINETEEN

K ate listened to the echo of her footsteps as she pace restlessly from room to room. The quiet house intensified her feelings of loneliness. Conner was with Janis. A moan escaped her as his image floated before her, as he'd looked when she left him. The huge eyes, gazing at her somberly, tears sitting on the edge of his eyelids, his face held in stern lines, and trying so hard to be a big boy.

Was he afraid she'd abandoned him? No, she decided, he trusted her. It was the pain of the separation that hurt him, and he loved Janis. "He'll be happier," Kate consoled herself. "I'm the one with the problems. I miss him and feel guilty about leaving him, but it's a good thing I've done, and I'll have to bear the loneliness for a short time, just until I get things settled here."

This would be a good time to take the key Jude had given her and see what it was meant for. Kate called Tippy and ran from the house. Almost immediately calm settled over he and she strolled along the forest path, savoring the warm air.

The fragrance of spring blossoms surrounded her, and she breathed deeply enjoying the beauty of the trees and the songs of the birds. Jude's spirit seemed to walk beside her, and she fancied him, as one of the trees, tall and straight, as he'd been on the inside.

She turned towards Jude's house, a chore she'd been dreading. Everything was as it had been, except Ben's belongings. He'd gone home to Georgia, much to Kate's dismay. The beds were made, even the stoves were filled with wood and paper, waiting for a match. Kate proceeded to light the stove in the front room. The crackle and hissing of the wood comforted her and she sank onto the sofa.

"I miss you, Jude," she said, remembering the many talks they'd had, the dreams they had shared. "I hate the Martins for what they did to you. You didn't deserve that. If only you could have told me, talked it out. I wanted to help you. Conner and I love you. You're part of our family and we will never forget you."

Unable to sit still, she paced around the room, gravitating to the desk Gus had given Jude. She tried to open the top. It was locked. So, this is what the key was for. She dug it out of her pocket and turned the lock. Everything was in its place except for an envelope laying in the workspace. She picked it up with trembling hands. Her name, Kate Willow Sutton, was written across the front in Jude's scrawling hand. She plopped heavily onto the wooden chair beside her, afraid to find out what Jude had written, but her eyes were inexorably drawn to the last written words of her brother and friend.

My dear Kate Willow,

I find it incredibly difficult to leave you without an explanation. I'm not able to speak of my reasons aloud, so have decided to write them, in the hope you will find this some day after I am gone. I won't be back, Kate, I will live out whatever time I have left at the county farm.

Ben has no doubt told you that Burt Martin was my father. I didn't believe Marcie when she told me, but the papers she shoved at me proved it to be true. I threw those papers in the stove, but the words are burned into my mind. It was my second birthday. Burt was visiting us, and Marcie coerced him into watching me while she ran to a shop to buy me a gift.

I can only assume I got into mischief. The report states that Burt knocked me off the table. I was unconscious for so long Burt decided I was dead. He carried me into the trees, dug a hole, and placed me in it, covering me with branches and leaves. When Marcie returned, he told her what had happened. He was afraid the truth would come out and he needed to protect himself. Marcie wrote she'd never witnessed such panic and fear as he displayed.

She evidently threatened him, and he showed her where he'd buried me. She dug me up and took me home, then called a doctor. I was conscious by the time he came. He wrote a report and called the police. Burt convinced them he believed I was dead, and they left, forgetting the report. I guess an ugly crippled kid like me didn't merit an investigation. Later that night I had my first seizure. The report itself was sparce, but my mother filled in the missing pieces and I have told you here what I know.

How you must have suffered at the whim of this monster I called my friend. When you told me what he'd done to you, I still found ways to excuse him. I believed in him, Kate, and he was my reason for living. I grieved for him when he was killed, and I put my life on the line to save his farm for Leon. Can you understand, Kate? I cannot live here anymore. He was my father. He denied me and he buried me alive. I can't describe the pain and horror I'm living with, since I have learned the truth and the bitter shame.

Goodbye, my dear Kate Willow. Remember, wherever I am, I am always with you. You and Conner are in my heart always.

Jude

Kate wept as she read the letter. What a tragedy, but also a victory of sorts, she mused. For Jude had clearly been a winner in all his transactions with life. He'd risen above his disabilities, cheated death at a young age, and grew mentally strong in spite of Burt's evil influence. He'd chosen the values of great men of the past, and educated himself to such a degree, had he been a healthy man, he could have written 'Professor' with his name.

Kate resolved to do something for Jude, to keep his memory alive, for death doesn't mean extinction of courage and hope. Somehow the name Jude Bainville would connote all that America stood for. He would be a beacon of light for the poor and the desolate.

The sunny day beckoned to her and she locked the door and began walking home. Her freedom to come and go as she pleased was the most prized privilege in her life. As so often happened, her mind darkened and the grim existence she'd endured threatened to cloud her emotions. With deliberate purpose, she forced her thoughts towards the future, and what would happen to her if she married Norm.

He'd proposed to her after the funeral, and instead of saying no, she'd asked for time to think about it. In a moment of weakness, devastated by Jude's death, she had almost succumbed to Norm's attractive description of a life as his wife.

Kate Larson, the doctor's wife. Would he allow her to go to teachers' college? She was startled by her own stupidity. When had she become so dependent upon him? No, there would be no wedding bells for her, not with Norm Larson. The thought of going to bed with him filled her with revulsion, and what about all the intimate things that must take place between husband and wife? Look how she reacted to Rob, she had a problem with intimacies, and it might be a long time before she was willing to try any serious romance.

Big John's image flashed through her mind, and again there was a yearning to see him, to be held by him. She imagined making love with him, and excitement filled her. The only man I've met I could be a real woman with, and he loves me like a sister, but she was heartened by the fact that she had met someone she wasn't averse to and there would be others.

When she came to the path that led to her house she turned east and walked to the main road. "Let's check the mail, Tippy, it's too nice to go in yet." She meandered along the gravel road wanting to prolong her activity so she wouldn't be faced with the coming darkness and the lonely night.

Kate shoved the mail in her pocket and settled herself on a large boulder that protruded from the ditch bank. Her eyes traveled over the acres of land. It would soon be time to plant the crops, and suddenly, instead of seeing herself doing the work, an image came to her mind of men, women and children, working, laughing, and playing on Burt's acres. The folks from the county farm! Caught up in the excitement of her new idea, she bounced off the rock and raced towards the house.

Plans and ideas flowed through her mind and she ran faster, her happiness so explosive she imagined firecrackers popping all around her.

Euphoria walked with her into the house, and she bustled about, gathering paper and pencils, and began writing her ideas in columns. More gas stoves would have to be brought into the house, and a new refrigerator added to the kitchen. Her mind raced, ideas coming, one after another. Grabbing a sheet of stationary, she wrote to Noah and Mandy, explaining in detail what she wanted to do. Then another one to Ben, asking him if he'd like to come back and oversee the farm. She also offered him Jude's house for his own along with the five acres. Satisfied she had done all she could for now, she ate a light snack and went to bed.

The full moon shone into the window over her bed. A short time ago she would have looked into the moon beams and retreated into a fairy world. Now, she simply closed her eyes and let sleep overtake her.

CHAPTER

TWENTY

J ohn Clayton rinsed the buckets at the well, relieved to be done with the chores for a few hours. Home for three days, and already tired of the constant grind of farm life. He walked to the corral and hung the pails on fence posts. He grinned and rubbed Beauty's ears. She was a damn good milker, and Gus' best cow. That Gus, he could really get excited about a good milk cow, or a prolific boar. A born farmer, he was, and Christine a perfect farmer's wife.

As much as he loved and respected them, their way of life seemed tedious to him. He sighed, wishing there was some way to make them understand or at least accept his passion for animal doctoring.

He'd spent a month with Dr. Reed, working with the veterinarian, assisting him on his calls, and had never been more fulfilled in his life.

Christine had suggested he try it before he gave up farming for school. It backfired on her as the work only reinforced the longing he'd had since he was a child. He remembered the livestock on his father's farm, the needless deaths and laming of good animals. He'd wanted, even then, to know what to do for them and he'd spent hours trying to cure a rotted hoof, pneumonia, or a sprain. He'd ordered books and pamphlets through the mail, and he tried the instructions on his father's livestock, learning as he went along. By the time he was in high school, neighbors were calling on him in times of crisis.

Yet, all the while he'd been away, it was like a magnet was pulling him home. He kept dreaming of Kate. His need for her baffled him. He'd finish up here and walk over to her place, say he was checking on the horses, or something.

Shit would hit the fan if he got tangled up with her, Christine had as much as told him Kate wouldn't be welcomed into the family. "Even if she isn't Burt's natural daughter, some of it was bound to rub off." He'd controlled his temper at her blind prejudice and tried to get Kate out of his mind.

She was just so damn sweet. Even when he'd first been aware she was living here, and he'd seen her for a few moments only, she stayed stuck in his mind. A big woman, she'd been then, dressed funny in an old gray dress that was too small, and a man's work shirt over the top. She'd opened the door as he was going up the steps, and their eyes met, her's bland as if she weren't seeing him, but as they gazed at each other, a spark of life had ignited them for just an instant, and he'd fallen into their depths and was still there; at least she was in his mind all the time.

You can't catch a fish if you don't go fishing, he told himself, and I want to catch Kate Willow.

He cut across the pasture and decided to take a gander at the horses on his way to the house. Quickening his stride, he hurried around the corner of the barn. Kate came around the corner at the same time.

"Oomph! Beg your pardon, Kate, are you hurt?"

"I'm fine. I wondered if you were back yet." She reached out her hands and he took hold of them. They stood taking each other's measure, until Kate smiled and said, "come in and eat with me. I left dinner stewing on the stove."

"Christine would be upset if I missed a meal at home. She's fixing her famous beef ribs." He had his head stuck down into his shoulders and his hands in his pockets. A pink tinge stained his cheeks as he spoke.

Why, he's shy, Kate realized. "I'll make you some baking powder biscuits," she teased. "High, golden brown, and light as a feather."

"Well, now, I can't turn that down. I'll just call home and tell them to go ahead without me."

Before the meal was over Kate had a new respect for the words 'hearty appetite'. John sure socked away the food. He was a big man, and it seemed natural to Kate that he would eat a lot. She scrutinized him carefully. About six foot two inches. Thick blond hair that turned colors according to the light and right now it cast reddish glints around his head. He wore it longer than the men here usually did, and she decided she liked it very much. Her eyes traveled across his broad shoulders and wide chest. Not an ounce of fat on him, all muscle and bone. He reminded her of the Vikings in her history book. His face was angular, the cheekbones high, eyes curving down, long and narrow, and vivid blue, like the color of the Montana sky on a sunny day, she thought.

"How old are you, John?"

"Older than I look. I'm twenty-five. You must be about sixteen." Her heart lurched as it always did when he looked into her eyes and grinned like that. Suddenly nervous, she began clearing the table, hoping he wouldn't see her trembling hands. She hated feeling self-conscious with him, they'd had such an easy friendship, and she was ruining it with her girlish notions.

John rose and started to help her, both of them reaching for the bowl of gravy and suddenly she was in his arms.

"Oh, Katie, I've wanted to hold you for so long," he whispered in a shaky voice. "I love you, Kate Willow. I love you so much."

"And I, you," she answered. "John, I didn't think I could ever love a man, not like this. She raised her lips to his and he placed his mouth on hers, teasing her with little nips and tickles, until she wanted to jump out of her skin. He groaned, "Kate, Kate." He lifted her in his arms and, with long strides, carried her into the studio, and placed her on the cot.

Her arms remained around his neck. The body she'd held in tight control for all her years was suddenly betraying her. She was all soft and wooshy, her legs weak and the most delicious feelings danced around on her insides. She couldn't get enough of his kisses ... kisses so warm, so sweet, more than she'd ever dreamed they could be. She was so hungry for his love. As if in a dream her legs opened wide and her arms pulled him close. The night was sprinkled with stardust. Kate and John spent it in paradise.

The day seemed to drag endlessly. She could think of nothing but John. He filled her mind as he'd filled her body. The overwhelming passion she had experienced stunned her. The aftereffects of their loving were still with her, tingling in her stomach, causing her legs to melt like butter on a hot roll. A rosy glow flushed across her face as images of her night with John passed through her mind. I'm a woman now, she mused, a real woman. It was a glorious discovery to know she had within her the ability to give and receive love. I'd never have guessed I could respond like that.

She paced in front of the window. When would he come? He'd been gone when she awoke this morning. In her hand was a dried flower he'd taken from the vase on the desk.

"The dishes need doing, the floor needs sweeping, the dog needs feeding, and I am not weeping, trala, trala." She sang and went about her work haphazardly, returning to the window often to look for John.

She continued to search the road and yard for him, until darkness closed her in. At ten o'clock she went to bed and lay there dry-eyed and numb, staring into the blackness.

"Good morning, guys," Christine greeted the men as they san down for breakfast. She watched John covertly, noticing the glad light in his eyes, and the way his chest expanded. *So!* she snorted to herself. *They've been at it.* She searched his face, and turned away, disgruntled. Poor slob, he doesn't know what hit him and he looks so … satisfied. Well, she'd better squash this before it got out of hand. She'd pretended to be asleep when he'd stolen into the house at three o'clock this morning and Gus, pretending he didn't know what was going on. 'Course Gus liked Kate, just like all the men, a pretty face and curvy figure, you could get by with murder, and maybe she did, Christine thought grimly. There was more than one reason to keep John away from that viper and she knew just hot to do it.

"Have you heard the latest? Seems our Kate and Norm are making wedding plans. Norm told me yesterday, when I was in town." She looked at Gus. "Could we throw them a party, honey? Just a small one." She sat, smiling cozily at them.

John was eating a strip of bacon when Christine made her announcement. At first it didn't penetrate his mind, and he repeated it over and over until it became real. The bacon became a fat blob in his mouth, and he couldn't swallow it, so he chewed and chewed until he thought he'd explode. Jumping up from the chair, he ran out to the barn, Gus close on his heels.

Christine cleared the table, satisfied she'd stopped what could have turned into a disaster. Besides they needed John to help work the farm. Without his help, they'd have a hard go of it.

In less than an hour they'd come back in the house and went up to John's room. Soon John came downstairs with his trunk on his back and Gus was carrying his suitcases. They loaded up the old trunk and John drove off. Christine watched while her stomach curled in fear.

"You see what your news did. John's gone, gone for good." Gus pulled on his work jacket. "It's just as well. He needed an excuse to get away from here, and you gave him the perfect one." He went out, slamming the door.

Kate spent four days wandering around the farm. She'd taken to climbing the stairs to her old room and watching the Clayton place through the little window. Gus and Christine puttered around the place, but there was no sign of John. He's gone, she thought dully. He used me. Shame washed over her when she remembered her wanton actions. Although she was skin and bones these days, the old Kate was in her body again. Ugly and useless. How could she have believed a man like John would love her? They all knew her story and no self-respecting man would saddle himself with the likes of her. She thought of her dream, of the ice filling the holes in her heart, and she shivered as she grew colder and more aloof each day.

It was time to finish her work here and get out. First, she would tell Norm marriage was out of the question. Why did he want to marry her anyway? But the answer was obvious. Being a doctor, he was no doubt hoping to cure her of her immaturity.

She dressed and drove to Ryan wanting to get it over with. To get all the odds and ends taken care of. Conner needed her, and she sure as hell needed him. "From now on, Conner, it's just you and me."

Norm greeted her happily, pulling her into his office. She backed away from him. "Please, I have something to say to you." She shook her head when he gestured for her to sit down. She could see he was excited, sensing she'd come to accept his proposal. She wanted to be kind, but her mind was wooden, her feelings jammed up; like she was at the bottom of the frozen river, staring at the world through the ice.

"I can't marry you. I thank you for the honor, but it's not possible."

"You can't mean that Kate. It's just that you're still upset over Jude's death. Give it time, dear." He reached for her hand, but she pulled back from him. Here he was again telling her how she was feeling.

She spoke, her voice cold, her eyes hard and lifeless. "Jude is well out of it. He's at peace. Truth to tell, he's the lucky one."

"Kate, this isn't like you." Suddenly he laughed, relieved. "You're having pre-wedding jitters, happens all the time."

It's impossible to tell him anything; he doesn't think I have a brain in my head. She turned to go, and he said, "Wait, Katie, I almost forgot. Christine is giving a party for us Saturday night. To make our engagement official. I'll pick you up at eight o'clock, Okay?"

"Don't you listen to me, Dr. Larson? I just said I won't marry you. I don't love you. Being your wife is the last thing on my mind. You had no right to tell people I accepted your proposal. Now, I have business to take care of. Good day."

The streets of Ryan were bustling with motor cars and teams and wagons, the country people bringing in their milk and butter, buying staples from the local mercantile. Half a dozen women hovered over the fabric counter, choosing light cottons and calicos for the hot days of summer. Kate noticed the gray nubby material Ma had used to make all her dresses. Her fingers subtly caressed the linen dress she had donned this morning. Store bought and expensive. Even if she were worthless these people would never know it to look at her.

She'd put off seeing Rob about her farm project because of embarrassment, but now it didn't matter to her. He'd stepped over the line with her and because she was too friendly. Never let it be said I don't learn from my mistakes, she thought grimly.

When she stepped into his office, he clambered to his feet. "Good to see you, Kate." He was awkward and ill at ease. "I have more information for you on those papers you found last winter. Please, sit down."

"I have a project I want your opinion on and, also, I need to know the legalities involved in what I have in mind. But let's begin with your news, shall we?"

Rob flushed; she had neatly put him in his place. He should apologize for taking liberties with her, scaring her like that, but he hadn't understood the extent of Kate's abuse by her family at that time. He began to say he was sorry, but the coldness of her demeanor, the hard look in her eyes, changed his mind. She's not open to my remorse, he decided, and began business at hand by clearing his throat.

"I checked out the property Burt purchased in Marshallville. Seventy-five acres on the south end of the city. I drove out and looked at it, it's a paradise, Kate, acres of prime lumber, a large lake, a creek running past what someone had staked out for a home site. Whether it was Burt who staked it out or the previous owner I don't know, but here's the surprise. Conner's name is on the deed. Along with Burt's. It's registered in the county courthouse there. At Burt's death, full ownership transferred to Conner." He searched in his desk and pulled out a paper.

"The taxes were delinquent, and I paid them for you." He handed her a receipt. Kate was speechless. What manner of man was Burt Martin? "I can't begin to understand his thinking. What do you think?"

"I didn't know him well, but I've wondered if he was protecting Conner from Leon when he put him in the orphans' home. It's all I can figure. He seems to have done right by him. Remember, he had three sons. Conner is the only who is sane, and healthy."

Kate wrote him a check for the taxes. "Tell me what else you've discovered about him. It's like I didn't know the man at all."

Rob fished around for the report his investigator had sent him and glanced over it. He picked up the yellow pencil and related the contents to Kate in his own words.

"A Mafia big shot was hiding in a hotel in Chicago. He caught influenza or some similar ailment and needed to be waited on day and night. The hotel had just hired a new man, a young guy with a baby daughter. He worked for room and board and a few extra dollars a month. They moved Burt and his baby into the connecting room and told him to nurse the guy." Rob began rolling the pencil between his fingers, Kate noticed a slight tremor and wondered if he was nervous or had partied the night before. At her nod he continued the tale.

"The mobster ran a high fever and became delirious, revealing where he kept a huge among of cash. By the time he recovered, Burt was gone with the money. He must have hidden out somewhere and waited for your mother to join him. They bought the farm here, and moved in, mother, father and baby. A regular family, it seemed. I don't suppose the mobster thought of looking for him in Montana. He dressed like a poor wretch, enhanced his Swedish accent, and it's unlikely they'd have recognized him anyway. He must have buried that money somewhere on your farm." She didn't respond, didn't blink an eye, but he knew everything he said was being filed away in her mind.

"People are interesting, aren't they Kate? Here's a man with half a million dollars buried in his yard, and he lived a miserable life, and his family with him. Then there's someone like Jude, who was happy just to hear a bird sing or see a fish swim."

"It would seem Jude had a good influence on many people." Kate said. "He's involved in what I'm going to do with the farm. But thanks, Rob, for reminding me of that." She smiled at him and saw an answering light in his eyes.

"I've decided to leave the farm, but I'm not turning it over to the Clayton's as everyone expects me to do. Rob, I've thought long and hard about this, and I have Noah's and Mandy's blessing." She struggled to come up with the right words to explain her idea. Finally, she threw the sheaf of papers on his desk, and said, "I want to close that wretched shelter Jude died in and bring the folks that are living there to Mandy's farm, and others who were ruined during the depression; people who need a hand up and are willing to work to achieve a new start." Kate paused, trying to decide what would sway Rob. He looked totally bewildered and it was for sure he didn't understand her reasoning.

"Rob, I saw families in that hovel, mothers giving their children their own food, starving themselves, and there were orphans, used for workers and they beat them, I saw the bruises. There's no school for the kids. They're growing up ignorant ..."

"Hush now, you're all wound up." Rob stepped around his desk and place a hand over her mouth. "If we're going to do this, I need all the facts, but slowly, Kate, and I want my secretary to write it down." He went to the door and came back with a woman he introduced as Margaret.

It took three hours to get Kate's plans organized. They decided to walk to Nellie's for coffee and sandwiches.

"Take the drawings for the renovations. We'll continue working while we eat." Kate nodded. Her plans were in motion and somehow she knew it would happen. It would be a kick to see Burt Martin's face if he knew what was happening to his Little Kingdom. The place wouldn't be known as Burt's much longer. Kate had designed a wooden sign, in the shape of a shield, to be placed at the entrance of the farm. 'Jude Bainville Memorial' would be carved across the top half of the shield, and underneath, in small letters, the dates of his birth and death. The words, 'A Man of Value' filled the bottom half and she planned to ask Ben, if he came back, to carve little animals and trees around the edges. The farm would be known as The Honor Ranch.

This was her way of bringing meaning to Jude's life. He, more than anyone, had shown her by his own convictions, how necessary it is to be true to one's self and even when he rode away in that old brown car, it was with grace and dignity and the kind of courage she couldn't begin to have herself. It was something to work towards, and she vowed to teach Conner these truths.

They chose a large table at the back of the café. When they finished eating the waitress filled their coffee cups and removed the plates. Kate and Margaret spread the diagrams out on the table.

"We forgot the plans to the main floor. I'll run back and get them." Margaret left and Rob and Kate studied the designs she'd drawn for the bathrooms.

"Are you sure you should be a teacher? You have a talent for drawing and designing. That's a lucrative field these days."

"I'm sure. It's the only thing in my life I am sure about."

219

"Kate, you seem different today. Like you're crawling back into your shell. I hope I'm not to blame. I'm really sorry I frightened you."

"I guess I'm wondering if there's something wrong with me. Why do … men, seem to have those ideas about me? Do I exude some kind of invitation?"

"No, of course not. You are the most honest woman I've ever known. It's not you, Kate, it's us, with our screwed up egos and our male prerogatives."

"You don't need to prove you're a man, do you Rob? I mean, you're successful, young, popular. Don't take the blame for something that's my fault."

"Don't blame yourself, it was me, I tell you. I've been running after women all my adult life."

Margaret returned and they dropped the conversation. Kate found her eyes returning to Rob, often, wondering what his story was and how he'd come to know himself and his failings so well. She was relieved they could work together and surprised she felt so comfortable with him. Whatever failings he had, he was a darn good attorney and that's what she needed to get this farm thing through.

TWENTY-ONE

S he peeped out the window and cursed. "Wind again!" Another year of wind and dust?" The past years had brought drought to the land, with the winds so strong and constant, it blew the soil right out of the fields. It won't be my problem anymore, she reminded herself. The new folks would be fighting the elements.

She had a busy day ahead of her, better get started and quit mooning around. She dressed carefully and went into the kitchen and baked two chocolate cakes.

After checking the barn to make sure the hired hands were on the job, she took her coffee out to the porch to read yesterday's mail. There was a letter from Janis, and she read that first.

Janis' Home Rejuvenation was doing a good business. She loved it with a passion and was making good money. The house was too big for her and Conner and they were waiting impatiently for her to join them. Phillip and Conner were fencing off the property so Tippy could run free. They had put in a rose garden and numerous flowerbeds. *They want you to love it, Kate. The truth is they don't want to go back to Ryan again. To live, that is. Conner really loves it here. He's doing well in school, has many good friends, and is becoming one of the most popular kids in the community. Hurry home to us, Kate, we miss you. This may surprise you, but Phillip is singing your praises to anyone who will listen. The neighbors all know you're going to be attending college. He is very proud of you. I think you finally have a real father.*

Panic touched her as the clock inexorably wound around to the time she had told the Gordons to expect her. Since they had no telephone, she'd sent them a note in the mail, stating she'd be there this morning at ten o'clock. Don't be such a dish rag, she scolded herself sternly, but she wished fervently she could back out of this visit.

She carried the frosted cakes to the car and drove slowly over the rutted lanes. There was the pile of rocks Leon had sheltered behind while he waited for Essie. She could easily picture him there, that horrible gleeful grimace on his face, avidly waiting to pounce on the little girl. If that had been her girl.

The Gordons stood in their front yard, waiting for her. Their tired faces set in chiseled unfriendly lines. Perhaps she should have left this alone. It was too painful for them, a forbidden subject. People didn't speak openly about these things, especially folks like the Gordons.

Holding the cake and handkerchief, she began walking towards them. Nervous tears ran down her cheeks and she couldn't wipe them away, or she'd drop the cake. Damn. She'd hoped to appear confident and mature.

Max Gordon spoke first. "Say your piece. We've work to do."

She offered them the cake, but they ignored it. Finally, embarrassed, she set it on a tree stump. Speaking softly, she said, "I know you've heard that Leon hurt your little girl. I've come to tell you it's true. We found this in his belongings." She held the handkerchief. Mrs. Gordon cried out and covered her face with her hands. Max stepped forward, threateningly.

"Please, let me finish. The Martins have caused you a lot of grief. I would give anything to be able to change that, but all I can do is apologize and offer to pay for therapy or anything Essie needs."

Max and his wife exchanged glances and Max said, "If you're apologizing then I guess we can talk." He picked up the cake and led the way to the kitchen.

Kate spent an hour convincing them that Essie needed treatment from a professional to help her work through her guilt and fear. Finally, in the face of their bullheadedness, she told them her own story. Hazel sighed, and looked defiantly at Max.

"Essie is fearful. She won't go to school. Just drags around, day after day. Her eyes, they don't say anything. She used to sparkle with life." Hazel tried to explain why she would accept Kate's money. It shamed them, but they must choose between pride and Essie. Max was tougher to convince.

"I don't hold with outsiders knowing our business. We're a God-fearing family, and this kind of thing shouldn't be bandied about." He looked at Kate and said sternly, "Don't you go around telling folks what you just told us. It makes them see you in a different light. Much as you'd like to think folks are big-hearted and understanding it just ain't so. I'm believing you because I feared Burt for some reason; he had a ruthless streak in him. After his funeral I had a run in with Leon. Sent goosebumps popping up all over me." He took a chaw from his plug of tobacco. "Always knew he had the heart of a weasel."

They made plans in earnest then, agreeing on a cash settlement, with the stipulation that Hazel and Essie would travel to Minnesota to see a Dr. Morris. "He's having a lot of success with children and women that have been in unfortunate circumstances." Kate knew she sounded stilted and stuffy, but you couldn't say the words that would explain it clearly. Max was too old fashioned.

"Dr. Larson told me about him," Kate said, "when I was concerned about Conner and Ellie."

"I don't see how our Essie can rest easy knowing the guy that did this is dead. I'd think she'd have to know he was punished for his wrong-doing." Max said bitterly, "I believe in an eye for an eye."

Kate knew her answer would make the difference between Essie getting help or remaining on the farm, her life a travesty, filled with guilt and fear.

"The fear is our real enemy. Until we win against it, Leon is still cracking the whip. He's dead, but his evil continues to rule us. Explain that to your little girl. Understanding it's the fear she must overcome will give her the will to fight. Her dignity and self-respect can be restored and she can look at herself as a winner. She's young and eventually the horror of the attack will dim."

She looked at Max and shook her head, "I wish you could have made Leon pay for what he did, but don't you see, if Essie recovers, it is the same thing, and never again will she have to wonder if he is around every rock and corner. We are all better off that he is dead."

Max nodded his head and Kate wrote the check. Hazel shook hands with Kate and left the room to tell Essie the news.

Max walked Kate to her car. As she was about to get in, he put his hand on her arm. "Tell me, Kate, about Jude. He was a good friend to us. It's been said you put him on the county farm."

"That isn't true, Max. For reasons of his own Jude had to go. Events that concerned himself and Burt. Have you heard what I'm doing with the farm?"

"Gus said you were bringing the hard-hit depression folks to live on it. Turning it into a haven for the destitute. Is that right?"

"Yes. I guess it could be explained that way, but they make it sound as if these people are undesirable. They're good people, just down on their luck."

"It could be us, you know, Kate, we just barely skimmed through ourselves. There was a time, a few years back, when we almost moved to the county farm. A good friend bailed us out. Good luck with your venture. I'll surely give them a hand if they need it."

"Thank you, that means a lot and don't hesitate to ask them for help or an extra hand if you need it." Kate started to get in her car again and then hesitated. "The farm is going to be called The Honor Farm in memory of Jude. He's my inspiration. It's all I could think to do for him, to give value to his life."

"He's the one who got the ball rolling to get Leon out of circulation. I'll never figure out how he crawled all that way." Max turned his head to spit.

"He pulled himself along, inch by inch. Using his right arm." Kate felt the wetness in her eyes. "He was a real hero. A man in the true sense of the word. Until his last days, he didn't know the meaning of defeat and as much as I hated Burt Martin before, after I found out what he'd done to Jude. I hated him more than ever. Turning his farm into The Honor Ranch is also a revenge against Burt. It shows that good is more lasting than the kind of evil he and Leon personified."

Kate realized she had said too much to Max and then decided to tell him Jude's reason for leaving them. When she'd finished with her story, Max shook her hand and said, "You can count on me to keep my neighbors thinkin' in the right direction. Good luck to you, girl, and keep in touch with us, please. Thanks for your help. Today's been an eye opener, in more ways than one."

Her next stop was at the Claytons. She forced herself to drive to their house, trying to keep her mind away from John. There were times she wanted to blame Christine for his absence, but that was ridiculous, what could she have to do with it?" No he'd just been an eager young stud, doing what young men seemed driven to do, and she'd been too naïve to know it.

They welcomed her warmly and accepted the cake with eager thanks. "Chocolate! It's been a long time since we could afford to buy it. Thanks so much, Kate, we'll enjoy every mouthful."

"I'll be leaving soon and wanted to thank you for being such a help to Angie and me. I don't know what we'd have done without you." She turned to Augusta. "Noah and Mandy want you to take two of the heifers and he said you can have the Case tractor. They're gifts to you, from Noah, for all your support."

Where is John? She wanted to ask. The words fought to get out, but she didn't say them. Pride was all she had left of the short affair. Her hurt was her own business, so she smiled and lifted her head high. She left amidst a profusion of thanks and goodbyes.

Now for her final trip of the day and most enjoyable one, she mused, as she turned the car north and headed to town. Ben and his wife would be at the train depot in half and hour. His letter had told her he'd married an old friend, and they were both eager to work on The Honor Ranch. *We'll do you proud,* he'd written. *My wife, Helen, is good with people and a good manager. She can run the business in the house, and I'll do the rest. We're grateful to be a part of this new idea. God bless you, Kate. Jude would be proud.*

The house was ready for its new occupants. Kate cast a disinterested eye around the upstairs bedroom. She went from room to room, checking for any personal items that might have been forgotten. Angie's room was plainer now, she'd sent the new bedroom furniture to Ben's. They'd set it up in Jude's large room along with the fine linens and spread. Kate had decided to leave the furniture in the house, except for the desk and Ma's cherrywood table. These she would save for Conner. Mandy would receive Angie's dressing table and her personal items.

For herself, she wanted nothing, especially not the memories. "I won't miss this house," she said aloud. "I hope the new families can fill it with laughter and purpose." For an instant an image floated through her mind of men and women dancing in the large living room and children playing games in the corner. She smiled wistfully and with a last cursory glance around, she sped down the stairs.

The boxes were stacked neatly on the front porch. Rob had offered to find someone to move her things to Marshallville and they would be picked up tomorrow. She sat on the steps waiting for Rob. He was going to take the Thoroughbreds to his parent's place. "These are prize mares," he'd told her, "they need to be worked daily. My dad is a trainer and he'll do good by you. Burt must have figured to race them." He pointed to Ginger Spice and Miss McTavish. "My guess is those two might make the big time." He'd called this dad and made arrangements for their board.

What would she have done without Rob? He'd helped her from the beginning to the end of her project. He'd known what to say to the County Commissioners and helped her prepare the speech she'd so earnestly given.

He'd asked for volunteers to help build two rooms onto the schoolhouse and presented the list to the school board. They'd agreed to hire two more teachers and to modernize the school.

Kate was amazed at the many sides of Rob she hadn't been aware of. She'd thought of him as the attorney, a studious guy, closed in by four walls all day, who, when he went home at night, was shut in, surrounded by his large law books and stacks of papers. Then there was the part of him that seduced women, the love 'em and leave 'em reputation Norm had told her about.

Now here he was, with four men, to load the horses. They knew what they were doing. She watched Rob as he ran across the corral and jumped on Ginger Spice, riding her bareback to the truck. He looked wonderful in his blue jeans and denim shirt. She liked the well-used cowboy boots, too. He was a charmer all right; she could see why he had so much trouble with the women. *I wonder who will end up with him.* She toyed with the idea of Margaret but dismissed it as nonsense. No, it was likely Rob would choose a flashy girl, maybe the party type.

Whoever she is, she'll know what she's getting, anyway. Rob was honest. Not like John. The hurt closed in on her again, and she rose and walked over to the barn to watch the action.

After Rob guided the trucks out of the corral, he walked over and joined her. They grinned at each other. "Rob, you're outstanding, you know that?"

"You're my inspirations, Kate." He shoved his hands in his pants' pockets, so he wouldn't grab her. *God, he would miss her, and he wanted her, as he'd never wanted another woman.* In fact, since she'd fought him off so fiercely, he'd been holding himself in check, afraid he'd frighten her off forever.

He'd found out from Betsey about the abuse she'd suffered from Burt and Leon. His heart cracked as she'd related the degradation and terror Kate had suffered. He honored her for her love of Conner, and for having the courage to make a life for them.

"I'm going to miss you."

She nodded, "Thank you for all you've done for me."

"If I should happen to be in Marshallville, could I stop by and see you?"

"Yes, I'd like that. I'll make sure you have my address. Rob, I'm going to miss you, too." She moved closer to him and put her hands on his arms. He gathered her to him and hugged her for long moments. "I might marry you some day, Katie," he teased. "After you're a teacher, of course, and you're able to trust me. I have a feeling you're going to be seeing a lot of me," he said, his voice husky with emotion.

Kate watched him drive away and wished she could love him with the same intensity she loved John, but her woman's heart told her John would be the only man for her. "I'll probably be a second Emily Lowell, and old spinster, with a hundred kids crowding my mind." Suddenly she knew if that was the case, it was all right. It would be enough.

TWENTY-TWO

The farm was silent. Never had Kate heard it so still. The animals were out to pasture, the hired men gone home. They had stayed around the clock during the calving and now were getting some well-earned rest.

The folks from the County Farm would be here soon. Kate looked around the barnyard, wondering what life would have been like here if her family had been different.

There was the chicken coop where Leon had grabbed an old setting hen and plucked it clean. The squawking had sent Kate running to see if a weasel had gotten into the henhouse and she had found Leon in the act of completing the cruel deed. He'd turned the bloody hen loose and she had run in circles, so frightened she had dropped dead within minutes.

There was the well, used for watering the stock, appearing very safe and well built with its platform and a red pump standing solid and strong. A large bucket stood beside it, a bucket big enough to hold a small child, a bucket strong enough to keep a little four-year old girl safe as she hung in the cold dank well for hours.

Leon had laughed his high-pitched whinny as he'd forced her struggling body into the pail and lowered her down the round enclosure. He'd tied the rope around the pump and gone away.

Ma found her when she'd come to rinse the milk buckets. By that time Kate had slipped into semi-consciousness from the fear. Ma said she shouldn't tell Pa and took Kate and put her to bed. It was the only time she'd seen fear on her Ma's face. Leon explained it was just a little joke, he hadn't meant to leave her there, but had forgotten.

Life had always been abnormal with Leon around. He had tied her up one afternoon and used the clippers on her. Her thick black hair lay in piles around the chair. Kate made not a sound when he shoved her in front of the looking glass, so horrified was she. He'd taken the cut right down to the scalp. All that was left was a short black bristle. School was another humiliation to be gotten through. She'd tried to disregard the taunts and giggles of the students, but it was an awful experience. Her teacher had pretended nothing was different and that was almost worse than the kids teasing her. Leon was gone for good and truth be told she was glad he was dead. Now she could live.

The new residents of The Honor Ranch would bring hope and happiness with them. They were so enthused and had told Kate of their plans for the farm. The future of the children was assured as the orphans were being split among the married couples.

"There you are. I was hoping you'd still be here. About ready to leave?" Ben came out from behind a stand of pine, smiling and holding a sack out to her. "Helen made you a lunch in case you get hungry on your trip. She put in a beef bone for Tippy, too."

They stood there, face to face, grinning at each other.

"Are you finding it comfortable in your new quarters?"

"Sure am. I find myself thinking of Jude a lot, though. I guess that will fade as time goes by."

"Ben, I wish Jude could see what is happening to the place. He would be so enthused with it all." She sat on a tree stump and patted the space beside her. After, Ben was seated she said, "I hope you and Helen will be happy here. I don't want you to stay if it is too laden with memories."

"It's possible that Jude is watching us, ya know. I believe in life after death. My folks raised me up as a Southern Baptist and I reckon I believe what they taught me. We like it here fine and want to stay. The memories are pleasant, really, except for that stint at the Poor Farm."

Ben stood up to leave and pulled Kate to her feet. "Gotta go, but I'll leave you with a thought. Helen feels a warmth in the house she says is spiritual, something new to her. I think it's Jude still bossing me around and trying to control things. You know Jude always had to have the last word. It's great, Katie, so don't you worry about us. Just take care of yourself."

TWENTY-THREE

The four friends sat dejectedly in the rickety chairs on Gus and Christine's front porch. They visited back and forth, but their eyes remained glued to the main road, watching the many trucks moving things in and out of the Martin place.

Norm pointed to a red truck. "That belongs to Rob. He's taking Burt's horses to his dad's ranch. She's really going through with this crazy idea, isn't she?" He shook his head, finding it hard to believe that one woman could cause so much controversy.

"She should have her head examined," Christine said, with bitter resignation. "The apple doesn't fall far from the tree." She tried to shake off the guilt that lived with her, wishing she'd let things run their course. Her actions had lost them a brother, a good farm hand, and probably the Martin place, too. There was no way Kate could know what she'd done, was there? Unless John had told her. She lifted herself from the chair abruptly and refilled the coffee cups.

"I can't believe she talked the county into closing down the Poor Farm. It was a mess, true, but it kept the riff raff from out doorsteps. Now they're right in the middle of us all and more coming in. They'll expect free medical care, I suppose." Norm felt cheated.

He'd really wanted to marry Kate. He'd seen himself as her savior, steering her along life's path, training her in the mode of genteel womanhood. He had to admit there wasn't much about Kate Willow that was genteel. She lived too much for the moment, but she had a dignity about her that made up for her impulsive actions.

"I talked to Rob yesterday. He's had his finger in this from the beginning," Norm pounded his knee in frustration. "Kate never mentioned to me how she felt about the county farm. I could have made things a little better there."

Gus was tired of Norm's holier than thou attitude. "These folks that are moving onto Burt's place, I hear they're just ordinary people that lost everything during the depression and drought. Down on their luck, looking for a way up." He chewed on his matchstick for a bit and continued. "I'm going to offer them a welcome. If we work together, it might not be as bad as you think. We could be in their predicament, you know."

"You'll welcome them over my dead body." Christine spat her words at Gus. "If Kate hadn't come up with this crazy idea, we would have had that farm and made some money for a change. Noah same as promised it to us."

Betsey's eyes glittered with anger as she leaned forward in her chair. "I like what Kate is doing. I especially like why she'd going it, not for fame or because she's running for office." She cast a baleful look at Norm. "She's doing it for Jude and for those people. Jude's life has to mean something you see. We've got to remember what he stood for. The Honor Ranch will do that for us. It's really for everyone."

Gus, Christine, and Norm stared at her, surprised. Betsey rarely spoke out about anything. They didn't consider her anything but a good nurse and she knew it. Well, it was time to stand up for herself.

"I've hung around you three all these years, not because you made me feel welcome, but because I was so in love with you," she nodded at Norm, "I'd have done anything to be near you. Kate and Jude helped me see that half a life is worse than no life at all. When Kate walked out of the asylum with her son and later Ellie you were all fluttering and gasping with your self-righteous hypocrisies. Personally, I thought it was a brave and wonderful thing for her to do. She's got more grit and gumption than all of us put together."

Betsey walked to the steps. "From now on I'm living the kind of life I believe in. If you don't like it, tough shit." She walked away, her head high, and spring in her steps.

Norm rubbed his head. He felt as if the sky had fallen on him. He looked at the road where Betsey was hiking. "I'm going to give her a lift. Eight miles is a long way for her to walk." He hurried to his car, anxious to reach her before one of the truck drivers offered her a ride.

Gus and Christine were quiet, watching as Norm caught up with Betsey and she finally accepted his offer of a ride to town. "We'll be having a wedding soon," Christine said, chewing on her bottom lip. "I wish I had not messed with John's attraction to Kate. God, Gus, I am so sorry. How will we manage with just the two of us?" She reached out her arms to him. Gus bent over and kissed her. "Just be glad this winter is over. As long as we have each other we'll do just fine." He left to finish the repairs on the barn.

Christine smiled. Gus was right. They had spent a most unlikely winter, one that would never be repeated, thank God. To think that Leon had murdered five people, his folks included. What if Angie had not come home and stirred things up? Would Kate be dead now? And whom else might he have slain? Suddenly she grabbed a jacket and followed Gus to the barn. Pounding a few nails would be a relief, maybe take her mind off the terror, or at least until June came home from 4-H. Maybe having The Honor Ranch next door would bring some excitement to the dull community. She'd always known if Kate broke loose from her shackles she'd set the world on fire.

TWENTY-FOUR

K ate drove steadily along the narrow road, not looking back. She passed the fields of fertile soil, where the newly plowed furrows lay waiting to receive the new seed that would take root deep within its rich, dark moistness and there was the rock where Leon had committed his heinous crime. She moved slowly past the hollow spot where Emily had hidden her schoolbooks.

When she came to the end of the road, she stopped and eyed the new entrance. The tall lodge poles had been put in the ground, one on each side of the road and one across the top. 'The Honor Ranch' was painted on the crossbeam. The plaque was still in the shop. Ben would affix it where he thought best. Her work here was done.

She called Tippy and opened the door so he could get into the car with her. "I hope you like your new home, boy." Tippy assured her with a big lick across her face.

Someday soon, little children would call her Teacher. Her years on this place would become dim memories. There was a whole new life for her, just ahead. A grin spread across her face and she drove into the sun, to the family that waited for her.

School vacation had begun. Conner and his friends were running and shouting in the back yard. Tippy raced along with them, barking joyfully. Spicy smells from the kitchen spread hints of good things to come throughout the rooms. A beautiful home, Kate acknowledged. Janis had decorated all the rooms with taste and ingenuity. Phillip called himself 'straw boss of the yards' and had a team of gardeners working twice a week. The landscape was a riot of vibrant spring blooms and colors. Everything was as she had dreamed it could be.

Tuesday morning Kate set out early to register for the spring quarter at the college. She would attend classes for three months, have the summer free, and begin again in the fall. In four years, she would have a Bachelor's Degree.

Montana would soon be passing a law that required teachers to attend four years of school. The thought of such an extensive education excited her, and she was anxious to begin her studies in earnest.

Janis slipped silently down the hallway, so as not to wake the others. She'd worked late and then spent some time with Jeffrey. Things weren't all that good between her and her sister, but she be darned if she'd give up her visits with her darling nephew. She came to her room and was about to go in when she saw Kate standing by the window, a look of profound sadness on her face. Janis became alarmed. "Has something bad happened?"

Kate started, "Oh, no. I'm not sleepy. All's well, really."

"Kate let's have a snack and talk. You've been brooding over something ever since you came home."

The steaming cups of coffee and warm gingerbread touched Kate's heart. Janis was the most giving person she'd ever come across. She watched her friend and saw the genuine look of concern on her face. "Janis, I am fine. I just happened to go and fall in love."

"You don't mean it. Who's the lucky guy?"

"Big John Clayton. He obviously didn't think he was so lucky. He loved me and left me."

"I want to hear what happened. Isn't he that good guy that helped you with the livestock?"

Kate nodded. "Yes, and he is a good person. I probably scared him to death. Anyway, we had a beautiful night together and I never saw him again. He left home." The tears streamed from her eyes. "There's other guys that like me, but I'm not able to respond to them. In fact, they frightened me. John's my man, there's no doubt about that. I am happy to know I can have normal feelings about love and sex, though. I thought I'd be scarred for the rest of my life. Now I know I can give and receive love with the right person."

"You're coming right along. I can see how much headway you've made, especially since Leon died. I mean, here you are enrolled in college, and look what you did with the farm." Janis leaned forward and added, "What you've done for me, I can never repay. I can't believe I'm earning a good living at something I love. You've made in indelible mark on my life. I can't image John would leave you without a good reason."

"I did think Christine might have had a hand in it, but that's a guess. I really don't know, and she wouldn't tell me where he went. Of course, I didn't ask outright, but a person would mention it in ordinary circumstances, don't you think so?"

"Yes, I do. I'm sure there's more to this then we know. Now we better get to bed. Morning comes early."

Janis canceled her appointments for the day and visited Phillip. He listened to her intently and she could see the wheels spinning in his head.

"I know John. He's crazy about our Kate. There's something behind this. We need to find him, Janis."

"He's planning on going to veterinarian school. If he's here in Marshallville he might have a job with one of the local doctors." Janis gripped Phillip's arm.

"Shall we go find him? Do we have the right?"

"I'm her father. Who has more right? I'll accept the consequences. If I didn't know this young man, I might chart a different course, but he's the one for Katie. They fit together, somehow."

They visited four clinics, but no John. "We're guessing he's in this area, but he could be in another town." Janis was losing hope.

"I think he's here. He worked for a Veterinarian last spring. If I could just remember the name. A famous doctor, Kate said. He was teaching somewhere on the side."

"Well, as it happens …" Janis laughed and pulled into the parking lot of the community college. "Wait here, I'll run in and see if he taught here. I have a feeling this is where we will find the mysterious doctor."

She came back, breathless, and excited. "John's with Dr. Morris. They're at the Parker ranch, pulling a calf." They spun out of the parking lot and drove into the country.

John stared at the sheet of paper and shook his head in disbelief. He'd been meaning to write a schedule for the treatment of the cow he was doctoring, instead he'd doodle Kate's name all over the page.

The night he'd spent with Kate was in his mind constantly, and he missed her more each day. He was afraid she was married to Norm by now. Afraid she'd used him as a distraction, but then her wide eyes, soft and surprised would come before him and he would once again believe in her honesty.

He'd known he wasn't first with her, but that didn't matter, as he had heard the story of Kate and the terrible way she'd been treated by Burt and Leon. What kind of man would rape an eleven-year-old girl? And especially one that supposedly was his daughter. And impregnate her, hide the child and then, to top it off, treat her as if it were her fault?

His mouth tightened as he realized the horror his Kate had endured with the crazy Martin men and how little she had been valued. He was just grateful their blood didn't run through her veins.

He wondered about Conner, though. He was a swell little fellow and seemed as normal as blueberry pie, but wasn't it possible that something could go haywire with him in later years, or in his own offspring? He'd seen it happen in animals and believed it was a cause of concern.

If he had his way, he would help raise Conner, along with the babes he and Kate would have. Had she married Norm? How could she? Maybe it was time to look the truth right in the face.

He would call Gus as soon as he was through with this job. His gut told him they were meant for each other. If he hadn't been so hurt and hot headed be would have checked the validity of Christine's announcement before he went off half-cocked.

It wasn't like Kate to be so devious. She was the most open, honest woman he'd ever known. Now that he'd decided to look for the truth he felt better and began again to write the course of treatment he was administering to the Parker cow:

Owner: George Parker, RR1, Horseshoe Trail

Breed: white-faced Hereford. Name: Melancholy the second. 3 years. Heavy producer. Calved at 10:15 A.M. Hard delivery, calf breeched.

Diagnoses: Mammitis {inflammation of the udder} came on four hours after calving

Treatment: check fever; support the udder by placing it in a sack suspended from the back

Physic: 1 lb. of Epsom salts dissolved in one-half gallon of water; give until bowels are loose.

Give 30 grains of nitrate of potash in one-half pint of water every four hours.

Milk cow several times a day and bathe udder with warm water. Apply ointment and massage teats. Continue treatment for several days.

Discontinue potash treatment on 2nd or 3rd day.

He signed his name to the chart and closed the book. A little shut eye sounded good and he turned the radio on to soothe him to sleep. He lay on the cot in his clothes so he would be ready to continue the treatment throughout the day and night. It was 4:30. He had time for a couple hours of sleep.

The Parkers had outfitted a small room in the barn loft and John was surprised how comfortable and homey it was. He had just dropped off when he heard a woman calling his name.

Sleep clutched him and his eyes kept closing while he struggled to wake up enough to answer the call. He was too tired to wonder who it was. Finally, he croaked out a "Hold your horses, I'm coming." He crawled down the ladder and looked at Janis inquiringly. Then he noticed Phillip standing outside the door.

"Hey, Phillip, what brings you here?" They were here about Kate, he was sure. His heart hammered so loud he put his hand over it to shut it down. Dear God, he prayed nothing had happened to her. Phillip introduced John and Janis then got right to the point.

"John, you might think me an interfering old fool, but my girl is unhappy. What happened with you two, anyway?"

"I did Kate wrong. I left because I thought she was promised to Norman Larson. Christine told me so and I took it as gospel. She didn't marry him, did she?"

"No, John, that was all one-sided. Oh, she kinda' thought about it at one point, right after Jude died, but soon came to her senses." Janis could see why Kate had fallen for him. They were alike in a lot of ways. An innocent gentleness clung to his personality, but you sensed the strength of him, too. Kate would be safe with him and he would likely be a good father to Conner.

John still couldn't figure out why they'd searched him out, unless Kate was ...

"Oh, my gosh, Kate, she isn't with child, is she?"

Janis could tell Phillip didn't like that question. He hadn't really known things had gone so far with them. She said quickly, "No, she is not, and she also has no idea we went searching for you. We did this because she seems so sad. If you think anything of her at all, couldn't you visit her and explain your behavior?"

"I have three days here before I can get to town but give me her address and I'll go to her as soon as my job is done. She means everything to me." He looked at Phillip and said, "I will never hurt her again, I promise you, but I must say I'm surprised to see you on a quest like this. Didn't you walk out on her too?"

Phillip's dignity almost deserted him. "I did at that," he said, "it is my cross to bear. Katie, Conner, myself and Janis are a family now. You'll see how things have changed for the better. I wish you luck with my daughter, but there is one thing you must bear in mind. She will be attending the university this fall, to get her teacher's degree. Nothing must stand in her way."

"I want that for her, too. I will see you all soon, then." They shook hands and Janice handed him a slip of paper with Kate's address. John knew the next three days would seem like three years, but he was happy. Kate must love him why else would Janis and Phillip go to all this trouble? He clicked his heels together and jumped high into the air.

Rob rang the doorbell and smiled broadly when Kate stood before him, her eyes wide with delight.

"Hello, Kate, just in the neighborhood, can I stay awhile?"

"Of course, Rob. It's so good to see you. Come, sit down, and tell me all the news." She pulled him into the kitchen and poured coffee before she remembered she should have taken him into the living room. No, this is who I am, a kitchen girl, take it or leave it, she thought.

"I wondered if you might go out with me. There's a good band playing at a place called 'Willies'."

"Thanks, Rob, but I don't date."

"Let's just go and hear the entertainment and dance a little. We won't call it a date, just friends going out together. You might be surprised and enjoy yourself."

"I don't want to hurt you, Rob, I like you so much, but the truth is I am in love with someone. It is over, but I need time to adjust to that." Their hands met over the tabletop and she was relieved to see he did understand.

"I always knew you weren't for me, but, well, I can't help wishing you were. Maybe I could make it with someone like you."

"What do you mean, you could make it with someone like me? You intrigue me, Rob. I think you are a mysterious outlaw, posing as an attorney." She laughed and sobered instantly as she noticed his serious expression.

"Believe it or not, I used to drink my way through the day. Every day. I've only been sober for about two years."

Kate didn't know what to say so she patted his hand and smiled. He nodded at her and said, "I wasn't a refined alcoholic, either. I was a falling down, gutter snipe drunk." Rob sat back and watched her reaction.

"I'm sorry, Rob. I had no idea. You always seem so put together and you must have done something right, after all you do have a very important profession, and you are good at it, too. Give yourself some credit."

"I give my folks the credit. They stood by me and never lost faith in me. These days, when I want a drink, I just have to remember the humiliation and heartache I put them through, and that drink doesn't seem so important anymore."

"It must be tough to fight an addiction like that. I had trouble with food, so I have an inkling of what you go through."

"I managed to quit drinking but kept on chasing women. I've gotten into some bad scrapes doing that. You cured me I think. I never had a pretty little gal sock me in the eye before." He gave her a rakish grin. "The way you fought for your honor showed me what a spoiled, selfish man I had become."

Janis and Phillip barged in as they were talking and when Rob again mentioned the dance Janis' eyes lit up. "Why don't you two go?" asked Kate. "I have a heap of work to do this afternoon and by tonight I'll be dead tired."

Rob turned to Janis and bowed, sweeping his Stetson through the air. "I'd be dee-lighted to escort such a charming maid as yourself. Would you accompany a buckaroo like myself?" Janis laughed at his antics and accepted. Rob left, promising to be back for dinner and his date.

Janis was sparkling and wanted to know everything about Rob. Kate cut her off and ran to answer the phone. It was Emily, coming to visit the day after tomorrow. Could Kate meet the train?

Marcie was at her wits end. She was broke and since Jude died she hadn't had a penny to her name. That girl of Burt's, Kate, Jude called her, had sent her the money found in Jude's possession, but it wasn't much and didn't last long. Her mouth twisted as she thought of what she had missed out on because Jude was too stupid to see what a goldmine he was sitting on.

There was no reason she couldn't cash in on it herself, though was there? Burt's girl was living it up, high and mighty in Marshallville and she could damn well split with her. Marcie got up and threw some clothes into a bag. She was on her way to the city to stick it to Jude's half-sister.

Life at 1900 Comanche Avenue took on a new glow. The house was filled with family and friends constantly coming and going. Emily and Phillip were stepping out together and Kate and Conner waited impatiently for them to announce wedding plans.

Rob and Janis got along famously and continued to go out to dance and eat. They were good for each other, one seeming to know how to keep the other in good spirits. Kate was happy for her friends. She loved her new life and sometimes when the ugly past reared its head, and she looked around her, she felt as though she'd been re-born.

The lessons she'd learned about human nature had astounded her, it seemed she wasn't so different as she had thought. Everyone had fears and felt inadequate at times.

Learning these things had given her more confidence and she was able to relate to people without thinking that she had to be so accommodating to them. Now she was more honest in her dealings with her new friends and neighbors. They liked her, too. Better get back to work, she told herself, and began writing.

The knock on the door startled Kate and she hastily wiped the ink from her fingers and went to answer it.

A woman stood there, looking for all the world like a caricature of a Dicken's novel, right down to the dingy bonnet slapped haphazardly on her blond-gray curls. At Kate's inquiring look, the woman stepped forward and said belligerently, "Marcie's my name. I'm Jude's mother. I've come to get what's rightfully mine."

"Oh, Marcie, I heard of you from Jude. Please, come in. I am so thrilled to meet you. We all miss Jude so much." Kate reached out and drew Marcie into the foyer, then helped her off with her coat. She was disturbed by the condition of Marcie's clothes and the unkempt appearance of her.

Marcie, at a loss for words, let Kate take over the meeting. She had barged in here with great plans, but the kindness and welcome from Kate bewildered her. She decided to attack again. "I came for what I got comin'. Jude should've had the farm. He was the oldest. Burt cheated him." Kate watched her, silent for the moment, trying to decide what kind of person Marcie really was. She sensed a false bravado in the woman's attack.

By the look of her she was down on her luck and needed more than a quickly written check. "Yes, of course, we will take care of all that. First, though, let's get you settled in the guest room, and you can refresh yourself after that long trip." The woman looked as if she'd walked all the way.

The truth was Marcie had hitched rides with truckers, going from one truck stop to another, using the old *my kid died* routine. Along with the free rides, she'd gotten a few dollars from the sympathetic drivers.

Now she was on her way down a softly lit hall in a splendid home, being treated like somebody special. She decided to go along with this Kate and milk her for all she could. Smiling her appreciation, she followed Kate into the bedroom. Kate ran and got a bathrobe and pajamas and told Marcie to use the tub and put the nightwear on. "When you are refreshed, we will have a snack and talk."

She left Marcie to take the first bath she'd had in weeks. Marcie loved the pajamas and robe and didn't mind bathing in exchange for them. The powders and lotions enticed her, too, and she smiled into the mirror. "I've landed on easy street." Her hands were trembling as she turned the faucets.

Marcie joined Kate at the kitchen table an hour later. Once they began talking sarcasm crept into Marcie's voice. Then she whined, "You don't know what it's like to be always in debt, to wonder how you're going to eat or pay the rent. I gotta have money. Jude paid me every month, but now he's gone, and I have no income." Her husky voice droned on and on.

Kate pretended interest, all the while keeping a close watch on Marcie's hands. A small silver ashtray disappeared into the pocket of the bathrobe. A silver spoon and letter opener followed. Marcie was so good at lifting the things, Kate couldn't actually see her take them. She only noticed they were gone after Marcie moved her hands.

Kate didn't need the rest of the family to tell her Marcie was a con. She'd learned enough about human nature to see it for herself and she found it hard to like this woman who had thrown her son away for those worthless men.

"I have decided to help you, Marcie. This is the deal. Take it or leave it." A grimness settled around Kate's mouth. Marcie was disconcerted to hear the rich snob talk so tough. She decided this was the time to use her ace in the hole.

"You have me to thank for your son. Burt brought him to me to feed and take care of while he found a place to take him. It ain't easy to take care of a newborn babe. He never paid me for it either." Kate kept quiet and listened. When Marcie ran out of steam, she continued as if there had been no interruption.

"First, let me tell you I don't believe for a minute you are due anything. Whether you took care of Conner or not is beside the point. You messed around with Burt, knowing he was a married man. He was unfaithful with you, unfaithful to my mother." Kate glared at her and had to sit on her hands so she wouldn't hit the woman. She despised Marcie, probably because of her Ma.

"You are the one that destroyed your son's life, the one who didn't protect him from those abusive men. When he ran away you didn't search for him. At least his father gave him a home and food to eat. As much as I hate Burt Martin, I have to admit he gave Jude back his self-respect. You, on the other hand have taken it from him. At the end, you destroyed him by giving him those papers."

She bent forward and put her face close to the astonished woman's. "Why couldn't you have left him alone? How could you not have cared enough about Jude to let him have his dreams? You killed him as sure as you're sitting in that chair."

Unable to bear the woman any longer she grabbed a checkbook from the desk behind her and quickly wrote a check. Handing it to Marcie, she said, "Here is $800.00. It's because of Jude I'm giving you anything at all. He was a better person that I am. I hope, for your son's sake you use it to start a decent life."

She started to mention The Honor Farm but changed her mind. Marcie would just be trouble. No, she would have to find her own way.

"Don't come back here looking for me to help you. This is it. Now go to your room and be ready to leave in the morning. Oh, before you go, empty your pockets. Stealing is a criminal offense."

Marcie silently left the house early the next morning. When Kate checked the room, the only thing missing were the pajamas and robe. Glad to forget the unpleasant encounter she walked to the mailbox.

There was a letter from Helen and she hurried back to the house to read the news from home.

She went into the back yard and sat at one of Phillip's rustic park areas with the wooden benches and round table. Her heart was pumping fast, it was a longer walk to the mailbox then she'd realized. Eagerly, she tore open the envelope.

Dear Kate,

I was fixin to get the mail and thought I'd drop you a line and catch you up on things here.

You never saw such a hustle and bustle of energy. The folks here sure love the place, and work hard, each trying to out do the next. They love the bathrooms. It's a good thing the water level is high. I never seen so many clean folks in one place in my life.

Ben and I have become parents, in a way. A young girl, she's fifteen, her name is Tansy. She remembers you from when you visited Jude. She'd the one that was in the room with him. She's taken to sewing and makes really nice clothes for herself and the other girls. Ben and I keep her with us a lot and are teaching her as much as we can.

The fields are planted. Ben says to tell you the livestock is thriving, and that the older men have planted a lawn and put in a small orchard of plums and crabapples. Also, they are getting the ground ready for a huge garden. We'll be canning plenty this fall.

Haven't had any trouble with the neighbors. Seems like they're taken to these people. Max Gordon is good about stopping by and Gus, too. Emily comes out twice a month. She's teaching the grown-ups to read and write and do sums. Including me. She says I need to learn fractions so I can keep the books in good order, but some can't read or write at all. Emily is in her glory and we all love her. I guess we will be losing her soon as the gossip is she will be marrying up with your dad.

We miss you here, Ben especially. Hope things are going your way over there. If you can, please write. Ben worries about you.

Love, Helen, Ben and the gang at The Honor Ranch

Happiness shone from Kate's eyes. She'd worried that so many people in one place would be a cause of friction, but they were pulling together, making a life for themselves. Jude's spirt lived on and it lived in Conner. She'd been startled at Conner's likeness to Jude. She hadn't noticed it until she'd come here after their separation, but there were the dark straight brows, the wide forehead, and the hair. Thick, with black wayward curls. His eyes and nose were her's and Phillips, his mouth and chin her mother's. He's the best of us all. He's got Jude's sensitivity. His kindness to all creatures, man or animal, surprised and frightened her. He trusted everyone.

When she admonished him, he had a way of gently smiling at her, like she was the child and he the elder. She was frightened for him. Some one could hurt him. When she tried to explain to him why she worried and wanted him to show more caution, he simply said, "The Lord is my shepherd. He watches over me. Don't worry, Mama." How could she argue with an answer like that?

One day she had asked him why he couldn't talk when she first met him. "I promised God if he would get me a family, I would only pray and not talk until He picked me out the right ones. I waited a long time, but you came for me. God got me a Mama." His little arms had reached around her, and his head burrowed into her apron.

She recalled the brown envelope Conner had kept hidden under his mattress. He'd shown it to her after they were settled in this house. He'd pulled a picture carefully from the brown envelop and said, "Mama, I can hang this up now. It belongs in this house." It was a picture of Jesus. Kate gulped when she'd seen the big bleeding heart exposed on his chest. "It's called 'The Sacred Heart of Jesus'," Conner had explained. The picture hung over his bed and she tried not to look at it when she cleaned up his room. Conner had confided he would be a priest one day. There was no way she could answer him, so she had started reading about the Church and learning all she could of his Catholic religion. It only raised many questions in her mind. Was one's life pre-ordained? Had Conner spent his first five years in a Catholic orphanage because he was fated to be a priest?

For now, she would let him explore his dreams, he was still a child, and would likely change his mind about many things before he settled into a profession. Maybe someday she would know the answers to his many questions. For now she could only read and search for life's truths.

While she learned to accept the strange notions that Conner had, she found it was an easy step to also accept the past. Forgiveness was in her nature and after sending Marcie off, her own past faded, hibernating deep inside her. Burt's influence on her thoughts receded and her memories of Leon became unimportant to her. It was as if she had lived through a horror movie and now only the raw edges of it remained.

Her world would be complete if she were with John. Things had never been better for her. Mandy was coming to stay for the next school year. She and Conner had made plans to help her feel at home. Conner had chosen her bedroom, a rosy room that looked out over the creek and beyond to a meadow. He'd seen deer and antelope grazing there and wanted Mandy to see them too.

Unconsciously she rubbed her thigh, humming softly. An image came into her mind; Big John was walking towards her, a smile on his face and love in his eyes. Alarmed, she tried to push the image from her, to keep her mind from blanking out the real world, but he came closer, close enough to lift her up and hold her. She smelled the masculine, spice scent of him, and the warm pressure of his arms. "It's really you. Oh, John, you've come back to me."

"I'm sorry I left you. Christine told me you were going to marry Norm and I couldn't handle that. I love you, Kate Willow. Will you marry me?" His hands gripped her shoulders.

She looked into his eyes for a long time, reading his love for her. She nodded her head.

"Come," she said, "let me show you the garden." She walked beside him, willing her weak legs to move. Truth to tell, she was as shaky as a beanstalk in a windstorm.

Edith Campbell-Murray

CPSIA information can be obtained
at www.ICGtesting.com
Printed in the USA
LVHW031128010421
683210LV00007B/176